October's
PROMISE

Marianne Garver

Bella
BOOKS
2009

Bella Books, Inc.
P.O. Box 10543
Tallahassee, FL 32302

Printed in the United States of America on acid-free paper
First Edition

Editor: Katherine Forrest
Cover Designer: Linda Callaghan

ISBN 10: 1-59493-145-3
ISBN 13:978-1-59493-145-1

Dedication

To Missy, who showed me that writing could be fun.

To Kimberly, who never stopped believing I could do it.

To Jeanne, who helped me to believe others might enjoy reading it.

But most of all to Melody, whose love opened my heart to all the possibilities.

Acknowledgments

Special thanks to Jeanne Westby who not only provided insight into what goes on behind the doors of an advertising agency, but also offered encouragement and counsel all along the bumpy road from rough draft to finished product.

The prospect of working with an editor was daunting enough for this first-timer, but the intimidation factor was multiplied tenfold when I learned the editor in question would be none other than Katherine V. Forrest. My thanks to Katherine for making the process as painless as possible (understanding now that pain-free was never an option) and for having more faith in me than I had in myself.

Finally, my deepest gratitude to my wife, Melody, for her unwavering emotional support and always being there with a hug when I needed it (not to mention making sure I had hot meals and clean underwear when I was too crazed with deadlines to see to such things myself).

About the Author

    Originally from Charlestown, New Hampshire, Marianne Garver now resides in South Texas with her partner, Melody, and two highly opinionated cats, Spooky and Mr. Stinky. She credits her mother for encouraging her love of books and her father for encouraging her love of writing when he presented her with her first typewriter (a portable electric Olivetti) when she was just twelve years old. *October's Promise* is Marianne's first published novel.

Chapter One

"You don't have to do this, you know."

Quinn Barnett tossed a duffel bag in next to the few cardboard boxes already in the back of the truck, pushed down on the lid of the ice chest to make sure it was shut, then lifted the tailgate. "I told you, I don't know how long I'm going to be. Could be a few weeks, could be…longer."

"And I told you I don't care how long it is." Arms folded across her ample chest, the manager of The Sizzlin' Skillet, a truck stop outside Reno, looked like she planned to win the way she won most arguments, simply by virtue of being the most stubborn. "You're one of the best cooks I've had here in a long time. Sure as hell the most dependable. I can get along without you as long as you need me to. I'd just like to know you're coming back."

"Joyce…" She heard the impatience in her own voice and made herself stop, take a breath and a mental step back. She considered telling her the truth. Once she said goodbye to a place, she just didn't go back. But Joyce would probably try to argue over the logic of that. She didn't have the time or the mood for that debate, so she opted instead for what was just another version of the truth.

1

"I appreciate that. I do. But I don't make promises I can't keep. I feel bad about leaving you, but I'd feel a whole lot worse about lying to you." She knew the woman's zero-tolerance policy for liars in general would make it impossible for her to argue with that. "If it makes you feel any better," she added grudgingly, "you're one of the best bosses I've ever had. I'm going to miss—"

"Don't think you're gonna win by making me cry," Joyce said sharply.

"Christ, I hope not. If you cried it might make me change my mind." She tried to look worried about the possibility, but the very notion of Joyce tearing up transformed it into an amused smirk.

As expected, Joyce's grin was immediate. "I guess you really are out of here then, aren't you?"

They both laughed, knowing their similar sensibilities were the main reason they'd gotten along so well for the past couple of years.

A few minutes later, she pulled out of the truck stop's parking lot, briefly returning Joyce's wave of goodbye before she raised the window and turned up the air conditioning.

She didn't have any misconception that they were friends and doubted Joyce did either. But they'd gotten along well, which was worth almost as much. No, what Joyce would miss was a hard worker who knew how to do what was expected of her without bitching and moaning, and Quinn would miss a job she'd enjoyed, working for a woman who didn't have her nose six inches up into everyone else's business.

A nosier woman might have pestered her with questions about what she planned to do about her apartment, or what should she tell anyone who came by looking for her. She hadn't worried for a minute about hearing any of that from Joyce.

Thankfully her landlord had taken readily to her suggestion that he keep her furniture and rent the upper level of the duplex as a furnished unit. He'd tried to push a couple hundred dollars into her hand, claiming he'd make that up in the first six months with the higher rent he'd be charging, but she'd refused to take it. It was all used furniture to begin with and probably not worth that much. If he hadn't been willing to let her leave it there, she'd have just called Goodwill to come get it.

Anything that remotely mattered to her was in the few boxes sitting in the back of the truck. It wasn't the first time she'd benefited from her minimalist views on the subject of personal possessions, and a similar attitude toward personal relationships pretty much guaranteed no one would be coming around looking for her anytime soon.

She turned on the radio, cranking up the volume on Nickelback to mask the sounds of yet another bridge burning behind her, and headed east.

Chapter Two

The setting sun cast the Manhattan skyline into a deepening silhouette against a twilight sky. Libby Jackson spent a moment absently admiring the familiar view from her office window before the significance of what she was looking at sank in.

A quick glance at the clock on her computer screen confirmed the time. Six forty-eight. *Crap.* She'd missed her step class. Again.

If she hurried, she might be able to get into the next class at seven, the one led by psycho-bitch Barbie. She was convinced the statuesque blonde with the buzz cut had been an Army drill sergeant in a previous life. But it was either put up with Barbie or wait until eight, and by then the gym would be crawling with everyone else who couldn't manage to drag themselves away from work at a decent hour.

Or—her index finger hovered over the key that would shut down her computer—she could just do what she'd done yesterday; skip it all together and promise herself she'd leave work on time tomorrow.

A familiar cadence of footsteps approaching her office made up her mind.

"I know, I know. I'm supposed to be gone already," she said, tapping the keyboard to power down just as Brian Galloway stepped through the door. Brian, as the firm's senior art director, was her immediate supervisor, but over the past few years they had also become good friends. "I was working on the Christopher Blue Jewelers layout and lost track of time. What's your excuse?"

She was reaching under her desk for her purse when she noticed that behind the fashionable, dark-framed glasses his blue eyes were too serious. "What's up?"

"Lady Belle."

Libby stared at him. "That's a done deal. Kevin said they loved the presentation," she said, referring to Kevin Finch, the account executive in charge of the Lady Belle Cosmetics campaign.

"Capshaw loved the presentation. It appears, however, that Capshaw was merely a flunky."

"Capshaw's their marketing exec," protested Libby weakly. "He's Elizabeth Belle's son!"

"Stepson," corrected Brian. "And since Daddy doesn't even own stock in the company, that's all he is now. Word is old lady Belle took one look at the video and fired Capshaw on the spot."

"She didn't like the campaign?"

Brian grinned without humor. "Hated it," he intoned.

Hated it? They'd worked their asses off on that campaign. Lady Belle Cosmetics had the potential to be the next bright star in the designer cosmetics industry and a successful campaign for Belle could put their own agency on the national advertising map.

"How'd Kevin take the news?"

"It wasn't pretty. He came as close to begging as I ever hope to hear. You know, I really thought I'd enjoy that a lot more, but it was actually kind of depressi—"

"Highlights, Brian, highlights," prompted Libby with an impatient little wave.

"I know, but haven't you ever—"

"*Brian*," she said, turning his name into a threat.

"Oh, all right. Belle's agreed to give us one more shot."

Something in his tone marred what should have been good news. "But? Quit stalling, Brian. Just give it to me straight."

"Is that supposed to be funny?" he asked, but the eyebrow Libby cocked at him was all the prompting he required to get to the point. "Kevin wants a new presentation ready by ten tomorrow morning."

"Is he *crazy*?" She shot up from her chair, but it was hard to storm around in less than ten square feet of walking space, especially with Brian taking up part of it, and she had to stop after only a few steps. "There's no way. It took us three weeks to put that together, finding the perfect model, the perfect music and now...now..." She stared at him. "Is he crazy?"

"I think that's where you started, dear, and if you don't calm down, I'm afraid you're going to start spitting." He put an arm around her shoulders and settled her back behind her desk. "It's all crazy if you ask me. If this afternoon is any indication, Kevin is on the verge of a breakdown so the least we can do is humor him. He wants to take another look at Larson's original idea, so it's not like we're starting from scratch. Not exactly," he added at Libby's withering look. "Alan and Kevin have a flight to Chicago tomorrow morning to meet with Belle herself. Look, they know it's going to be a rough presentation. I'm sure we're just talking about getting some storyboards together. So conference room in ten minutes, okay? If it makes you feel any better," he added on his way out, "they're having some Chinese brought in. I went ahead and ordered for you. Hope you're in the mood for spicy."

Two hours later everyone on the creative team that had put together the Lady Belle campaign was still gathered in the firm's main conference room. The table was littered with the remnants of Chinese takeout and cups of cold coffee, and an industrial-size bottle of antacid tablets was gradually making its way around the room. The tension level in the room had kicked up another notch when Alan Pfeiffer, the firm's managing partner, had joined them. Unlike the rest of them, he looked as fresh as he did on any given day when he arrived at the office at seven fifteen. His hair, a sandy blond that hid the gray unless you were really looking for it, was perfectly combed and he hadn't so much as loosened his tie. His only concession to the day's stress and the late hour was the suit jacket he'd hung on the back of his chair, but even that struck Libby as something of an affectation. *See folks? Here I am, slogging through the swamp with you mere mortals.*

"I know no one wants to hear this," said Libby, ignoring a muffled *again* that reached her ears, "but if Belle hated our presentation enough to fire her marketing exec over it, how can we expect her to go for this?"

Her question was answered by a silent chorus of scowls and one not-so-muffled groan that came from Kevin's general direction. He sat at the far end of the table, shirtsleeves haphazardly rolled up, the tie he'd been wearing an hour earlier lying in a plate of mushu pork where he'd flung it during a fit of exasperation. His disheveled brown hair betrayed how often he'd dragged his hands through it.

"She understands it won't be a fully developed presentation. All we have to do tomorrow is tickle her imagination. If we can do that, we can get another week to sex it up and—"

"But this isn't *going* to tickle her imagination," Libby interrupted, frustration overriding good sense. In the silence that followed, she took a breath and held it, fixing her gaze on an empty fried rice container that sat halfway across the table. "Look, I'm not saying our original concept wasn't any good. I liked it. I still believe it would sell the product. But all that matters now is that the client *didn't* like it."

"But we're not talking about—"

"You're right," agreed Libby, cutting Kevin off. "What we're talking about," she said, snatching up the photocopied sheets of the notes from their brainstorming session weeks ago, "was the jumping off point for that concept. This is what we started with before we spent three weeks making it *good*. If we go in there trying to resell it"—she flung the papers back down on the table—"she's going to recognize it. The implication will be we

7

were counting on her being too stupid to see it for what it is, and whatever happens after that...well, it'll be even worse than the first time."

She could see in Kevin's eyes that he knew she was right and for one brief moment thought he might actually back her up on this one, but all he said was, "If you have a better idea, Libby, I, for one, would be delighted to hear it."

"I—well, no. Not yet. But that's my point. We don't have enough time to waste half of it tweaking what we already know isn't going to work. If we're going to save this, we need to come up with something—different," she said, at the last minute catching herself before she said "better."

"I have an idea," said Lori Hernsman. Libby's gaze shifted to the quiet young intern who had apparently made the announcement with more enthusiasm than she felt the idea merited, because as soon as everyone's eyes turned toward her she shrank visibly in her seat.

"I just thought, well, what if we have the agency send over a model to go with you tomorrow for the presentation? You know, use a live model wearing Lady Belle instead of just storyboards. Maybe it wouldn't be so...flat."

The suggestion was met with a beat of dead silence. "All right," said Kevin slowly. "That's an idea."

Yeah, thought Libby. *A bad one.* But Kevin's acknowledgment, while noticeably less than enthusiastic, was enough to trigger a scattered murmur of agreement.

"Do we have any idea who might be available?" asked Audrey, one of the senior copywriters.

"Darla Haynes is coming in for the Flemming shoot in the morning," Lori offered, her confidence returning in light of the positive response to her suggestion. "Maybe we could reschedule the shoot and you could use her."

"Darla's a little ordinary looking, don't you think?" someone else commented. "We need someone more exotic. Maybe Tonya Aguilar?"

Wondering why Alan wasn't nipping this in the bud, Libby

stared at the rice container and tried to tune them all out. You didn't march into a presentation with a model unless you planned to pitch her for the campaign spokesperson. Tonya Aguilar was so wrong for this it wasn't funny, and while Libby didn't think Darla Haynes was at all ordinary-looking, she was as dumb as a post. It was one thing to use her in a video, but to bring her to Elizabeth Belle's office was tantamount to saying *this* is the image Lady Belle needs to project and the moment Darla opened her mouth—and being Darla she'd *have* to open her mouth—that alone would be the beginning of the end.

Although Libby had never met Elizabeth Belle, she'd gotten a feel for the woman behind Lady Belle Cosmetics from an article published in *Today's Entrepreneur*. A strong-willed, highly opinionated southern woman, Belle was zealously proud of the fact that she'd been born and raised in Atlanta, Georgia, as had generations of her family before her. She'd married a widower from Chicago and allowed herself to be transported north, but continued to maintain her family homestead in Atlanta and visited there several times a year. Clearly, from the brief snippets of the interview quoted in the article, Belle's roots and her heart remained in the South and she viewed all Northerners—Yankees, Libby corrected herself—with a suspicion that bordered on disdain.

Possibly with good reason, judging from the discussion going on around her. Not for the first time this evening, she found herself wondering what the hell was wrong with Alan.

Everyone at Pfeiffer, Strausburg & Finch was aware of how much pressure he'd been under since his father and founding partner of the agency retired last year, but that didn't explain why he seemed to be almost intentionally allowing Kevin to drop the ball on this one. Losing one account, even this one, would not ruin PS&F. But Alan had made too big a deal of what Lady Belle could mean for the future of the agency to let it slip through his fingers without someone taking the fall. While Alan would have no qualms about accepting all of the credit, he sure as hell wouldn't be taking any of the blame. So was all this just Alan giving Kevin a couple more feet of rope to hang himself with?

A pale pink antacid tablet, pinged across the table hockey puck style by Brian, ricocheted off her arm and startled her from her musings. Chairs were being shoved back and people were moving.

"All right people," Kevin was saying. "We'll meet back here in—" He glanced at his watch. "—six hours to see where things stand."

She glanced at Brian wondering what she'd missed. Evidently aware that her mind had been elsewhere, he winked at her. "You're with me, kid."

Wincing at the perfectly awful Bogie imitation, Libby rose to follow him. As an afterthought she reached back to snag the pink hockey puck and popped it in her mouth. She had a hunch before the night was over she was going to need a lot more of these.

Chapter Three

The stench of rotting garbage assaulted Quinn's nose the moment she opened the back door, effectively negating any relief the air conditioning provided from the dry, west Texas heat.

She stepped inside, concentrating on breathing through her mouth. The table was still set with the molding remains of breakfast.

"Jesus H. Christ," said Rafael Cruz as he came in the door behind her. "Smells like something died in—" He caught himself, the look on his face equal parts embarrassment and disgust, but remained standing close to the door, head angled to breathe as much from the outside air as possible.

Pretending she hadn't heard, Quinn picked up one of the pots on the stove, glancing at the clump of congealed grits inside. She dumped it, pot and all, into the trash, dislodging some of the squirming white creatures that clung to the black plastic liner.

"I probably should have sent someone over to check on the place," Cruz said, apology implicit in his tone.

Torn between agreeing and not caring, she said nothing. It was only because of Cruz that she was here, but she hadn't yet decided whether that called for gratitude or retaliation. Cruz had served under her father for years before being promoted to Chief of Police. The position afforded him the means to track her down, but she was surprised he'd bothered to do so. She doubted anyone else would have.

She glanced around the kitchen. Someone else might find the yellow café curtains with the daisy border to be cheerful. She knew that the same curtains had hung on these windows for at least thirty years. Same curtains, same mustard yellow Melamine dishes that were even uglier than she remembered. And it might have been her imagination, but even the faded rooster on the dishtowel tucked over the handle of the oven seemed painfully familiar.

Her gaze fell on the ceramic maple leaf salt and pepper shakers on the back of the stove. Three holes in the yellow leaf for salt. Two holes in the red leaf for pepper. Without thinking, she picked one up and was instantly twelve years old again and standing in Wilson's Department Store. They'd been her mother's birthday gift that year. They looked pretty kitschy now. Hell, they'd probably been just as kitschy back then, but her mother had loved them, just as a twelve-year-old Quinn was sure she would. A much older Quinn wanted to believe they were still here because they'd continued to hold some sentimental value for her mother, but she suspected they were like the curtains and the dishtowel—merely functional props her mother had stopped looking at or caring about a long time ago.

The floor creaked when Cruz braved another step into the kitchen behind her. "So you got any ideas about what you're going to do with the place?"

She put the red maple leaf back down on the stove before casting one more look around the room. "You can burn it to the ground for all I care."

Stepping around a startled Cruz, she walked out and didn't look back.

Twenty minutes later, she found herself parked in front of the two-bedroom house where Guadalupe Hinojosa used to live. She didn't bother cutting the engine. The place had obviously been derelict for quite a while. Overgrown grass and weeds obscured the steps to the front door. It looked like a fire had taken out a section of the roof and, with that left unrepaired, nature did the rest. Probably with a little help from kids, she decided, noting the broken windows and remembering what used to pass for entertainment on a Friday night in Flat Rock.

It surprised her a little, how sorry she was to see what had become of the place. She hadn't thought about Lupe in years, but now that she was here, it was easy to remember the hours she'd spent sitting on the bed in the room Lupe shared with her two older sisters and their infant brother. Mostly she and Lupe had talked about their mutual dream of one day getting out of Flat Rock. Where they would live, the lives they would lead. How fast her car would be. How many babies Lupe wanted. Lupe loved babies, and she'd wanted a lot of them. She'd even had the names picked out. Quinn hadn't understood the fascination, but she'd enjoyed listening to Lupe talk about it. Hell, she'd enjoyed listening to Lupe talk about almost anything.

She watched a scruffy looking yellow tabby saunter down the sidewalk before it vanished into the jungle of weeds that used to be Lupe's front yard.

What had she hoped to accomplish by coming over here? It wasn't like she'd expected Lupe to be around.

"If I ever hear you've been sniffing around that Hinojosa bitch again—"

She shook her head as if she could dislodge the memory of her father's voice, but the effort proved as futile as her attempt to defend her friend had been all those years ago. She remembered all too vividly how her stomach had dropped and the smile that appeared on his face.

"Did you really think I didn't know about that? Little girl, I know everything that goes on in this town."

"You leave her alone. If you touch her, I'll—"

"Touch her?" His laugh was an ugly sound. "I'm probably the only one around here who hasn't touched her."

"That's a lie!"

"Don't kid yourself. That slut's spread her legs for every tomcat in town and everybody knows it."

"Shut up! You don't know anything about her!"

"I know what I need to know. So if you can't stay away from her, you just tell me right now, and I'll be more than happy to remove temptation from your path."

She took a step toward him, her young hands balled into fists. "If you do anything to her, I swear I'll—" Blinded by her own fury, she never even saw the blow coming until it knocked her off her feet. Her face struck the corner of the coffee table as she went down. She cried out at the sharp and sudden pain, furious with herself for giving him the satisfaction.

"Young lady, I'll do whatever's necessary, and there's not a good goddamn thing you can do about it."

She'd been so careful not to give Lupe any reason to suspect that her feelings went beyond friendship, but somehow her father had known and his threat, however vague, had been sufficient motivation to push away the one best friend she'd ever had.

Lupe had tried to get her to talk, to say what she'd done to make her so angry. She'd begged for some explanation of why Quinn didn't want to be her friend anymore. But she couldn't risk letting Lupe know the truth, so she'd simply ignored her. Eventually Lupe stopped asking.

A few months later, shortly before Lupe's sixteenth birthday, she'd seen a pair of silver earrings on sale at Wilson's. She'd bought them, knowing that she shouldn't, and wrapped the small box carefully in pink tissue paper, Lupe's favorite color. On the day of Lupe's birthday, she'd slipped the gift into Lupe's gym bag with no card, no note.

The next day she'd come to school sick to her stomach with anticipation. Would Lupe be wearing the earrings? She'd imagined how pretty they'd look on her, shining brightly against the backdrop of Lupe's long black hair. Would she have guessed they were from Quinn? What would she say if Lupe asked her? She couldn't let on, of course. But Lupe would know anyway, and then she'd understand that Quinn didn't really hate her, and that she must have a very good reason for acting the way she did.

But Lupe wasn't at school the next day, or the day after that, or the week after that. Quinn never saw her again.

It took a couple weeks for the rumor to surface that Lupe had gotten pregnant and been sent by her mother to live with relatives in Matamoras. At fifteen, Quinn wasn't naive enough to think that couldn't have happened, but the coincidence of timing made it hard to swallow. She'd almost made herself sick wishing she hadn't bought the earrings, wishing that somehow Lupe would know she didn't hate her, that she loved her. Hoping that Lupe really was just pregnant, because then she could have the baby and come back home. But of course that hadn't happened.

Why would she have come back here anyway? This place had never really been home, not for either of them. Home was somewhere you were wanted, and where you wanted to be. Some place you felt safe, maybe even loved. At least most of the time. When she was younger, she hadn't understood why that was too much to ask. Now, with thirty-two years in the rear-view, she'd glimpsed enough of other lives to be convinced it was mostly just a matter of luck. And like good luck, if you weren't born with it, you'd better learn to live without it. Because just wishing for it…

She pulled away from curb, leaving Flat Rock and her memories of Lupe behind her for the last time.

Wishing never you got you anything.

Chapter Four

It was a little after nine in the morning when Libby climbed the four flights of stairs to her East Side apartment. She knew she'd be skipping the gym for the third time this week, but she was too tired to feel guilty about it. Her knapsack landed with a soft thunk on the hardwood floor, and she kicked off her heels before flipping the deadbolts. A hot shower might help the stiffness in her neck and shoulders, but she doubted she had the energy left to stay on her feet for that long.

She headed for the bedroom, unzipping her skirt as she went and walking out of the puddle of teal fabric when it slid to the floor. Her blouse followed in short order and a few minutes later she was asleep, hugging a feather pillow to her chest and oblivious to the distant rolls of thunder.

She awoke with a headache raging in the back of her skull. With a little groan, she rolled onto her back, dragging the pillow with her to cover her face. She stayed that way for a long moment before reluctantly lifting the edge of the pillow.

The light seeping in along the edge of the blinds was thick and gray. Rain beat a light staccato against the window and added a wet, hissing sound to the noise of traffic rising up from the street below. Her eyes shifted to check the clock on the night stand. Six eighteen. She let the pillow flop back onto her face and then resolutely pushed it away and sat up, a move that sent the pain in the back of her skull exploding upward.

In the bathroom she pulled on the sweatpants she'd left hanging over the shower rod and rifled through the medicine cabinet for the bottle of ibuprofen. Tossing back two of the pills, she helped them down with a scooped handful of water from the bathroom sink and splashed another couple of handfuls against her face.

Returning to the bedroom, she pulled a T-shirt from the dresser and found herself wishing it were cold enough to bundle up in a sweatshirt or a thick cable-knit sweater and some nice cushy socks, her clothing version of comfort food—wearable meatloaf and mashed potatoes. Her stomach growled with the thought. It was almost twenty-four hours since she'd eaten, probably why her head was killing her. Eating something might make the pills kick in a little faster.

In her refrigerator were the wilted, browning remains of a bag of mixed lettuce and a tomato that left the better part of itself on the shelf when she tried to pick it up. A Styrofoam takeout tray looked promising until she opened it. Holding the container at arm's length, she dropped the mutating science project into the trash can.

She was flipping through her stash of take-out menus and trying to decide who might have the fastest delivery on a rainy Tuesday evening when the door buzzer sounded.

A six-pack of Sam Adams filled the view from the peephole. She flung open the door. "What the hell took you so long?" she demanded, and grinning, she claimed the beer.

"Your gratitude is seriously underwhelming," Brian told her. Elbowing the door shut, he set a damp pizza box down on the coffee table before peeling off his jacket.

"Hey, if you saw what I was contemplating eating before you got here, you'd know how grateful I am." She carried the beer into the kitchen where she pried the caps off two bottles and set the rest in the refrigerator.

Plopping down on the sofa next to him, she raised the lid of the pizza box, releasing the aroma of spicy Italian sausage and a hint of sweet basil that already had her mouth watering. She pulled out a slice, plucking a fat piece of sausage from the top and popping it into her mouth.

"So'd you hear the news yet?" Brian asked.

"News?" she said, eyeing him warily, pizza only inches from her mouth.

"Old lady Belle cancelled the meeting."

"What?" The hand holding the pizza dropped toward her lap. "When did this happen?"

"Fortunately, right before anyone got on the plane to fly out there."

"Well, that didn't take long, did it? Do we know who she went with?"

"Oh, that's not why she cancelled. She had to fly to Atlanta," Brian said affecting an exaggerated Southern drawl, "for the birth of her great-great-grand-niece." The fake accent faded. "Or grand-grand-great-niece. Something like that. One of those relationships only Southerners have."

"I'm pretty sure anybody with a sibling can have a niece," she said dryly, "but I don't think even Elizabeth Belle is old enough to have the one you just described."

"*Any*way," continued Brian, with a you-know-what-I-mean look, "she's still going to meet with them, but not until after she gets back."

"Which will be..."

"No idea," he said around a mouthful of pizza. "Few days. A week." He paused to take a swig of beer before continuing. "A month. She told Kevin that family comes before business and she'd be staying in Atlanta for as long as they needed her."

She brightened. "So we're going to have some more time to work on the campaign after all."

"Yeah, but not in the way you probably mean. We're going

forward with what we started on last night. Don't give me that look. It wasn't my call. But with no guarantee of how much more time we're going to have..." He shrugged.

Disgusted, she tossed the slice of pizza back down in the box. "Okay, is it just me, or has Alan lost his fucking mind?"

Brian looked more amused than shocked. "I don't know, but I'm surprised you didn't ask him yourself last night. What was up with you, anyway? Kevin's on the verge of losing it, Alan's wound so tight it's not funny, and you decide it's a good time to poke that mad dog with a stick. Talk about losing your mind." He picked up the slice of pizza she'd thrown down and put it back in her hand. "Eat."

"I just don't see what the point was of Kevin selling his pride for another shot at this if we weren't actually going to *take* it," she said before taking a halfhearted bite of pizza. As soon as the mix of flavors hit her tongue, she closed her eyes with a little moan of appreciation. She took a couple more bites in quick succession. "Maybe it's time for a change. Maybe I'll give up advertising and open my own pizzeria."

Brian snorted. "Oh yeah, I can see you tossing a pizza. You can't even boil an egg without burning it."

She scowled, but knew she couldn't really argue that point. Okay, so maybe not a pizzeria. But that didn't alter the fact that something had to change. The certainty of that had been with her for a while now, despite her best efforts to ignore it.

It had first crossed her mind a couple of years ago, after she'd spent the weekend at her family's home in Hartford to celebrate her stepdad's fiftieth birthday. She'd arrived back in New York to discover that Amanda, her partner of almost four years, had, in her absence, packed up and moved out. No warning. No explanation. No apology. Just scattered empty spots, like the corner where a schefflera plant used to be.

It had been a week before Amanda would even answer her cell phone, and even then all she could get out of her was, "We've just run our course, Libby. Nothing lasts forever. And you and I, well, we want different things."

She'd hung up, crying, before Amanda could dredge up too many more bad clichés. Evidently they *had* wanted different things. She'd wanted Amanda, and Amanda had wanted the new waitress at the coffee shop where they used to go for breakfast Sunday mornings.

It was during the weeks of depression that followed that she first thought of leaving New York, but even then she'd recognized the idea was more escape than plan, merely an attempt to avoid the painful memories that seemed to be lurking around every corner. So she'd stuck it out, found a new coffee shop, and thrown herself into her work in an ironic attempt to distract herself from the fact work was all she had. But she liked her job, and since it often required long hours no one thought it unusual if she was there late into the night or on the weekend. Every weekend.

A few months later, when her stepfather, Harry, was killed in an automobile accident involving a patch of black ice, she'd considered moving back to Hartford to be closer to her mom. She might have gone through with it then, if not for a particularly memorable conversation in which her mother had thanked God for the fact that Libby would never have to go through losing a spouse. That's when she'd decided moving back to Hartford was not going to be an option.

Thankfully she still had her job, but lately even that wasn't providing as much satisfaction as it once had. The discontent seemed to be coming to a head since Alan Senior retired and handed off the reins to his son. Even before his father's retirement, Junior made no secret of the fact that when he took over the firm he planned to "bring PS&F into the twenty-first century." She couldn't really fault his ambition, but Alan's casual disregard for his father's accomplishments had bothered her more than it seemed to bother his father. While she had nothing but respect for her former boss, she did not have anything close to the same regard for his son. She'd worried that it would be difficult to work for someone she did not respect. What hadn't occurred to her was how difficult it might be working for someone who didn't respect her.

Brian's amused expression was drifting toward one of concern. She took another swallow of beer and forced a smile. "You're probably right. You know me. I go too long without eating and my brain cells go all wonky. So quit hogging the pizza and slide that box back over here."

An hour later, three slices of pizza remained in the box and they were working on the last two bottles of beer. Libby, comfortably mellowed by food and nearly half a six-pack, sat sprawled out with her back against one arm of the couch, her feet in Brian's lap at the other end. Holding his almost empty beer bottle against his lower lip, Brian blew into it while the thumb of his free hand absently rubbed little circles on the sole of Libby's left foot.

"Keep doing that and you're going to put me to sleep," she warned, letting her head loll backward in mock unconsciousness. "Hey," she exclaimed, her head popping back up, "my headache's gone."

"You get headaches?" said Brian, looking surprised. "I thought you were just a carrier."

Libby narrowed her eyes at him. "Just for that," she said, wagging an imperious index finger toward her feet, "rub."

"No," said Brian, slapping the bottom of her foot. He finished his beer and set the empty bottle down on the end table. "I didn't come here to put you to sleep. Let's do something. Get dressed. We'll go dancing."

With a whiny sound of protest, Libby let her head fall backward again. "I don't feel like dancing. I'm too tired. Too old and tired."

"Shut *up*," demanded Brian in a lilting tone that was completely out of character.

There was a moment of silence before Libby, her head still hanging backward over the arm of the couch, giggled. "That sounded so gay."

"I am gay."

"I know, but you don't usually *sound* gay." Another giggle erupted before she could stop it, followed by an immediate and sobering sense of remorse. She raised her head to look at him. "I'm sorry. Am I offending you?"

Brian was shaking his head. "You are completely wasted on three bottles of beer."

She scowled. "I am not."

"You am too," he said, returning her scowl with a fond smile. "And although I'm pretty sure it would only improve your dancing, I couldn't possibly be seen with you in public with your feet looking like this."

"What's wrong with my feet?"

"For starters, when was the last time you had a pedicure? And what is this color all about anyway?"

She flexed her feet to look at the pearlescent green that decorated her toenails. "It's just something Brenda left here."

"Brenda? Christ, don't tell me you're seeing her again," said Brian, all traces of good humor gone.

After witnessing the twenty-something bike messenger flirting with Libby during one of her visits to PS&F, Brian had convinced Libby to go out with her. She was pretty sure all he had in mind was a quick fling with as much sex as possible to get her back in the swing of things. Brenda, it turned out, had been a perfect choice for the as-much-sex-as-possible part, although her chief motivation turned out to be landing herself a meal ticket and a nice roof over her head while she pursued an acting career. The affair had ended as abruptly as it began when she'd found Brenda, by then an understudy in an off-off-Broadway production, rehearsing with the play's leading lady—in Libby's bed.

"*No*, I'm not seeing Brenda again." She yanked her feet out of his lap, not sure if she was more hurt or angry to know Brian thought she could—*would*—make that kind of mistake twice. "How stupid do you think I am?"

"I know you're not stupid," he said defensively, "but you haven't been getting out much lately and—"

"That's by choice, Brian," she reminded him.

"I know it is. But don't you ever just get...lonely?"

"No," she said, probably too quickly to be convincing. Sure, she was feeling a little unsettled lately. But that was work related. "But even if I was, I mean, come on. *Brenda*?"

"Okay, so she wouldn't be my first choice, but you said the sex was—"

She threw a hand up, stopping him. "It was sex, and that's *all* it was." The fact that she'd ever believed it could be otherwise was humiliating enough without having to fine-point it with Brian.

"So you said," he admitted, but then his mouth crooked in a puckish grin. "Just sex. Just *good* sex. Wild, crazy, *monkey* se—"

She reached for a throw pillow and flung it at him. "Will you *stop*! God, you're worse than a little brother! I never said any of that, and you know it." He only laughed and tossed the pillow back at her. She hugged it to her chest. "Why are we even *talking* about this anyway?" she grumbled.

"Because you're wearing her nail polish."

"Oh, for God's sake! It's not her nail polish, it's *my* nail polish. I mean it was hers, but she left it here—*eight months ago*," she added, for emphasis, "so now it's mine. And what's wrong with it?" she asked, looking at her toes again and starting to hate the color herself. What the hell had she been thinking when she put it on? It looked ridiculous, not that she was about to admit it. Not to him anyway.

"What's wrong with it? It's *green*. What you need is some serious fuck me red. And don't tell me you don't have any back there."

"Of course I have red." Nothing *but* red. Which, if she wanted to analyze it—and she did not—was probably what had made the single bottle of green so appealing.

"Get it then. Don't argue with me." He made a little shooing motion. "Go."

She rose from the couch and had to stand there for a second to give the room time to stop spinning. Okay, maybe she was just a tiny bit wasted. Note to self: Next time pizza first, then beer.

Brian was busy gathering their empty bottles, so maybe he didn't notice when she listed just enough to knock a stack of unread mail from the end table. She paused briefly with the thought of picking it up, but there was a slim chance she might end up on the floor if she tried. Best to just keep moving.

She felt better after splashing a little cold water on her face in the bathroom. By the time she returned to the living room, Brian had cleared away the pizza box and empty beer bottles and was gathering the mail she'd knocked to the floor.

"Okay," said Libby, rifling through the basket of tiny bottles, "I've got Riviera Red, Strawberry Wine, Last—"

"What's this?" Brian passed her a thin white envelope. *Law Offices of Darryl Latham* was imprinted in the upper left corner.

"Junk mail," she declared after a quick glance at the return address. "Have you been injured at work? Would you *like* to injure someone at work?" She sent the envelope flying, Frisbee like, in no particular direction and returned her attention to the basket of polish.

"Last Tango Red, Candied Apple—" She looked up at the sound of paper tearing and pointed a finger at Brian. "You're opening my mail. That's a felony, mister."

"You threw it away. That makes it trash. It's not a felony to open someone's trash."

"I didn't throw it away, I just threw it. Technically it wasn't trash yet. Still a felony. I should report you to the authorities. You'll go to jail and become some bad man's bitch."

"Promises, promises." Brian scanned the single sheet of paper. "Libby, I don't think this is junk mail." He passed the letter to her. "Well?" he finally prompted.

"I don't know." She read the letter again, certain she was missing something.

...naming you sole beneficiary of the Estate of Mark Shepherd.

"I don't know who he is," she said.

Brian plucked the page from her hand. "Sole beneficiary," he read aloud and then looked at her over the top of the letter. "This guy leaves you everything he's got and you're telling me you don't even know who he is? Come on. You must have some idea."

"Not a clue. Besides, everything he's got may not be enough to fill up a shoe box, for all we know."

"Hey, if it's a shoe box filled with the right stuff..." He scanned the letter again. "You really don't know the guy?"

She thought about it again and shook her head. "There must be a dozen Libby Jacksons in New York. They probably just sent it to the wrong one."

"But it's not addressed to Libby Jackson. It's addressed to Liberty Jackson. Liberty *L.* Jackson," he added as if noticing that for the first time. "You might not remember the guy, but he obviously knew you. Hey," he said, snapping his fingers. "Maybe one of those bums you're always handing money to was really a rich old—"

She snatched the letter back from him. "You watch too many movies. Besides, it's not like I give them a business card with my name on it." She looked at the letter again, paying attention to the letterhead for the first time. "This is obviously a mistake. The guy wasn't even from here. This came from New Hampshire."

"So?"

"So I've never even *been* to..." A mental flash of something too quick to latch onto. Just...trees. Seen through a car window.

"What?" prompted Brian.

She was in the backseat of her parents' car, staring out at an endless blur of brown and green along the highway.

"You're remembering something, I can tell."

"I don't know. It's probably nothing." She sat down on the edge of the coffee table, trying to capture the images and associated emotions flitting through her mind. A feeling of childish boredom. Nothing to do. Nothing interesting to look at, just trees and more trees. Then a flash of excitement at what looked like water just on the other side of them. A lake?

"When I was little, I think we went camping one summer. It might have been New Hampshire, but..." She shook her head. "It could have been Vermont. Or Maine. They all look alike, don't they?" She caught Brian's exasperated look. "Hey, I was a just a kid. All I know is it was a long drive. And there was definitely a lake. And turtles," she remembered, a smile blossoming.

"Turtles?"

"Yeah. You know. Little turtles," she said, holding her thumb and forefinger a couple of inches apart. "Harry helped me catch them. And there was a slide in the lake—actually out *in* the water," she remembered. "I had this little plastic sandpail, and we'd carry them up to the top of the slide and then I'd wash them back down into the lake one at a time. Wow. I'd forgotten all about that."

Grinning at the rediscovered memory, she looked over at Brian to find him staring at her like she'd sprouted a second head. "Okay, so it sounds kind of weird now," she admitted, "but back then I thought we were all having a good time. But I still don't remember where it was."

"Sure sounds like it could have been Turtle Cove."

"Very funny."

"No, that's the address," said Brian, tapping his finger against the letter. "Turtle Cove, New Hampshire."

"But—" She stared at the letter. "That can't be it. That was more twenty years ago."

"I think you should call him."

"It's too late to get anyone on the phone tonight."

"Well, call your mother then."

"You think my mother's going to know why some guy left his estate to a kid he didn't even know?"

"Maybe not, but she's bound to remember the place better than you do. She'll at least know why you went there to begin with."

"There's only one reason I can imagine. It had to be Harry's idea. And the fact that we never went back tells me it didn't score very high on mother's list of vacation destinations." Not that she was surprised. She couldn't imagine how Harry had talked her mother into it to begin with, let alone what made him think she'd enjoy it.

"You're not trying to talk her into going back, you just need to find out what she remembers. If it was Harry's idea to go up there, maybe this Shepherd guy was some friend of his."

That was possible. Even plausible.

"Well, what are you waiting for? Call her."

"I can't. She's on a cruise," she added when the look on Brian's face accused her of stalling. "She went with some ladies from her bridge club. They won't be back until next week."

"Libby, we could die of curiosity before then."

"No," she said laughing at him, "*you* could die of curiosity."

"You know," began Brian.

"I am not calling the ship," she said firmly. "The best I could hope to accomplish would be to leave a message for her to call back, and do you have any idea what those ship-to-shore calls cost? Besides, if she gets a message from me, she's going to think it's some kind of emergency, and I'm not going to do that to her." Her relationship with her disapproving mother was strained at best, but this was first time the woman had shown any sign of life since Harry died. She wasn't about to interrupt her trip with questions about some possible friend of his.

Because there wasn't much else they could do given the late hour, they'd gotten online and Googled Mark Shepherd. The search turned up nothing they could be sure related to the man in question. A similarly fruitless search for Turtle Cove suggested the town wasn't big enough to be considered much of a tourist attraction, although they did find a New England travel site that made brief mention of the Turtle Cove Tomato Festival. She wasn't sure if that was charming or a little disturbing.

She shooed him out the door a little before eleven and started turning out lights. The basket of nail polish was still sitting on the coffee table. It wasn't too late to get rid of this ridiculous looking green, she decided. Grabbing the bottle of nail polish remover and a handful of cotton balls, she carried them to the bedroom and went to work.

When she was finished, she tossed the last of the green-smeared pieces of cotton in the trash can next to the bed and then, wiggling her toes, admired her handiwork.

Naked toes. That was definitely different.

But still not the sort of change she was looking for.

Chapter Five

Any notion she was still clinging to that she was the wrong Libby Jackson was quickly put to rest when she called the lawyer the next morning. He confirmed that her date and place of birth matched that listed in his file. In return for the information, she learned that Shepherd's property consisted of a residence and a few small rental cottages situated on approximately ten acres of land at Lake Tolba, a few miles outside of Turtle Cove.

Unfortunately, he hadn't able to tell her much more than that. He hadn't known Mark Shepherd personally. The Will had been drawn up nine years earlier by another lawyer, Michael Ferris, who'd since retired after selling his practice to Latham. The fact that Libby didn't know the man either didn't seem to bother him at all.

"Miss Jackson, I've been in this business for more than thirty years and I assure you, this is far from being the most unusual bequest I've seen. I've known people to leave thousands—even millions—to their cat."

"At least it was *their* cat," she pointed out, but when he chuckled, she knew he'd missed her point entirely.

Although the necessary paperwork could be handled long-distance, he'd encouraged her to come up and view the property before she made any decision about what to do with it, suggesting a visit within the next few weeks would allow her to catch some spectacular fall foliage.

Having lived all of her life in the Northeast, she was no stranger to fall foliage, but she didn't see the point in putting the trip off any longer than necessary.

Getting time off from work on such short notice proved to be unsettlingly easy.

"A few days off might be just what you need," Alan told her, and suggested, a little too casually, that she use the time to get some perspective on where exactly she saw her job with PS&F taking her. The implied threat might have carried more impact if she hadn't already been doing that.

The beauty of New England that Latham had carried on about was difficult to appreciate in the unrelenting rain that plagued her all the way through Connecticut and beyond. The hills on either side of the New Hampshire highway had been a nice change from the flatness of Massachusetts, but more often than not they'd been barely visible in the downpour.

She'd hoped the drive would trigger more forgotten memories of that long-ago vacation, but after twenty years it was probably silly to think anything might seem familiar. All she'd managed to dredge up was a scattering of mental images of what had been significant to a child of five or six. The curious thrill of getting up while it was still dark because Harry wanted to get an early start. Her fascination with being able to look down into the thick fog hiding the valleys on either side of the highway until the sun finally made its appearance and burned it off. She remembered a couple stops when she'd gathered pinecones and acorns. Being heartbroken when her mother refused to let her bring her treasures back into the car. Her stepfather, as usual, had saved the day when he tucked them all safely into the trunk for her to retrieve later.

In the here and now, she'd define treasure as a hot cup

of coffee and some lunch, but she was too close to stop now. Another hour, she estimated, glancing at the map unfolded on the passenger seat and then back to the highway in time to see something small and dark in the middle of the road. Hitting the brakes, she fishtailed on the slick highway before skidding to a stop on the muddy shoulder of the road.

Heart pounding, she took a deep breath and relaxed her death grip on the steering wheel. In the side mirror, she saw the dog still sitting on the road about forty feet behind her. She'd managed not to hit it, but someone before her may have. If it could move, surely it would have made some attempt to get out of her way.

She couldn't just drive off. But if the dog was injured what was she going to do with it? She wasn't even sure where she was, let alone where to find help. Besides, wounded animals could be dangerous. What if it bit her?

She shifted the car into reverse, stopping when she was still a good distance away to avoid scaring the dog any more than it probably was. She turned on the flashers and then retrieved the jacket that she'd tossed into the backseat earlier.

The dog wasn't very big. Fifteen pounds, maybe. Definitely a mutt, but with a lot of terrier in him. Mostly black, he had patches of white on his chest and around his muzzle and two bristly white bands over his eyes like twin eyebrows. The coarse, wiry white hair that suggested terrier also brought to mind a whiskered old man.

The dog stared back at her, panting slightly, but with no obvious sign of aggression. She squatted down a few feet away, trying to ignore the cold trickles of rain soaking into her hair and running down her neck.

"Hey there, fella," she said softly. "You're not going to bite me are you?" She stretched a hand out to get a sense for his reaction. "That's a good—"

When the dog leaped to his feet, she recoiled at the unexpected movement, lost her balance and landed flat on her backside on the wet pavement. A flash of fur had her scrambling to get to her feet before she realized the dog wasn't running at her but around her, heading for the open door of the car.

"Hey, don't— No! Stop! *Stay!*"

By the time she got her feet under her, the dog was staring at her from the driver's seat and his panting now looked more like laughter.

Clawing wet hair out of her face, she strode toward the car, any fear of getting bitten lost in her outrage at being outwitted by a dog. A soaking wet, undoubtedly smelly, and apparently uninjured dog, who was now sitting behind the wheel of her car as though he belonged there.

"Out!" she demanded, jabbing a finger toward the pavement. The silent laughter stopped, but he didn't move. "Go on. Out of my seat." Obediently the little dog wiggled backward onto the passenger seat, soaking and tearing the map as he backed over it.

"Oh, no you don't." No longer fearful of the animal, she reached into the car intending to grab him and pull him out, but he lay down on the seat, brown eyes staring up at her from under those bushy white eyebrows. His woeful look made her hesitate, giving him just enough time to add a whimper.

She narrowed her eyes at him. "That was a nice touch, but a little too calculated. Now get your ass out of my car you furry little con artist." She pointed toward the pavement again. "Out. *Now.*"

Head hanging in defeat, the little dog obeyed and hopped down to the pavement.

She got in the car, grimacing at the wet dog smell he left behind, and sent an irritated look in his direction. Soulful brown eyes held her gaze for a moment before he turned and walked away.

She slammed the door shut, watching him in the side mirror as he headed back down the highway, the very picture of dejection.

As if on cue, thunder rumbled overhead, and the rain began falling harder than before.

She dropped her head back against the headrest, wondering

how long it was going to take her to regret this. She looked again in the side mirror, but could no longer see him. Using the electronic control, she adjusted the angle of the mirror trying to see where he'd gone to and discovered him sitting just next the rear of her car. Waiting. For a moment, it almost seemed as if he was watching *her* in the mirror, and when he stood, his short tail drawing loopy little circles in the air, she was sure of it.

"Oh, all *right*," she said, opening the door for him. "Get in." He leapt up, leaving muddy paw prints across her lap before reclaiming his previous spot on the demolished roadmap.

She started driving again, confident that she was close enough to her destination to find it without the map. What to do with the dog was another matter. She wasn't going to bring him home with her. She couldn't dump him back on the side of the road again either. Maybe there'd be an animal shelter in Turtle Cove that would take him. But would they find him a home, or just put him to sleep if no one came to claim him?

She glanced down to find him watching her with a look that made her feel guilty for even thinking about dumping him in a shelter.

"It was only a thought," she told him. "I didn't say I was going to do it." He continued to stare at her. "I'm not going to do it, okay? I promise."

She'd only been driving for a few more minutes when he stood in the seat to stretch and then almost tumbled onto the floorboard when he lifted a hind leg to scratch behind one ear. Regaining his balance, he planted his front paws against the dashboard, then looked at Libby and offered a soft whine. Just ahead, a solitary figure walked along the edge of the road, looking like some character from a country music video in the cowboy hat and jeans, shoulders hunched against the rain in a loose fitting jacket.

The dog yipped excitedly as they approached, and when she didn't slow down, he began to whine, his anxious gaze alternating between the pedestrian and Libby. When she passed the figure on the side of the road, he darted between the split front seats into the back. The sound of his agitated barking filled the small car.

Libby was braking even before the idea was fully formed. As soon as the car stopped, his barking ceased. He must have recognized his owner walking along the highway. Relieved to know she wouldn't have to figure out what to do with him after all, she released her seatbelt and reached across the seat to push open the passenger door.

"There you go. Hey!" She whistled sharply. "Open door here." His attention remained stubbornly focused on the rain-obscured rear window. With an agitated sigh, she climbed to her knees to reach into the backseat. "Come on, you. I said it's time to *go*."

Quinn watched the blue sedan that had just passed her come to a stop on the shoulder of the road a hundred yards or so ahead.

She slowed her stride, due in part to healthy suspicion of anyone who'd offer a ride to a stranger, especially one who hadn't been hitchhiking to begin with. It was a tempting thought though. She was sick to death of this rain and not really sure how much farther it was to town. When the passenger door was pushed open in silent invitation, she made up her mind and broke into a jog. As she drew closer, a woman's voice from within the car demanded, "Get over here, damn it!"

One hand on the open passenger door, she peered inside, trying to decide if getting out of the rain would be worth biting her tongue against the heated retort that sprang to mind. For a moment she was too distracted by the length of thigh exposed by the short denim skirt to wonder what the woman was doing, awkwardly straddling the front seats to reach into the back of the car. When she saw her lifting a furry shape from the backseat, she realized the *Get over here, damn it* had not been directed at her after all and that the woman may have pulled over for some other reason than to offer her a ride.

"Sorry," she said, preparing to back away from the car. "I

thought you—"

The woman started at the sound of Quinn's voice, smacking her head against the dome light inside the car and uttering a brief expletive before she turned and looked at Quinn.

Quinn knew she was staring, but she couldn't help it. The woman's eyes were amazing. A little wide with surprise, they seemed to fill up her face. And the color—the color reminded her of the raw honey old Mr. Coleman used to give her for helping him with his hives. For a moment she was transported out of the cold New Hampshire rain and back to a hot Texas afternoon, licking the sweet stuff from her fingers and feeling sure there wasn't anything better in life.

"Sorry," said the driver, rubbing the back of her head, and Quinn wondered what she was apologizing for. "I thought you were—I mean I was just trying to...uh..." Sinking back onto her knees in the front seat, she pushed her hair away from her face. "Did you need a ride?"

"I thought that's why you stopped," admitted Quinn, "but it looks like you were just having trouble with your—" She glanced into the backseat where a familiar furry face stared back at her. "Well, I'll be damned. I wondered where you'd disappeared to."

"Here, let me just get this out of the way."

When the driver, still kneeling, grabbed at a knapsack on the passenger side floorboard and pitched it unceremoniously into the backseat, she realized she was going to get a ride after all. The tattered remains of a map and a crumpled Almond Joy wrapper followed it before she was able to get in, ducking when she realized there wasn't enough room for both her head and her hat.

"Mind if I set this in the back here?" she asked, not waiting for a response before she dropped the hat onto the backseat which the dog had already abandoned in favor of her lap.

"Hey, you." She scratched his ears vigorously. "Bailed on me last night, the little traitor," she commented. "Must've known what was coming."

"What was coming?"

"All this damn rain. I was camping last night," she explained. "Woke up around four this morning to this big ass clap of thunder about thirty seconds before the sky opened up. And PJ here—" She grabbed the dog's muzzle playfully "—was nowhere to be found. I spent the rest of the night in my truck and this morning the damn thing wouldn't start. I was beginning to think I'd drown before I got back to town."

She realized she was staring again only because the other woman was staring back, with the sort of indefinable directness that always triggered a little ping on her radar. In her experience, straight women rarely maintained eye contact with another woman in quite that way. Not that she was in the market this trip, but a little harmless recreational flirting might be just what she needed to take her mind off the leaden weight that had taken up residence in her gut of late.

"Thanks for the ride, by the way. Name's Quinn." She was holding out her hand before she noticed how much dog fur was clinging to it. "Sorry," she muttered, wiping her hand on her jeans. *Smooth, Barnett. Real smooth.*

The undisguised amusement on the driver's face might have added insult to injury if not for the way it sparkled in those honey-colored eyes. "Why don't you tell me your name so I at least know who's laughing at me," she suggested as they pulled back onto the highway.

"It's Libby."

Quinn waited until her silence drew the driver's glance her way. "Sorry, I thought you were going to say something else. Maybe, oh, I don't know. I wasn't laughing at you. Whatever gave you that idea?"

The woman's lips curved, but all she said was, "Where are you headed?"

"Just up to Turtle Cove. However close you can get me is good enough."

"I can do better than close. That's where I'm going."

Maybe her luck was going to turn after all. "So what brings you up this way?"

"Oh, just some personal business." Libby's tone was dismissive, suggesting nothing interesting to be talked about there, but then her expression turned guarded. "How did you know I don't live here?"

"Just a wild guess," she said, trying to toss it off with a shrug, but the woman's expression remained suspicious enough to almost make her laugh. "You're driving a car with New York plates. You don't get in a stranger's car without noticing a few things."

"I'm from New York. I wouldn't *get* in a stranger's car."

"But you'd let one into yours." The contradiction left her grinning.

"Well, he wasn't going anywhere," Libby said, glancing briefly at the dog, "so it only made sense to let you in."

She looked at the dog zonked out in her lap, doubtful of how much protection the little guy really provided. It didn't seem to be in her best interest to point out the flaws in Libby's security system, however, so she decided to bypass that subject and move on to another. "New York, huh? City or state?"

"City."

"And what do you have going on in New York City that makes it worth staying there?"

"Not a fan of the Big Apple, I take it?" Libby said with an indulgent smile. "Well, I'm in advertising, so it kind of makes sense for me."

"Oh yeah? Anything I might be familiar with?" she asked, mainly because it seemed safer than admitting she thought "commercial" was a synonym for "mute button."

"Probably not. We don't handle a lot of national accounts." It almost had the sound of an apology. "We did design a print ad for Gionelli Timepieces last year."

Quinn shook her head. Libby named a brand of work boots. "Owned a pair once, but can't say I ever saw an ad for them."

Libby was silent for a moment before glancing over at her with a vaguely speculative look. "Salem's Brew?"

She started to shake her head. "Wait a minute. That's a beer, right? Was that the one with the witches?" She'd seen that ad.

Some crowded bar with a guy too involved in the hockey game playing on the television to notice the bored look on his girlfriend's face or give more than a distracted nod when she excused herself from the table. She walked through a door marked "Ladies" but instead of the bathroom you were expecting, the door opened onto a moonlit clearing in the woods where three women in slinky black outfits stood around a cauldron with thick curls of mist pouring over the edge. The witch in the middle—a blonde, she remembered, only because she'd never really been partial to blondes but this one was exceptionally hot—said, "Join us, sister" in that smoke and whiskey kind of voice that had a way of going straight to your crotch, and then reached into the cauldron and pulled out a tray holding bottles of beer. By the end of the commercial, all the guys in the bar were looking around like a bunch of dumb asses, having finally noticed that all their dates were gone, and then you saw the women in the clearing, dancing and laughing and holding bottles of Salem's Brew.

"Man, I loved that commercial," she said, trying to think back to when she might have seen it. It must have been a few years ago when a cohort from her days in the army had organized a little reunion group to meet in Provincetown during the women's festival.

"What was that line at the end? Say goodbye to the ordinary and—"

"Discover the magic taste of Salem's Brew," they finished together.

"Wow. So that was one of yours, huh?"

"Well, I can't take all the credit," said Libby, but her modest smile suggested she could take a good bit of it.

Grinning in appreciation, she mentally checked off another box in the *We Are Family* probability column. She could be wrong, but it was hard to imagine anyone other than a lesbian coming up with that one. "You know, I think that was the only time I've seen a beer commercial aimed specifically at, uh, women." God, had she really just used "women" as a euphemism for "lesbians"?

"Well, it's what the client wanted."

"Is it still around?"

"The beer, not the commercial. They've got a microbrewery in, well, Salem. These two women started it in their garage and it kind of took off with the local crowd. They were hoping to expand their market a little. Unfortunately they had a hard time finding local stations that would run the ad, and most of the ones that did pulled it when they started getting complaints, either from nut cases who thought they were actually promoting witchcraft or people who thought the subtext wasn't quite subtle enough."

That would have been the perfect opening to pursue the subject, but just then they passed the sign for Turtle Cove. "I think you want to take this right coming up here."

A two-lane road split the trees to take them on a winding descent into Turtle Cove. The snow-white spires of at least three churches rose up along the main street. An expanse of lush green around an oversized gazebo was obviously a park, while playground equipment and a baseball diamond suggested that a trim brick building was an elementary school.

She noticed that the car was slowing, but a glance at Libby told her the other woman was just admiring the view. "First time here?" she guessed.

"I was here once, but it was a long time ago."

She watched Libby's eyes scanning the horizon as if looking for something.

"There should be a lake around here somewhere..."

"Yeah, Lake Tolba. It's back that way," said Quinn, stabbing a thumb over her shoulder. She'd been camping there for the past few days. "Are you going to be staying out there?"

"No," said Libby as she resumed their descent into town. "But I think that's where my family stayed when I was a kid. I'll probably take a drive out there before I leave town."

Quinn spotted a service station up ahead on the right. "You can just drop me off over there," she said, gesturing.

"Do you want me to wait?" Libby asked. "Just in case they can't help you. You don't want to be walking all over town looking for another service station."

Amused by the suggestion, she aimed a deliberate glance down the short length of the town's main street. "Oh yeah. Like that could take a whole ten minutes."

"Sorry," said Libby with a wry smile. "Guess I'm used to thinking on a slightly larger scale."

"I'm sure this one will be fine. Thanks for the offer, though." She stroked a hand over the sleeping dog's head, and then patted him on the rump to roust him. "And for the ride," she added as she got out of the car and turned to settle the waking dog onto the seat she'd just vacated. "You're a lifesaver."

"What are you doing?" said Libby.

Quinn stared at her blankly. "What do you mean?"

"Aren't you going to take him with you?"

Confused, she looked down at the dog. "Why would I take your dog?"

"He's not my dog, he's your dog," said Libby, looking at her like she was the one who was nuts.

And this, she reminded herself, is why you never accept rides from strangers. "He was in your car when you stopped to pick me up," she pointed out carefully.

"But—he knew you. You knew *him*. You called him by name, for God's sake!"

That's what this was all about? "It's on his tag," she pointed out. When Libby's gaze dropped toward the animal in her passenger seat, she took a quick step back away from the car.

"But don't you—no, don't—just…will you *wait*," Libby said, fumbling with her seatbelt. "You said he'd wandered off last night, remember?"

"Yeah. Same way he wandered *in* last night. I'd never seen him before that. Sorry," she said before she closed the door, but she was looking at the dog when she said it.

Chapter Six

Libby watched Quinn disappear into the service station without a backward glance. The dog was happily thumping the seat with his tail but stopped abruptly when Libby looked at him.

"You did that on purpose," she said, not caring how crazy it sounded, even to her own ears. Frowning, she reached over to lift the tiny oval hanging from his thin, black collar. No address, no phone number. Just "PJ." How the hell had she missed that? Of course, she hadn't gotten close enough to him to even look for a collar, and almost as soon as he got in the car he'd curled up and fallen asleep. Still...

Sparing another brief glance back toward the service station entrance, Libby put the car in gear. She did not want to be still sitting here when Quinn came back out.

After talking to the lawyer the other day, she'd gone online to discover there were no hotels listed in Turtle Cove. She'd had better luck searching for bed-and-breakfasts, but when she called she quickly discovered that rooms were already getting scarce, many having been snatched up as long as a year ago by tourists planning a trip with no certainty of when the foliage would actually kick in. Thanks to someone's last-minute cancellation, she'd managed to snag what might be the last room in town at a place called The Cobbler's Inn. It was only available for two nights, but she couldn't imagine she'd need more time to accomplish what she needed to do.

With its white clapboard siding, slate-blue shutters and gable roof, the inn virtually reeked of New England. The wide flat arms of Adirondack chairs on the porch invited you to relax with a cup of coffee and admire the flowerbeds that, even in late September, offered an amazing festival of color with purple delphinium, scarlet and yellow snapdragons and deep red and golden chrysanthemum.

She retrieved her suitcase from the trunk, explaining to PJ—all the while feeling a little foolish for talking to a dog—that this was going to be a quick stop, and while he was free to go on his way, if he did decide to wait for her, she'd get them both something to eat when they left here.

Fat chance of that, she decided as she headed up the walkway. With all the squirrels running around here, he'd be off chasing one of them in no time and long gone before she came back out.

All she could think of, walking up the stairs to her room on the second floor, was a hot shower, dry clothes and food, in that order. Maybe not in quite that order she decided, setting her suitcase down and snatching up the small maple candy she found waiting on the bed pillow.

Savoring the sweetness and waiting for the sugar rush to kick in, she glanced around the room. It was on the small side, with enough room for the double bed, nightstand and a small upholstered chair in the corner beside a narrow writing desk. Decorated in soft shades of green and lavender, the place felt cozy rather than cramped and the lace-covered windows provided a view of the flowerbeds out front.

If she'd been here for a vacation she probably would have enjoyed it more, but she was anxious to get on with the business at hand. Digging Latham's phone number out of her purse, she noticed for the first time that there was no phone in the room. One hundred twenty-five dollars a night and no phone or television. *Thank God for cells*, she thought, retrieving hers from her bag.

She hadn't made an appointment because she wasn't sure what time she'd arrive, but glancing at the time on her cell phone she worried it might already be too late to get in to see him today. She was surprised when he answered the phone himself and, rather than offering her an appointment, simply assured her he would be there all evening. He gave her directions and said she should just stop by at her convenience.

Her idea of a quick shower was derailed when she stepped into the bathroom and saw the claw-foot tub and ridiculously thick, irresistibly soft, pale lavender towels waiting there. Rather than hurrying through a shower, she'd wait and indulge in a long, hot soak when she got back.

After hurriedly freshening up at the sink, she dusted on a little blusher and added some lip gloss and then dressed for the meeting in brown wool slacks and a cream-colored silk blouse. She slipped her feet into leather loafers, then gave herself one last look in the mirror while putting on simple pearl earrings, ran her fingers through her hair, and was ready to go.

PJ appeared to be dozing in one of the Adirondack chairs out front. He jumped down and followed her to the car without any prompting, taking his former place on the passenger seat as soon as she opened the car door.

Although Latham had insisted there was no hurry, she didn't feel comfortable with the idea of dawdling over a leisurely meal. Besides, with the dog to think of, a drive-through was probably the best bet. She made her way back to Main Street to a cute little fast-food place called Burger Depot. The building was designed to resemble a train car, and the drive-through menu offered items such as a Smokestack BBQ Burger, Choo-Choo Chili and a Little Caboose children's meal. She left the drive-through a few minutes later with a paper sack on the floorboard and drove to the park she had seen on the way into town.

The benches scattered around the park were still wet from

the recent rain, so she and the dog ate sitting in the car with the windows rolled down. PJ plowed through his burger in short order and then managed to sweet talk her out of a few of her fries before she let him out to amuse himself while she finished her meal at a more leisurely pace.

She stuffed the wrapper and napkins back into the paper sack. As an afterthought, she turned to retrieve the torn map and candy wrappers from the backseat and saw Quinn's hat.

Even after a quick glance around to confirm she was quite alone, she still felt a little self-conscious as she placed the hat on her head. She angled the rearview mirror to study the effect.

Not quite the same. She wasn't really surprised. Black had never been her best color, but even so, she wasn't the urban cowgirl type. She'd never imagined that a cowgirl, urban or otherwise, might be her type, but she couldn't deny she'd found something seriously sexy about this hat when it was on Quinn. Probably the fact that Quinn was under it.

She removed the hat, brushing away a bit of dog hair clinging to the brim. Quinn would probably still be at the service station. She could swing by there on the way to the lawyer's office, return the hat, maybe even straighten out that embarrassing confusion about the dog…

You mean the dog you said wasn't yours but that you're still driving around with?

She looked to see where he'd wandered to and spotted him a few feet away from a squirrel, the two of them eyeing each other with equal parts wariness and curiosity.

Oh, yeah. That was a *great* plan. Quinn would probably take one look at him—at her *with* him—and take off running in the other direction.

Leaning her head out the car window, she whistled the universally recognized signal for hey-dog-come-here. He hesitated for only a fraction of a second, just long enough to betray some mixed feelings about leaving the squirrel, but then tore across the park and bounded up onto the passenger seat beside her.

Since he had a tag, maybe one of the local vets would know who he belonged to. She'd make a few calls later and see. For now, since she was still driving around with the dog she'd insisted was not hers, the potential for further embarrassment was more than she felt like dealing with at the moment. With a little sigh, she returned the hat to the backseat.

Quinn would just have to live without it.

The attorney's office was not difficult to find. The reason Darryl Latham answered his own phone became clear as soon as she turned the corner and found herself in a residential neighborhood. He worked out of his home. She parked in the driveway behind a late model SUV and left PJ in the car with the front windows rolled down.

"You know the drill," she told him. "You can wait if you want to. I may be a while. If you're not here when I get back, I won't be looking for you."

PJ's response was an exaggerated yawn before he curled up on the seat. He would wait.

Lush green ferns spilled out of clay pots on either side of the wooden steps leading up to the gray, two-story house. More plants in oversized ceramic pots and hanging baskets kept company with cushioned white wicker furniture on the front porch. At the far end of the porch, a wooden swing hung suspended by chains from a beam overhead. A coffee cup sitting on the floor next to the swing suggested someone had been sitting out here earlier. She might have been tempted to sit down on the swing for a minute herself if Latham hadn't answered the door just then.

He looked older than he'd sounded on the phone. In his early to mid-sixties she guessed, with snow-white hair that was a stark contrast to his thick, black eyebrows. He was wearing a white shirt and blue paisley tie, and the cloth napkin crumpled in his hand told her she'd interrupted his dinner.

"Mr. Latham? I'm—"

"Miss Jackson," he said, shaking her hand. His grip was firm, short but enthusiastic. "Come in, come in." He stepped back, waving her into the house. "You caught me finishing my supper," he said closing the door behind them. "Have you eaten yet?"

"Yes, thank you. I stopped for something on the way over."

"I would have asked you to join me, but I'm fending for myself in the kitchen these days. I do all right, but nothing really fit for company if you know what I mean. Well, let's see if we can't get you taken care of."

She followed him into an office which, at a glance, seemed a study in controlled chaos. The surface of his oversized cherry desk was covered with short stacks of files. Behind the desk, taller stacks tilted precariously on a matching credenza. In one corner, a wingback chair sat next to a small, round table. There was barely enough room for the lamp and the half dozen or so law books stacked next to it, leaving a coffee mug perched perilously close to the edge. A few more books were strewn on the floor next to the chair along with several yellow legal pads covered with scribbled handwriting.

He gestured her into one of the two chairs in front of his desk as he sat down behind it. Slipping a pair of reading glasses from his shirt pocket, he reached for a manila folder that had a sheet of handwritten notes clipped to the front.

"After we spoke on the phone the other day, I made a few discreet inquiries. No one I spoke with had any recollection of Mr. Shepherd ever mentioning any family. I really don't think you need to be concerned with anyone disputing your claim to the property."

"But I don't *have* any claim to the property. Other than the Will, of course," she added, to save Latham from having to make that obvious point.

"In the eyes of the law, that's all you need."

"But surely there's some—"

"Miss Jackson, I do appreciate your confusion, and I sincerely wish I had answers for you, but I don't. All I can tell you is that the property is legally yours."

She'd expected there would be some kind of deed transferring title to the property, but Latham explained that everything was held in trust with her as the named beneficiary and could remain in the trust. He would simply resign as trustee and appoint her, or the fiduciary of her choosing, as his successor, in the same way Mr. Ferris had appointed him earlier. Alternatively, he told her she could petition the court to terminate the trust, but said he didn't see much point in going to the expense of doing that until she'd decided what she wanted to do with the property. Either way, he said, there could be benefits to leaving it in the trust and suggested she discuss it with her own attorney before making any decision.

He spent a few minutes going over with her the general status of the Estate accounts. There'd been sufficient cash to pay Mr. Shepherd's final expenses, the estate taxes and administrative fees. The remaining cash, he assured her, would be more than sufficient to the task of getting the property either back up and running or in shape to be put on the market.

"Why don't you just drive out there and take a look at the place," he told her. "I'll warn you, it's been closed up for a while. Mr. Shepherd had his stroke and went into the nursing home about two, maybe three years ago, if memory serves. A place stays empty that long around these parts, you're bound to have mice in the cellar, chipmunks in the attic, that sort of thing. Still, it's a prime bit of real estate. If you're inclined to sell it, you won't be lacking for offers, I can promise you that."

Libby hadn't begun to think that far ahead, but she nodded and accepted the envelope, fat with keys, that Latham slid across the desk toward her.

The road heading toward the lake felt narrow, probably due to the towering pine, birch and maple trees that closely bordered either side of the two-lane highway and filtered the late afternoon sun into a dapple of green-gold light. The going was slower than she'd anticipated due to the endless twists and turns, but it was easier to appreciate the beauty of the area when you weren't whizzing past everything at sixty miles an hour.

She could see why her stepfather would have liked it up here, for many of the same reasons her mother would not. While no one would ever have accused the slightly overweight insurance adjuster with the seriously receding hairline of being a great outdoorsman, he'd always shown an appreciation of nature his wife hadn't shared. For the most part, a vase of fresh-cut flowers on the dining room table was as close to nature as Madeline needed to be. She had no qualms about having them delivered by the local florist, but for Harry, it had been a matter of pride that they frequently came from the flowerbeds he spent his weekends diligently tending.

After his death, Madeline hired a yardman to maintain the lawn. It was several more months before she began to miss the frivolous pleasure of cut flowers, but when she did, she went back to getting weekly deliveries from the florist. The beds around the house still sported color from Harry's carefully chosen perennials, but they were not the explosions of color they had once been and it was hard to look at them without feeling like even the flowers missed Harry and his tender loving care.

Harry was not her biological father, but she'd been only three when he and her mother married. She'd loved him more than anything, but there was a part of her that had always believed if he loved her, truly loved her like a daughter, he would have adopted her.

When she turned eighteen she'd finally worked up the nerve to ask him. At first, the look on his face had her wishing she could go back and erase the question, but then he'd patted the seat next to him, and she'd sat down.

"I love you, Libby, like you were my very own. Always have. I'm sorry if anything I've done—or haven't done—ever made you doubt that. In my heart, I am your father. And a father's love runs deep. If I died tomorrow, sweetheart, I'd take that love with me to the grave and I'd still be loving you from the other side. That's how I know your real dad still loves you, too. I just could never bring myself to take the credit away from him for the most beautiful thing he left behind in this world. You have all the love in my heart, baby girl, and you always will. But you should be proud to carry your father's name, because that's all he

had time to give you."

Although she still found no real comfort in a gift from a man she never knew, she'd found some comfort that night in finally knowing Harry's reasoning.

"I miss you, Pops," she whispered aloud, and then closed the door on those memories as she saw the sign ahead marking the entrance to Shepherd's private drive.

She followed a gravel-strewn driveway for about twenty yards through the trees until a slight curve brought her first view of the lake and rekindled the enthusiasm of her youth. For a moment she was again that little girl, thrilled with all the adventure that woods and water might offer. How could she have forgotten about this place, she wondered, when being here again brought back such a flood of pure, unadulterated joy? Apparently sharing her excitement, PJ stood on the seat next to her, his tail swishing furiously.

The driveway opened onto an area large enough to accommodate a detached two-car garage as well as parking for the guest cottages that could only be reached beyond here by foot.

When she opened her door, PJ leapt across her lap and out of the car. She followed him, pausing to inhale deeply, savoring the sharp fragrance of pine and the pleasantly musty scent of rain-dampened earth. The surface of Lake Tolba rippled darkly in the setting sun. On the other side of the garage, nestled against the woods, was a modest Cape Cod house with a screened porch. Both the house and garage were covered in wood shingle siding with weathered white trim. Farther down, through the trees, she could just make out one of the guest cottages, its shingled exterior and white trim mimicking that of the main house.

She stood there for a long moment, undecided about which direction to go first, but in the end it was the wooden dock extending out over the water that finally drew her.

Lake Tolba, she knew from her excursion online, was an oddly shaped body of water approximately two miles long and a little more than half that at its widest point. Shepherd's property was at the north end of the lake where the water carved out a small, private cove against the heavily wooded landscape.

Kneeling at the edge of the dock, she reached down to trail her fingers through the water. There should be a boat here, she thought, standing and shaking cold droplets from her hand. A rowboat. Or a canoe. There used to be, she knew, having a vague memory of Harry taking her and her mother out in one. After a bit of pleading and over her mother's objections, he'd let her try her hand at rowing, an experiment she quickly lost interest in when she found out she didn't have enough muscle for it.

Turning from the lake brought the house back into view. Like the painted trim, the wood shingle siding that had probably once been stained a rich brown was faded after at least a few years of abuse by the rain and winter weather. There were some holes in the screen around the porch and a couple places where the corners were loose and flapping in the breeze, but for the most part it appeared to be in pretty good shape, considering.

The raucous cry of a crow overhead drew her attention to the chimney on the far side of the house. That meant a fireplace, and brought to mind an image of the lake frozen over as it would be in winter. Everything covered in white. The wind whipping through the pines. Shepherd snug in his house with a fire burning in the fireplace and a pot of stew on the stove. A small pot, she thought, for a man with no family.

The cozy little image suddenly seemed a sad one as she thought of him spending long winter nights alone in that house. The summers may have been busy with guests staying in the cabins, but the winters...

She let the porch's screen door swing shut behind her just for the nostalgic sound of wood striking wood. The porch floor was scuffed and marred except for a discolored rectangular patch at the door, evidence of a mat that must have sat there for many years. She spotted it in a corner next to an old coffee can that was half-filled with sand topped with cigarette butts. An empty beer bottle with the label half peeled off and a few dented Coke cans were scattered around along with crumpled food wrappers and one worn navy KED with a hole in the toe. Local kids, she deduced. She wasn't surprised. If this place had been empty for two or three years, it had probably become a prime location for hookups among the local teens.

PJ sat patiently by her feet, his tail sweeping the floor as she worked her way through the various keys Latham had given her until she found one that fit the deadbolt. There was a little bit of resistance when she turned the knob and pushed, but with a nudge of her shoulder against the door, it opened. A beeping noise reminded her of the alarm system and she punched in the numbers Latham had given her to silence it.

"Now don't go getting yourself into trouble," she cautioned PJ as he dashed past her. She flipped the light switch inside the door and when nothing happened she pushed the door open wide to let in as much of the fading light as possible.

To the left of the entry, a swinging door led to the kitchen where she almost tripped over a broom lying across the floor. She picked it up and leaned it against the wall before setting her purse down. She pushed back the curtain covering the window over the sink and found herself looking out at the lake. Even cast into shadows by the setting sun, it looked lovely and peaceful and provided a view that would make having to stand here doing dishes bearable.

The kitchen was large enough to accommodate an oak pedestal table at one end. Pots and pans hung from an iron rack suspended above a work island. The refrigerator was modern and generally nondescript, but the stove—the stove was remarkable even to a layman like her. White and black porcelain, it had chrome levers, six gas burners and two ovens. It looked ancient and probably weighed a ton. A spice rack hanging on the wall over the stove displayed a collection of delightfully kitsch salt and pepper shakers while several vintage cookie jars were displayed along the tops of the cabinets.

The overall effect was one of warmth and charm and efficiency, but it was a bit of a shock. She'd been expecting an empty house. Of course, if she was the only beneficiary of the estate, there would have been no one else to do anything with the contents of the house. Still it added to her feeling of trespassing and the sense that any moment now someone might walk in and demand to know what she was doing here.

Opposite the kitchen, on the southeast corner of the house, the living room seemed part library, part art gallery. Floor-to-ceiling bookshelves, already heavily burdened with books, also displayed an eclectic collection of curios and objets d'art. The rest of the wall space held what appeared to be original paintings. Mostly watercolors, they had a decidedly regional feel, all of them scenes of rural or coastal New England and fiery displays of fall foliage. The furniture, upholstered in warm earth tones and comfortably worn from years of use, was of the fat and friendly overstuffed variety that begged to be sat on.

At the back of the house, two bedrooms shared a single large bath. One of the bedrooms, cozily cluttered with a small roll top desk and more books and mementos, was obviously Shepherd's. The other, while pleasantly furnished, was a little generic looking, suggesting it might have been used as a guest room.

The tiny click of claws caught her ear. She turned and followed the sound back to what she had decided was Shepherd's bedroom.

"PJ?" It took a few seconds before she spotted his little face peeking out at her from under the edge of the quilted bedspread.

"Come on, fella. Time to go."

In response, the spread dropped as he moved back under the bed. "PJ," she said, exasperated. "Come on, we don't have time for this. *PJ,*" she said sharply. "I mean it. Come out of there." He emerged to give her a look that was all too easy to interpret: *You're no fun.*

"So I've been told," she told him. "Come on, it's going to be getting dark soon and I want to get out of here while I can still see."

Returning to the kitchen to retrieve her bag, she noticed a door she'd missed when she'd been in there earlier, next to the refrigerator. A broom closet, she speculated, or maybe a pantry.

The hinges squeaked in mild protest as she opened the door and found a flight of wooden stairs leading down into the cellar. Stepping onto the landing, she peered down into the darkness, inhaling the cool, slightly musty scent that brought back memories of summer visits to Harry's parents' house and afternoons spent playing in the basement when it was too wet to go outside. It had been a wondrous place to her as a child, with shelves stocked with jars of vegetables, fruit preserves and cinnamon apples Nana Peerman canned herself, and a chest freezer that seemed to contain an endless supply of Libby's favorite fudge ripple ice cream.

Sentimental memories of her grandparents' magical cellar tweaked her curiosity about what she might find in this one. Probably no cinnamon apples, she knew. Still...

Without expectation, she flipped the light switch on and off a few times, vexed by the lack of electricity. Then she remembered her flashlight.

Stepping back into the kitchen, she dug through her knapsack for the rubbery little penlight and squeezed it experimentally. It didn't give off much light and was probably better suited for what she typically used it for—rummaging around in the bottomless pit of a knapsack she called a purse—but it was enough to afford her a quick peek and take the edge off her curiosity.

The temperature dropped a few degrees as she descended into the basement. She could easily make out a washer and dryer next to a utility sink and an empty upright freezer with the door blocked open. Air ducts snaked out along the ceiling from an oil furnace in the corner. Pretty standard fare as cellars went and not a cinnamon apple in sight. There were several cardboard boxes in one corner, though, some of them fairly large, which might be interesting to investigate after the electricity was turned on.

She'd turned to head back upstairs, but moved a little faster when she heard PJ's nails clicking across the vinyl floor of the kitchen overhead. There wasn't much trouble he could get into down here, but she didn't relish playing hide-and-seek with him in the dark.

She heard more sounds coming from the door above. Sniffing, snorting. A couple of canine sneezes followed by a familiar creaking that didn't fully register until a split second before the cellar door banged shut, cutting off what little light had been coming in.

Now that her penlight wasn't competing with the light coming down from the kitchen, it cut a slightly stronger path through the darkness. She reached the top of the stairs, turned the doorknob and pushed. The door opened less than inch before stopping abruptly. She shoved harder with no better result. *What the hell...?*

Peering through the small crack of open door only afforded her a view of the back corner of the refrigerator, but something down at the floor caught her eye. She squatted down to get a closer look, aiming the flashlight at it.

The broom handle.

The broom she'd propped up in the corner had fallen over and was lying in front of the cellar door. She shoved at the door again, but with the broom handle apparently anchored behind the refrigerator, no matter how hard she pushed, the door wouldn't budge.

She tried to get a finger under the broom handle to lift it, but the gap in the door didn't allow it past the knuckle and she could barely flick the handle with her fingertip. Even as she thought about using something else—A key? A pen?—to reach through, she remembered her purse was sitting on the kitchen counter. As if on cue, her cell phone rang inside it. After a few rings, the call kicked over to voice mail. In the silence that followed, she heard a soft whine and the tip of PJ's dark, wet nose appeared at the narrow opening.

"Hey, little guy," she said, kneeling down to put her fingers to the opening, momentarily cheered by the companionship, such as it was. "I don't suppose you have any bright ideas for how to get me out of here?"

The nose disappeared.

"PJ?"

The delicate clicking sound of claws traveled across the floor, then a muted thunka-thunka-thunka sound as the door to the hallway swung shut after PJ apparently pushed his way through. A moment later she heard the muffled wooden bang of the porch's screen door closing.

"I'll take that as a no." Okay, so it was up to her to get herself out of here, which meant finding a way to move that broom.

Without her purse, what did she have to work with? She was in a cellar. Time to take a closer look.

Starting over by the washer, she found half empty bottles of laundry soap and fabric softener. A chipped coffee cup on the back of the utility sink held a hodgepodge of things, probably retrieved from pockets before laundering. She scattered the contents in the sink. Coins, screws and buttons. A few thumbtacks. Ticket stubs and a couple of batteries. Two pen caps, but no pen.

In the cabinet under the sink she found spare lightbulbs, a hot water bottle, dog shampoo and flea dip. When she moved aside a replacement pad for a sponge mop, a fat, brown spider skittered away and she almost dropped the penlight in her hasty retreat from the sink.

"Okay, okay," she said out loud. "It's just a bug." Just an icky, disgusting, creepy crawly...she couldn't prevent a quick shudder of disgust.

She eyed the boxes. They were sealed with packing tape that proved difficult to peel back, but eventually she got one open. She pulled out the bristly green object lying on top.

Branches to an artificial Christmas tree.

Great. If she was still stuck down here come Christmas, she could decorate. She tossed the branch back in and moved on to the next box.

Two more boxes of artificial tree limbs had her opening a fourth simply because she couldn't believe it would contain yet another Christmas tree.

It did.

She swept the beam of light over the remaining boxes, easily fifteen or twenty of them. Was it possible? Three boxes later she decided it might be. Tiny ones, tall ones. Bushy ones, scrawny ones. Even one silver one. But Christmas trees, all.

She was wondering if there was anything to be gained in opening any more boxes when her penlight winked out. She shook it, squeezed again and was rewarded with less than a couple of seconds of feeble, fading light and then nothing.

She stood there, panic bubbling up for a long, paralyzing moment until the sound of her cell phone ringing again snapped her out of it.

"Libby Jackson, you get a grip," she commanded herself aloud. Panic was not an option. She needed to stay calm. She needed to think. What would get her out of here? Something thin enough to slip through the crack in the door. Something long enough and strong enough to lift the broom out of the way. A hanger or a screwdriver. Even a pen would probably do the trick. Just a *stick*, for God's sake. Just a simple…stick.

She felt around to find one of the open boxes. Pulling out a branch, she ran her hand down to the end where a two-or three-inch length of stiff wire would attach the artificial branch to a hole drilled into an artificial trunk.

Her urge to race to the door was frustrated not just by the darkness, but by the realization she was no longer sure where the door was. In searching through the boxes and moving them aside, she'd completely lost her sense of direction in the cellar.

The boxes had been stacked in the far left corner as she came down the stairs. Stretching out her hand, she felt around until she found a stack of still-sealed boxes. That meant the stairs—she turned slowly, focusing on a mental picture of what she'd seen before her flashlight died—had to be somewhere in…this direction.

With slow, shuffling steps, she moved toward where she envisioned the stairs to be. One step…two…three… Nothing. Another few steps and she walked face first into a whispery stickiness that her skin recognized even before her brain identified it as spider web. She jerked back reflexively, catching her heel on a rough patch in the concrete floor. Arms flailing, she went down, her right hand striking something hard as she fell.

"Son of a *bitch*!" Her right arm was tingling from her hand up to her elbow. She flexed her fingers experimentally, relieved that nothing seemed to be broken, then sat there for a long moment, wiping bits of a spider web from her face.

This sucked. Totally and completely *sucked*.

But on the bright side…

She patted the floor next to her and found the bottom step that she'd struck when she fell. Retrieving the branch, she hauled herself to her feet and headed up the stairs.

Night was falling. There was little difference in the light coming through the slim crack and the darkness of the cellar. She wondered how long she had been stuck there, but pushed the thought aside. All that mattered was that she was getting out now. She turned the branch around to poke the wire end through the opening and under the broom handle. Lifting it, she felt the broom handle move. Yes! Just a few more inches…

The broom struck something and stopped moving.

No! No, no, *no*! She tried to force it, but the broom wouldn't budge. "*Damn* it!" Without thinking, she banged at the door with her injured hand, a mistake that brought a flash of pain and tears to her eyes. She dropped the useless branch and heard the broom handle fall to the floor.

The doorknob. She couldn't lift the broom because the doorknob was in the way.

As the seriousness of her situation hit her, she felt real panic begin to set in. No one even knew she was here. When he didn't hear from her, Latham would probably get curious, but how long would that take? If the woman at the bed-and-breakfast even noticed she didn't come back tonight, she probably wouldn't think anything about it. And if she did begin to wonder, what would she do? Call the police? Except for Latham, no one here knew anything about her that would connect her to this house, and no one would know to ask Latham anything. She'd put her home number on the registration form at the inn, but if they called all they'd get was her voice on the answering machine.

Her cell phone rang again and she wanted to scream.

If she only had some *light*. How the hell was she supposed to find anything down here to help her out of this mess if she couldn't even see her hand in front of her face? Too bad she didn't smoke, she thought bitterly. Then she'd at least have a lighter or some matches. *Yeah, and those would probably be in your purse too.* But thinking about cigarettes reminded her about the coffee can turned ashtray out on the porch which in turn reminded her of the other evidence that someone had been using this place as a hangout, possibly in the not-too-distant past. Which meant they might come back. And she'd left the door open. If nothing else, curiosity at the open door would bring them inside, right? She only had to wait. The logical side of her brain knew that the likelihood of anyone coming tonight, just when she needed them, was slim, but the part of her brain busy with trying not to think about hunger and thirst and the things she couldn't see crawling toward her in the dark teased her with the thought that rescue could be only moments away if she just stayed alert and listened for it.

She sat down on the top step with her back against the door. Eventually she closed her eyes just to stop herself from straining to see into the impenetrable darkness, but still, she listened. She listened until the silence weighed on her eardrums like a tangible force.

Eventually, leaning against the door, she slept.

Chapter Seven

Quinn stared with unseeing eyes into the flames of her campfire, close enough to feel the skin on her face tightening in the heat generated by the blaze. The warmth of the fire was mirrored by the slow burn of tequila sliding down her throat.

The fire reached a pocket of sap inside one of the logs. It sizzled and popped, and the logs shifted slightly sending up a small shower of sparks.

It had been a mistake coming here like this, all purpose and no plan. It was too early to do what she wanted to do, but too late to consider doing anything else because she'd already decided this was the right thing, and probably her best chance of making some kind of peace with her past.

She drained the contents of her coffee mug then poured another couple of inches from the uncapped bottle sitting in the dirt next to her. There were a lot of things you couldn't count on in life, but hootch, even the cheap stuff, was always reliable in a pinch. Just the ticket when you needed to turn off for a while. Quit thinking about all the things you'd done wrong. All the things you could never make right. All the years when she hadn't cared one way or the other.

Frustrated with the direction of her thoughts, she picked up a small stone lying on the ground next to her and flicked it angrily into the fire.

"Baby, why are you trying to hurt that poor tree?"

"It's just a fucking tree," she said, teeth clenched to hold back what felt dangerously close to being a sob. She let loose another softball-sized rock that struck the trunk with enough force to send bits of bark flying. "You can't hurt a fucking tree."

"Quinn Rochelle, you watch your mouth." Her mother's voice was gentle but firm, as was the hand that captured hers when she hauled back intending to let another rock fly. "And you're wrong, baby. A tree's a living thing. Anything that lives can be hurt." She took the rock from Quinn's unresisting fingers. It landed with a dull thud in the dirt. "Just because it can't hurt you back, doesn't give you the right."

"Then what gives him *the right?" She clenched her fists, wishing for the rock back because she needed to throw something. She wanted to push, to hit, to hurt—something. "How come he gets to hurt everyone and everything and no one ever makes* him *stop?" Her angry shout turned into a broken sob. "Why don't you ever make* him *stop?"*

Instead of answering, her mother simply pulled her into her arms. Torn between needing to hang on and wanting to push her away, she simply stood there crying and ashamed of her own tears.

"Tell me what happened, Quinn." Her mother's voice, gentle and low, seemed to promise that it was all going to be all right, but she was long past being comforted by that sort of childish illusion.

"She's gone, Mom. Lupe's gone and I didn't even get to tell her goodbye. She thought I hated her, and I didn't even get to tell her goodbye."

"Baby, she knows you don't hate her." Her mother's words, while spoken soothingly, sounded too mechanical to be comforting. It was only further proof that she really didn't understand what was going on.

"No she doesn't. *I had to let her think that. I had to* make *her think that. And I did." Choking on tears, she could barely get the words out. "I did what he wanted, but he took her away anyway. I hate him. I hate him!"*

"Oh, baby," crooned her mother, stroking her hair back from her damp face. "I know it hurts now, but you've got to trust me when I tell you she wasn't right for you."

She did push away then, devastated by the sound of those words coming from her mother's mouth. "You sound just like him! It wasn't true, what he said about her! I know she—"

"Quinn, no." Her mother caught her face in her hands, holding her there to look in her eyes. "I don't mean she wasn't good enough for you. I mean she just wasn't the right one for you. She wasn't ever going to love you the way you needed her to, Quinn, because she still needed someone to love her."

"But I did love her. I do love her. That's why he made her leave." Why couldn't she see? Why wouldn't she listen?

"I know you believe that, baby. Maybe even he believes that. But it wasn't your father that made her leave. It was just…" Her mother seemed to be searching for words. "Life. Her life called to her, and when that happens…well, you just have to follow. You'll understand that one day."

"No I won't, because he's not ever going to let me have my life," she said, resigned to the certainty of it. But her mother had only smiled, her fingers lightly sweeping away the trail of her daughter's tears.

"Baby, when the time comes, he won't be able to stop you."

It hadn't been long after that she'd tried to run away for the first time. She hadn't really had a plan then either, just a desperate need to get gone and a juvenile certainty that *the time had come.* But she hadn't realized how difficult it would be for the only child of the town's chief of police to run away when there were just too many folks eager to ingratiate themselves with her father by being the one to bring her back. It had taken two more similarly thwarted attempts that same year before she accepted the futility of trying to escape.

After that, she'd worked very hard for a while at keeping her head down and her mouth shut, encouraging her father to believe he'd broken her. It wasn't a hard act to pull off, really, once she realized she had only to follow her mother's example. Except her mother's subservience wasn't an act, and Quinn's emotions toward her those last few years had fluctuated wildly between love and hate, pity and contempt, sometimes on a daily basis, and she hadn't particularly cared if her mother knew it.

Thinking about it now only brought on a refreshed sense of guilt and that was an emotion she couldn't handle anymore, not tonight. If she could just quit *thinking* about it, maybe she could get some sleep and when she woke up...well, she'd get through tomorrow when it got here. At the moment all she wanted was to quit thinking about all the things she'd done wrong, all the things she could never make right. Because caring about it now... well, that was just too little, too late, wasn't it?

Raising the mug to her lips, she inhaled the sweet, sharp scent that offered a chance to forget, if only for a little while.

Then, with a resigned sigh, she turned it over and poured forgetfulness out onto the dirt.

She did the same thing with the bottle, watching the rest of the amber liquid soak into the ground before she tossed the bottle aside. That was when she noticed the somber brown eyes staring at her from the edge of the clearing.

Libby awoke with the sensation of falling, unable to catch herself before the back of her head slammed against the floor. She yelped, more in surprise than from any real pain, but before her mind could register where she was or what had just happened, she was blinded by a bright light shining in her face.

A firm hand on her shoulder pressed her back down. She struck out at the dark shape hovering over her only to have her wrist caught in a vise-like grip.

"Will you stop?" demanded an exasperated voice. "I just want to make sure you aren't hurt."

She stopped struggling because the voice was...familiar. "I'm fine," she said hoarsely, squinting again as the flashlight was aimed directly into her eyes.

"Quit squinting so I can see your eyes."

"Quit shining the damn light in my face and I'll quit squinting."

Above her, Quinn sighed heavily, but aimed the flashlight away from her face.

"I'm fine, but the doorjamb is digging into my back. Will you just let me up, please?" She released a short hiss of pain when Quinn took her hand to help her.

"I thought you said you weren't hurt?" It sounded more like an accusation than a question.

"I'm not," she insisted, getting to her feet. "I just banged my hand on something down there. Nothing's broken, it's just sore."

"Let me see it," Quinn said in a tone that didn't suffer arguing.

She held her hand out, looking at it herself for the first time as the beam of the flashlight revealed an ugly bruise already taking shape along the outer edge.

"Can you move your fingers?"

She wiggled her fingers, tentatively at first, then with more enthusiasm. "See? Fine, just like I said." She looked at Quinn, her told-you-so smile slipping a bit. "What are you doing here?"

Quinn's eyebrows lifted. "Besides rescuing you, you mean?"

"Yes. I mean, no. I mean—look, don't think I'm not grateful," she managed finally. "It's just, how did you know?"

"Why don't you ask him," suggested Quinn.

Libby's gaze followed the tilt of her head to see PJ sitting by the refrigerator staring back at her. Her eyes traveled from Quinn to PJ and back again, skepticism giving way to patent disbelief. "Oh, come on. You don't really expect me to believe…" She couldn't even finish the question, it was just too ridiculous. "How would he even know where to find you?"

Quinn offered a careless shrug. "Same place he found me last night."

"But how would he—I mean, *why* would he—" The question along with her curiosity faded when Quinn removed her jacket and wrapped it around her shoulders.

She'd obviously looked cold, but she hadn't realized how cold she was until the jacket, warmed by Quinn's body heat, enveloped her. She closed her eyes, savoring the sudden comfort of it, and it was in that moment of hedonistic bliss that her stomach chose to issue an exceptionally loud and astonishingly prolonged gurgle.

"How long were you stuck down there anyway?"

"What time is it?"

Quinn consulted her watch. "A little past midnight."

Not as long as she'd feared it was going to be. Still, "Too long." Her stomach echoed the sentiment with enthusiasm. She pulled the jacket tight around her, hoping to muffle the sound. Quinn's amusement appeared to be on par with her embarrassment. "I'll grab something when I get back to town."

"Hate to break it to you," said Quinn, "but everything's going to be closed."

Closed? Everything?

Quinn's smile was sympathetic. "Don't worry, I've got stuff back at my camp I can fix for you."

"Oh, no, I couldn't. Really, you've gone to more than enough trouble already. I'm sure I'll be able to get something at the inn." She would, even if she had to sneak into the kitchen to do it. Although that presented yet another problem.

"It's no trouble," Quinn said from behind her.

When she'd checked in, she'd been told they locked the door at midnight and to just let them know if she was going to be later than that. At the time she hadn't thought it would be an issue. Maybe it still wasn't too late. She retrieved her cell phone from her bag on the counter. Dead.

"Just consider it a thank you for the ride you're going to give me."

She had to be a good twenty minutes away from town, but maybe if she hurried—

She looked at Quinn. "They weren't able to fix your truck?"

"No, they fixed it," said Quinn. "It just would have been a little tricky trying to follow fur face through the woods in it."

Oh. Right.

"Hey, if it's a problem…" said Quinn, obviously noticing a hesitation on her part.

"Don't be silly, that's the least I can do," she assured her, meaning it. She'd worry about getting back into the inn later.

Quinn and PJ waited on the porch steps while she locked the front door.

"So is this where you stayed last time you were here?" Quinn asked as they got into the car. Quinn tried to shoo PJ into the backseat, but he only wiggled back once she had her seatbelt fastened to take up residence in her lap.

"Yes and no. There's a few guest cottages over there," she explained with a nod in the general direction, although nothing more than trees was visible.

"Doesn't look like it's been open for a while," Quinn noted.

She followed Quinn's gaze back to the house which, even in the dark, was obviously in mild disrepair. "Yeah, it's been a few years."

They were at the end of the drive before she realized how incongruous the situation must seem when only a few hours earlier she hadn't even known where the lake was and said she hadn't been here in years.

"I just found out this week that I inherited the place. That's why I came up here, to check it out. I really only intended to take a quick look around tonight, but..." Well, they both knew how that had turned out. "Lucky for me you were still around."

"Oh, I think PJ deserves most of the credit on this one," Quinn told her. "Not like I would've wandered out this way without him."

Following Quinn's directions, she drove them to Quinn's campsite, turning off onto an unmarked road she would have missed in the dark if Quinn hadn't pointed it out. After a few hundred yards it opened onto a clearing at the edge of the lake. She pulled in behind the truck that was parked there, a sleek black model with a matching camper shell and Nevada plates. Black was obviously her color. Reminded of the hat, she retrieved it from the backseat and brought it over to Quinn who'd already dropped the tailgate and was pulling a big red and white ice chest forward.

She set the hat down on the tailgate.

"Hey, thanks," said Quinn, who was cleaning her hands disinfectant gel. She pulled a loaf of bread and a package of luncheon meat from the ice chest, and then angled the flashlight on the tailgate to better see what she was doing.

She liked Quinn's hands, she decided, watching her put together a sandwich with quiet efficiency. The way the tendons and veins shifted under the skin to create shadowed ridges in the beam of the flashlight. Like her eyes, Quinn's close-cropped hair was dark brown. It looked like it might be a little curly if she let it get long enough, which could be precisely why she didn't. Everything about her suggested she valued function over form, from the scuffed but sturdy-looking hiking boots to the faded Levi's. She'd bet there wasn't a pair of designer jeans anywhere in the woman's closet. Even her sweatshirt was simply a sweatshirt, with no sports logo or clever saying splashed across the front. No frills. Practical. Yet all that practicality came together to form a rather striking package. Even her name...

"Quinn." She didn't realize she'd said it aloud until Quinn looked at her expectantly. "Is that—short for something?"

"Nope. Just Quinn." When PJ jumped up and bounced against her leg, she obliged him by dropping a piece of ham which he caught out of the air.

"It suits you."

"Suits me?" said Quinn, digging around in the ice chest and fishing out a package of cheese.

"I think so. Slightly exotic. A little sharp around the edges."

"Exotic?"

"I said slightly exotic," she reminded her, making a note of the fact that Quinn didn't question sharp around the edges. "You've got to admit, it's not like, say..." She hesitated, trying to summon the most vanilla name she could think of.

"Libby?" suggested Quinn.

"Actually, I was going to say Jane," she informed her, a bit stung. "And for your information, my name's not really Libby."

Quinn passed her the sandwich. "An alias? I'm intrigued."

"Very funny. It's short for Liberty."

"Liberty," Quinn said like she was trying it on for size.

"Liberty Larue Jackson. Not quite as exotic as yours, maybe, but..." She shrugged, raising the sandwich to take a bite, but stopped, distracted by the look on Quinn's face. "What?"

"Liberty Larue?"

"Larue was my mother's maiden name."

Quinn turned her face away, but not before Libby saw the smirk she was trying to hide.

"Why is that funny?" she demanded.

"Well, it's—not," said Quinn, obviously changing her mind in mid-sentence. She nodded toward the sandwich in Libby's hand. "I thought you were hungry. You going to eat that or hold it?"

"I'm not doing anything until you tell me why you're laughing at me."

Quinn managed to look a little shocked. "I wasn't laughing at you. Whatever gave you that idea?" Her lips curved. "See how that works?"

Refusing to be distracted by that slightly crooked smile that already felt warmly familiar, she deliberately arched one eyebrow toward her hairline and held it there until Quinn caved. It didn't take nearly as long as she'd expected.

"It's just...Liberty Larue." Something about the way she said it seemed to imply *isn't it obvious*? "It sounds like a stripper's name."

Libby could only stare for a moment. "It does not."

"I'm not talking about some sleazy topless dancer in a back street bar. I mean, you know—one of those classy strippers."

"Classy stripper," she repeated, carefully enunciating each syllable to be sure she'd heard correctly.

"Yeah. You know—what did they call it, back in the fifties? Burlesque. That'd be a hell of a stage name, don't you think? Liberty Larue. I can see you now, wearing some strapless gown slit up to here and those stockings with that little garter belt gizmo. Your hair all gathered up," she said, one hand making a vague swirling motion, "so you could just pull out a pin or two and shake it down. Maybe some of those long satin gloves to peel off nice and slow and then toss to some poor schmuck to make him think he'd caught your eye." Quinn's gaze slid toward Libby's feet and then back up again. "Oh yeah. I can definitely see it," she said around a shameless grin.

"Really," Libby said dryly. "Got a thing for strippers, do you?" She was a little shocked by how normal her voice sounded considering she was pretty certain Quinn had just succeeded in dressing and undressing her. It was hard to know whether to feel insulted or flattered when at the moment all she really felt was... hot.

Quinn laughed, her bawdy grin melting into one of simple amusement that seemed directed more at herself than at Libby. "No, not especially. But that name," she said, shaking her head with a look that insisted she knew what she was talking about. "That's a stripper's name." She only laughed again when Libby, rather than arguing, narrowed her eyes and took a very deliberate bite out of the sandwich.

"Oh my God." She covered her mouth with one hand to hide the fact she was talking with her mouth full. "This is *so* good." Ham and swiss with too much mustard, but it was the most delicious sandwich she'd ever eaten in her life and she took another bite before she'd even swallowed the first. "God, I was hungry. Thank you!"

Quinn gave a brief nod of you're welcome and then turned back to the ice chest. "I'm afraid your choices are beer or water," she said, holding up a bottle of each.

"Beer's good."

Quinn twisted off the cap before handing it to her. She put the bottle of water back in the ice chest, seemed to hesitate for a second, and then pulled it back out again to set it on the tailgate while she repacked the ice chest.

PJ, evidently understanding that the food was about to disappear, pounced against Quinn's leg again. She tossed one more piece of ham down to him. "Now that's it," she said firmly, and closed the ice chest before shoving it back in the bed of the truck. "Why don't you go get something to drink," she said when PJ continued to dance at her feet. She waved her hand in the direction of the lake. "Go on."

Obediently, PJ turned and trotted off toward the water. Quinn hopped up to sit on the tailgate and uncapped the bottle of water.

"I think you should keep him," said Libby who'd been watching the exchange with a bemused smile on her face.

"What?"

"PJ," she said, taking a seat on the tailgate next to Quinn. "I think you should keep him. He likes you."

Quinn snorted. "He's a dog. He'd like anyone who tossed a little meat his way."

"That's not true."

Quinn looked at her.

"Okay, it's probably true. But I really do think he likes you." She watched him for a moment, sniffing along the water's edge. "You want to know the real reason I stopped the car this afternoon?" She went on to explain how PJ had come to be in her car in the first place and his reaction when he'd spotted Quinn. "I, of course, came to the brilliant conclusion that he recognized you. It never occurred to me you'd think I was stopping to pick you up."

"So when I recognized him—"

"*And* called him by name," she reminded her. "It just made sense. At least until you got out of the car and I realized you weren't taking him with you."

Quinn choked out a short bark of laughter. "Oh my God. I thought you were nuts."

"I kind of picked up on that."

"Hell, I almost took him just because I was afraid to leave him with you."

"Good thing you didn't. I'd still be stuck in that damn cellar." She heard herself saying it, but still couldn't quite believe it.

Quinn must have seen the doubt on her face, because she

said, "Yes, he really came and got me. Did the whole barking and tugging on my pant leg bit. He was a very determined little guy." She paused to take a sip of her water. "Personally, I can't believe you're trying to get rid of him."

"I'm not. I mean, he's not mine to get rid of."

Quinn looked at her. "Excuse me, but were you or were you not just trying to give him to me?"

"I wasn't trying to *give* him to you. I just said you should keep him."

"So you're giving away someone *else's* dog."

Libby tried but quickly gave up any attempt at looking offended. "Well, he seems kind of determined to be with one of us, and I certainly can't keep him. I've got a fourth floor walk-up, and I'm not about to walk the streets of New York carrying a bag of dog poop."

"Well, sorry to break it to you, but pets are not on my to do list this lifetime."

"Why not?"

"What difference does it make? You said they're not on yours either."

"I didn't say that. I just don't think an apartment in the city would be a good environment for a dog that's used to living free and loose in the country."

"But that's not what you said."

"It's what I meant." Well, that and the dog poop thing.

There was a moment of silence while Libby chewed a bite of her sandwich and Quinn sipped her water. Libby assumed the subject was closed and decided it was probably just as well. But then Quinn, who'd apparently continued to think about it, said, "That is not what you meant. You meant—"

"I just don't know how you can expect me to believe you don't like dogs," said Libby, cutting her off, "when I've seen how good you are with this one."

"I never said I didn't *like* dogs."

"Well, if you like—"

"No," said Quinn.

"But don't you think—"

"*No*," said Quinn.

When Libby fell silent, Quinn couldn't help feeling a smug thrill of victory for having won the argument, even though the look on Libby's face didn't exactly concede defeat. The pouting little scowl disappeared, though, when Libby took another bite of the sandwich.

She doubted that Wonder Bread sandwiches and Budweiser were Libby's standard dinner fare. No, she looked like she was probably more accustomed to sipping white wine at expensive restaurants where Quinn couldn't have pronounced half the things on the menu. Still, she'd taken to this impromptu tailgate party enthusiastically enough. Had to give her credit for that.

At just that moment, Libby popped the last of the sandwich into her mouth, her shoulders lifting on what sounded like a sigh of satisfaction. Quinn took a sip of water to hide her smile.

"I'd be glad to make you another if you want," she offered. Libby smiled and for a second she thought she might say yes.

"No, but thank you."

"You sure? I got two rides, seems only fair you get two sandwiches," she teased.

"I'm sure." Libby smiled. "Rain check?"

Quinn nodded, knowing that was one rain check that would never be collected on.

Libby reached up to tuck a few stray strands of hair behind her ear. "I guess I should get going."

"You don't have to rush off." The words flew out of her mouth without warning, with an earnestness that embarrassed her and seemed to surprise Libby. She just didn't want her to go. Not yet. Not when she was just starting to enjoy the company. She didn't, as a rule, enjoy people. It was usually more a matter of tolerating them and lately she hadn't even done much of that.

Still, she probably shouldn't have said anything. After driving half the day and being camped out in some cold cellar half the night, Libby didn't need to spend the other half sitting on some hard, cold tailgate.

Suddenly realizing what was missing, Quinn hopped off the tailgate. "Why don't I get the fire going?"

"Oh God, why didn't you say something?"

She looked back and saw Libby taking off her jacket.

"Put that back on."

"Seriously," said Libby following her. "Mine's in the car. I wasn't even thinking. Why didn't you say something?"

"I need to get this started anyway," said Quinn, squatting down beside the small circle of stones. Before she'd taken off after the dog earlier, she had extinguished the fire by unceremoniously throwing a bucket of lake water on the blaze. What she had now was a mess of soggy ashes and wet wood. She removed the wet, charred wood and set it aside, then arranged fresh kindling, adding branches as the dry bits of wood caught flame.

She stood, and turning stumbled into Libby. An automatic step backward threatened to put her in the campfire. Libby's hand shot out to stop her, and Quinn's fingers reflexively closed around her arm, reclaiming her balance.

"I'm so sorry!" said Libby, wide-eyed. "That was completely my fault."

"It's okay. I just didn't realize you were right behind me." She released Libby's arm and saw the hand-sized black smear of soot she left on the sleeve of Libby's pretty-sure-it's-silk, probably-cost-more-than-one-of-my-tires blouse. *Shit.* "Sorry, looks like I, uh…"

A brief grimace betrayed Libby's dismay before she caught herself and turned it into a weak smile. "Hey, it's just a shirt," she said, and brushing at her sleeve succeeded only in transferring some of the soot to her own hand.

She felt bad about the blouse, she really did. But there was something about the sight of Libby standing there looking more annoyed by her blackened fingers than by the ruined blouse that made her want to laugh, and a little snicker escaped before she could stop herself.

Libby's eyes and one eyebrow lifted in her direction.

"You think this is funny, do you?" A glimmer of humor in her eyes belied the implied threat in her tone.

"Well, it does kind of complete the look."

"And what look would that be?"

"Oh, you know. This whole street urchin, chimney sweep thing you've got going on. Spider webs in your hair," she said, reaching out to remove a bit of the sticky stuff. "And I don't know what all was in that cellar, but you brought enough of it out on your face to start a new one." She rubbed a thumb over Libby's cheek as if to remove the light smudge there, deliberately replacing it with a darker smear of soot.

Too late, Libby batted her hand away. She wiped at where Quinn's finger had trailed over her face, smearing it even more with her own dirtied fingers.

"Oh yeah, that's much better. Draws attention away from the spider webs in your hair."

"I don't have— Do I?" Libby demanded, brushing at her hair with just enough anxiety to suggest a slight case of arachnophobia.

"I said spider *web*, not spiders. See?" She tugged at Libby's hair to retrieve another bit of the stuff to hold up for Libby's inspection.

"Stop that!" Libby backed away a step, bringing Quinn's jacket up in front of her like a shield.

Quinn only smiled. "It washes," she said, continuing her slow advance. It was a silly game. A spin on fifth-grade recess, when boys chased girls without a clue about what to do if they caught one. But even in the fifth grade, Quinn knew she preferred chasing girls and had some pretty definite ideas about what she wanted to do when she caught one.

PJ, understanding only that some game was afoot, ran at their feet, barking encouragement.

"You stay out of this," Libby warned him. "She doesn't need a cheering section." When she turned to look behind her, obviously worried about stumbling over the dog, Quinn seized the opening and darted forward. Libby's startled shriek incited another round of manic barking as she propelled Libby backward the last few feet to pin her against the side of the truck, her jacket lying on the ground where Libby had dropped it.

"You're getting that crap all over me," complained Libby, breathless from laughter, but lacking her former conviction.

She'd won their little game, hadn't she? Caught Libby fair and square. And anyone who'd ever played the game knew there was only one thing to do when you caught the girl. Back on familiar ground and confident of what to do and just how to do it, Quinn felt the unsettling concerns of a few minutes ago slipping away. She slid her fingers into the silky mass of Libby's hair and heard Libby's breath quicken when she tightened her fist around a handful.

Lowering her head, she slid her lips across Libby's to feel the softness of them, teasing them with the tip of her tongue until Libby's lips parted to welcome her into the sweet, moist heat of her mouth.

She'd wanted to possess, but Libby's mouth, soft and yielding under hers, only fueled her hunger and left her wanting more. Craving more. She angled her head to take the kiss deeper and lost herself. She felt more than heard a rumbling moan of desire, but simultaneous with the hot flash of satisfaction came the realization that the sound had come not from Libby, but from herself. With characteristic arrogance, she'd intended to take Libby's breath away. She hadn't counted on having the favor returned, and the shock of her own reaction had her pulling away with what felt like panic pounding in her chest.

No, not panic, she told herself. Just her heart beating. But good Christ, how it was beating. She watched the slow curving smile of satisfaction on Libby's face, heard her softly murmured, "Wow."

Wow? Holy shit was more like it. Forgetting for the moment that the—what had she called it? Harmless recreational flirting?—had been her idea, she reached for the closest thing to cold water she could think of. Taking Libby's jaw in her hand, she tilted her head back to study her with a deliberately detached look. "Well, maybe not *all* over you." She watched Libby's eyes grow dark

73

with a different kind of heat.

Shoving with considerably more strength than Quinn was expecting, Libby sent her staggering back a step, then scrubbed a hand across her cheek, not really improving the situation.

Quinn tapped her own face. "You, uh, missed a little on your chin there."

"You are evil and must be destroyed," Libby declared, but with a glimmer in her eye that betrayed some appreciation of the fact. She held her hands away from her to avoid touching anything else and released a sigh that sounded a lot like surrender. "Okay, now how am I supposed to get this off me? Where do you wash up around here?"

"Right over there," said Quinn, indicating the lake. "Jump on in. The water's fine."

"You're out of your mind. That water's freezing."

"Wimp," accused Quinn, but without any real antagonism. "Oh, all right. Just hold on a second."

Funny, she thought, as she retrieved a small plastic bucket from the back of the truck, a little cold water sounded like just the ticket right now. She grabbed a towel that she slung over her shoulder and a bottle of liquid soap that she tossed to Libby before going to the edge of the lake. She returned with the bucket half filled with water and set it down on the ground.

Libby looked down at the bucket and then up at Quinn. "Wouldn't it heat up faster if you put it, you know, more in the fire?"

Was she serious? "It's a plastic bucket. It'll *melt* if I put it in the fire."

"I know that," said Libby too quickly.

"Libby, the water is going to be cold. If you want a hot bath, you need to hop in your car and drive on back to your hotel. I thought you just wanted to get your hands cleaned off." Saying that, she shoved up the sleeves of her sweatshirt and plucked the soap from Libby's hand to wash her own.

While she dried her hands on the towel, she watched Libby crouch in front of the bucket, washing her hands before making an effort to clean her face, but the water was cold and Libby was obviously trying not to get any more of it on herself or her clothes than was absolutely necessary.

Standing, Libby shook the water from her hands and reached out to Quinn for the towel, but instead of handing it to her, Quinn dipped one end of it in the bucket and then squirted some soap on it. "Come here."

"Why?"

"Your face," said Quinn.

"I already washed my face."

"Yeah, well, you missed. Come here."

Libby only wiggled her fingers in an impatient little give-it-to-me gesture. "Just give me the—"

"You can't even see where the dirt is," she said, and ignoring Libby's sputtered sound of protest cupped her hand at the back of Libby's neck and wiped the smears of soot from her cheeks and nose.

"Quinn, come on, this feels too much like my mother cleaning my face with spit on a tissue."

"Trust me, the last thing I'm feeling toward you right now is maternal." She made another pass across Libby's forehead just because she wasn't quite ready to stop looking at her yet. "There, all better," she said, slinging the towel over her shoulder.

Libby snatched the towel back and pressed the dry end to her face before throwing it back at Quinn. She cast a comically dangerous glance around the campsite. "So where'd your cohort disappear to?"

Quinn bent to retrieve her jacket from the ground. "Obviously he understands the value of a timely exit." That dog might be even smarter than she'd given him credit for.

"You don't suppose he would have gone in the water, do you?"

"I doubt it." She scanned the water, but saw only reflections of moonlight dancing on the rippled surface. "Besides, we'd have heard him."

"PJ," Libby called again.

"Look, he's a dog, with a dog's nose. Probably picked up some irresistible scent that he's chasing through the woods. Hell, for all we know his owner's got a swank little home right here on the lake somewhere. He probably runs around like a little hobo during the day, hitting the tourists up for scraps, and then heads home at night and sleeps nice and snug in his little doggie bed."

"You're probably right. Guess we don't have to argue about who gets to keep him now."

"I'm sure his owner would be relieved to hear that." She'd hoped for at least a little smile, but Libby still looked worried.

"I don't know why I'm upset," Libby admitted, angling her face away as if embarrassed. "God, now you're really going to think I'm nuts." She stuffed her hands in her jeans pockets, hunching her shoulders as a stiff breeze blew across the water.

"Hey, you care about the little guy. Why would I think that was nuts?" If anything, she thought it was sweet, and it made her wonder whether Libby might be more inclined to bring the dog home with her more than she'd care to admit. She wrapped her jacket back around Libby's shoulders, catching the lapels to hold it in place when Libby would have shrugged it off again.

"Quinn, put your coat back on. It's cold."

"Funny," murmured Quinn, using her grip on the lapels to draw Libby closer, "I don't seem to be feeling the cold much at all tonight." Any other protest Libby might have made was swallowed when Quinn's mouth covered hers.

How could she possibly be expected to feel cold when there was so much heat? It flared even higher a moment later when she felt Libby's arms wrapping around her waist to pull her closer.

Don't let go. It was the closest thing to a rational thought her mind seemed capable of. But this time she was prepared for the rush that filled her, and she had no intention of letting go. Slipping her hands under the coat, she took them on a slow tour over the trim line of Libby's waist and down the sloping small of her back, pressing Libby closer as she used the advantage of her height to push her thigh more firmly between Libby's legs. When Libby's head fell back on a low moan, Quinn turned her attention to the exposed skin of her throat, soft and pale in the moonlight. She lingered there, encouraged by the way Libby angled her neck in silent invitation, allowing the sweet, humming sound of Libby's pleasure to guide her lips and teeth until fingers again tangled in her hair to drag her mouth back to Libby's.

Their kisses grew more demanding, as did the subtly insistent pressure of Libby's pelvis against her thigh. The silky material of Libby's blouse slid free of her slacks with little resistance. Heedless of the jacket that fell from Libby's shoulders, she released the clasp of Libby's bra before sliding her hand between them to free Libby's breasts from the lacy constraint.

She closed her hand over Libby's breast and felt it come alive under her palm. When she slid her thumb across the nipple, Libby groaned and arched against her hand, simultaneously yielding and demanding, and Quinn felt her own hunger rising to meet the delicious, perfectly feminine contradiction of it.

"Oh, God," Libby said on a moan, and then again, which seemed like a good sign until she followed it with, "I can't do this."

What?

Libby stepped back out of reach. "I can't do this." She started to tug her bra back into place but then quit and folded her arms across her breasts instead.

"What's wrong? Did I—"

"No," Libby's eyes darted back to hers briefly before looking away again. "No, it's me. I just… I thought I could, but I can't. I just—can't. I'm sorry."

She frowned, trying to figure out what the hell had just happened, but Libby would barely look at her. Seeing her standing there like that, hugging herself and looking like she'd crawl into a hole if there was one handy… Hell, you'd almost think she'd never—

The answer that suggested itself was a splash of cold against her insides.

"I'm sorry," Libby was saying again. "I honestly didn't mean for things to—"

"No," she said quickly, stopping her apology. "It wasn't—I just didn't realize that you—I mean—" She clamped her jaw shut to silence her own babbling. What the hell did she mean? Sorry, I don't fuck straight chicks. *That's* what she meant. What the hell had she been thinking? "Libby, I'm sorry. I was way out of line. I guess I got a little…carried away."

"I think it's fair to say we both did," Libby admitted. She looked like she was going to say something else, but she didn't.

Quinn wanted to say something, but didn't know what to say.

Libby took a half step in the general direction of her car. "I…think I'm just going to go now."

"You sure you're okay to drive?"

Libby nodded, already looking less frazzled once she was sitting behind the wheel of her car. "Thank you again, for getting me out of that cellar. I owe you one."

"Not really," she said. "But hey, if I ever find myself stuck in a cellar, I may look to collect anyway." Grateful for Libby's attempt at a smile, she returned it with a slightly forced one of her own. Then, because there really didn't seem to be anything left to say, she watched silently as Libby drove away.

Chapter Eight

Quinn awoke early the next morning, if you could even call it morning, still being dark at—she squinted at her watch—five forty-seven. She blamed her foul mood on the fact that she hadn't slept worth a damn, and the reason for that wasn't anything she wanted to think about. Only one thing seemed obvious: it was time to get the hell out of Turtle Cove.

The lake had turned out to be a nice place to camp, but she was only here by an accident of timing. She'd have left yesterday if not for the starter going out, but now that everything was working again there was no reason to stay. She discarded the image of Libby that sprang to mind, not sure if her subconscious presented it as encouragement to stay or a reason not to.

If the town of Turtle Cove seemed to withdraw into its collective shell at sundown, it certainly awoke before the dawn. There was easily more than a dozen vehicles already parked in front of Quimby's Diner when she pulled up shortly after six thirty.

An annoying electronic chime announced her entrance, but finding herself immediately enveloped by the aromas of coffee, smoky bacon and rich maple syrup, her mood lifted a notch in spite of herself.

A stout waitress with wildly curly hair a shade of red not to be found in nature came out from behind the counter carrying a coffeepot in each hand. She slowed only long enough to nod toward a stack of menus on a table next to the entrance.

"Just grab yourself a menu and a seat and I'll be right with you."

Quinn slid one of the laminated sheets from the stack of menus and headed to an empty booth at the back of the diner. She'd barely taken a seat before the waitress—Rhonda, according to the name tag pinned to front of her black and white *Quimby's* T-shirt—was there, turning over one of the four coffee cups waiting upside down in their saucers.

"Leaded or unleaded?" Her eyes flicked briefly toward Quinn and she began pouring without waiting for a response. "You need leaded, I can tell. Rough night?"

It hadn't occurred to her to take the time to look in a mirror, and she wondered now if that had been a mistake. She gave Rhonda a reluctant half nod, not wanting to encourage conversation but smart enough not to be rude to a waitress who'd done nothing to deserve it. "Something like that."

"Well, don't fret about it now. You got yourself a brand new day," she said brightly, "time to make some fresh mistakes. So, what sounds good this morning?"

She glanced down at the menu that she hadn't really had a chance to look at yet and made a quick decision. "Cheese omelet, I guess."

"Better make that a Western," said Rhonda as she jotted on her little notepad. "You look like you need something with a little meat in it. You want toast or an English muffin with that?"

"Toast?" she said, annoyed with herself when it came out sounding more like a question than a response, and not at all certain Rhonda wasn't going to countermand her decision and make it an English muffin.

Rhonda nodded approvingly and said, "We'll make it wheat.

A little fiber's always good for what ails you. I'll get this right out to you," she promised and then earned herself a generous tip when she turned over a second cup on the table and filled it. "Don't worry, we'll get you powered up before you leave here," she told Quinn with a wink.

She drained the first cup of coffee almost as soon as Rhonda walked off and reached gratefully for the second. Stifling a yawn, she angled her body so she could lean back in the corner of the booth's seat, and closed her eyes, allowing the hubbub of conversation and rattle of kitchen noises to flow over her.

"Rhonda, you know I don't like my bacon this crisp," an anonymous male voice grumbled from a few booths away. "Might as well just set it on fire and be done with it."

"And you ought to know by now that's how Frank cooks bacon," responded Rhonda's already familiar voice. "You want it cooked different, you need to order it someplace different."

"These eggs are over medium," came another complaint, this one more whine than grumble. "I said sunny-side up."

"Raw eggs'll kill you," was Rhonda's matter-of-fact response. "I'm only looking out for your health."

She was trying not to worry that her toast would be burnt to a crisp if Rhonda happened to believe burnt toast aided digestion when another snippet of conversation and the words "New York" caught her ear. Although she knew there could be a hundred reasons why someone might be mentioning New York, she couldn't help but zero in on the voices nonetheless.

"—got here yesterday afternoon, I heard," an older man was saying, except with his broad New England accent it came out more like *yestuhday ahftuhnoon*.

"Lookin' to buy Shepherd's place?" a second man asked.

"No, not to buy it. The one he left it to is who I'm talking about."

"You don't say."

"I *do* say."

"Where'd you hear this?"

"Charlie Parkhurst who got it straight from Meredith. Said

Darryl met with her yesterday and handed her the keys, just like that."

"Now that you mention it," a woman's voice piped in, "when I called Bernie this morning to see how many cinnamon rolls she was going to need, she mentioned that someone from New York had checked in yesterday. Told Bernie she was up here on personal business," she added, her tone implying something inherently suspect in that statement. "Bernie said she took off right after she checked in and never did come back last night."

Never came back? She opened her eyes, but all she saw was Rhonda approaching with a coffeepot in one hand and a plate in the other. She caught only the word "midnight" before Rhonda was at the booth, setting down the plate and refilling her coffee cup at the same time.

Forced to abandon her eavesdropping for the moment, she eyed an omelet golden with cheese scattered over the top and small chunks of ham, onion and bell pepper tumbling out from the sides. And the toast looked perfect. "Looks good," she said, forgetting to hide her surprise.

"Of course it's good. What'd you expect, I'd burn your toast or something?" Seeing her guilty look, Rhonda appeared puzzled for a moment before realization dawned. "Don't pay them any mind," she said, waving a dismissive hand. "One's my ex-husband, the other used to be my son-in-law. I figure I'm duty bound to make their lives miserable. You have to earn a spot on that list before I start messing with your breakfast. Now eat that while it's hot."

Her eyes tracked Rhonda's departure and then scanned the occupants of nearby booths hoping to pick up again on the conversation she felt sure had been about Libby. None of the booths had the right combination of occupants—at least two men and a woman—but a kid who couldn't be more than sixteen wearing an already-dirty apron was busy clearing a booth that had been occupied when she first sat down.

It didn't matter, she told herself. It was just gossip. Idle, small town gossip. They probably got folks from New York up here all the time. Just because they were talking about a woman didn't mean it was Libby. And just because this other woman was here because she'd inherited property from—what had they said his name was? Shepherd? That still didn't mean...

Who the hell was she trying to kid? There was only so much she could write off to coincidence. Of course it was Libby. Who else could it be? And if they had that much right, they might be right about her not going back to the hotel last night too.

Quinn picked up her fork and poked at the omelet. Why hadn't Libby gone back to her hotel? Scooping some of the omelet onto her fork, she swallowed without tasting it. Maybe she was one of those people who liked to drive when she was worked up. Except she knew Libby had to have been nearly exhausted.

Libby was a grown woman. If she'd decided to spend the rest of the night driving around, that was her own damn business. Hell, if she decided to drive all the way back to New York last night, that was her own damn business too. It didn't make any difference one way or the other. Except these roads were like a damn roller coaster, nothing but twists and turns and hills and what with Libby not knowing her way around and as tired as she'd been...

Shit. I should have made her stay.

But she'd asked her. She'd asked if she was okay to drive and Libby said yes.

Of course she said yes. After what had happened, what else was she supposed to say?

A grown woman wants to leave, you let her leave. Especially when she herself had wanted Libby gone as much as Libby seemed ready to be gone.

Still, the question remained. Gone where?

Libby awoke with a seatbelt buckle digging into her hip, a kink in her neck and a disturbingly bad taste in her mouth. She sat up, shrugging her shoulders and twisting her neck to see how stubborn the kink was going to be.

Very stubborn, she decided. Probably served her right for

sleeping in the car when she could have been stretched out on a bed, but it had been pitch black when she'd returned here with nothing but a dead flashlight in her pocket, and the idea of fighting with unfamiliar keys to stumble through a strange house in the dark hadn't seemed all that appealing. It still felt too much like trespassing and more than a little creepy. Besides, she'd been so exhausted by the time she got back here, sleeping in the car hadn't seemed like such a bad idea. But waking up in a car—well, that was another matter entirely.

She shoved the car door open, letting in a wash of chilled morning air, and got out to stretch her back while she contemplated her situation. She could probably get into her room at the inn by now, but after spending an evening in a cellar and sleeping half the night in her car, walking in there wasn't going to be pretty. On the other hand, that's where all her clothes were. And her makeup. And that nice big bathtub, she remembered with a sigh.

Retrieving her bag that had served as a very lumpy pillow, she fished out her keys to let herself back into Shepherd's house.

The face that greeted her in the bathroom mirror was not encouraging. While the jacket hid her wrinkled and soot-stained shirt, there was no way to hide her eyes, puffy and slightly bloodshot from lack of sleep. Her hair was pretty ratty looking on the side where it had been smashed into the makeshift pillow during the night. She worked at it for a minute with her fingers to untangle and smooth it and then considered the results in the mirror. She looked...

Almost as bad as she felt. She pulled her hair back experimentally, wondering if she had a rubber band in her purse.

After she'd left Quinn last night, she'd tried to sleep—wanted to sleep—but hadn't been able to settle her mind down long enough to drift off. Instead, she'd chased her imagination down endless avenues of what if's and if only's. She'd hoped to find some degree of cold comfort in being certain she'd done the right thing. However tempting it might have been in the heat of the moment, one night's pleasure was simply not what she was looking for. And that's all it would have been, there was no reason to think otherwise. Not that Quinn had *tried* to make her think otherwise. But that only meant she had no one but herself to blame for letting it go as far as it had. If she hadn't come to her senses, in another minute they'd have been—

Okay, she was *not* going to think about that right now, because something inside her still throbbed just a little at the thought of what she'd walked away from. The idea was to know she'd done the right thing, not wonder whether she'd made a mistake.

Giving up the ponytail idea, she took a deep breath and released it through pursed lips.

She should probably blame Brian for at least some of this, with all his talk of crazy monkey sex. God, where did he come *up* with that stuff? Anyway, sex was not what she wanted. Okay, not *just* sex. If all she wanted was an orgasm, well, she could take care of that herself couldn't she? No, what she wanted was someone she could count on to be there the next day. The day after that, and the day after *that*. What she wanted was not to have to worry when she walked out the door in the morning what she might be coming home to that night. Was that too much to ask for?

She didn't care if it was. It's what she wanted. It might be a fantasy, but it was her fantasy and a woman was entitled to her own fantasies wasn't she? She wasn't going to make the mistake of settling for less, no matter *how* good the sex was—or would have been.

It *would* have been good, too. As good as this morning was bad, she was sure of it. For a moment, just the mere memory of Quinn's hand on her breast brought back an echo of the lightheaded, weak-kneed, blood warming pulse of—

"Okay, just *stop* it!" she commanded herself. Then, deciding the image in the mirror, bad as it was, was as good as it was going to get, she stepped out of the bathroom and almost walked straight into Quinn.

"Jesus!" She stumbled back a step in surprise. "What are you doing here?" she demanded, not sure whether she should be alarmed or annoyed.

Quinn held up a white paper sack and a large take-out cup. "Breakfast?"

She hesitated, not sure it was in her best interest to cave in so quickly, but the lure of caffeine proved too much for her. She reached for the cup with a grudging look of gratitude. "You keep this up and I'm going to start thinking you've got wings tucked up under your shirt."

"Excuse me?"

She allowed herself a moment to enjoy Quinn's baffled look. "You've come to my rescue twice in less than twenty-four hours so I can only assume you're some kind of guardian angel. Don't make that face. I could've said fairy godmother." She took a sip of the coffee that was still hot enough to be enjoyable. "Either way, I figure there have to be wings involved."

"Torn up old bat wings maybe," muttered Quinn. She handed her the sack. "It's probably still warm," she said, following Libby to the kitchen. "An omelet. I had one. They're not bad."

"You can sit down, you know," Libby told her when Quinn remained standing just inside the door. She tore open the little cellophane packet of plasticware and dug into the omelet with a little moan of appreciation. "Oh, this is way better than not bad," she said, taking another bite. She washed it down with some coffee while eyeing Quinn who had moved farther into the room but still looked like she was angling for an escape.

"So how do I rate all this? Not that I'm complaining, mind you. I just didn't expect to see you again after…uh…" Okay. Awkward moment. With a conscious effort, she pushed past her embarrassment. "How'd you know I'd be here?"

Quinn shrugged, her eyes everywhere but on Libby. "It's a long story."

"I love long stories." Libby nudged the leg of the chair opposite where she sat at the table.

After a moment's hesitation, Quinn pulled out the proffered chair and sat down.

"I had to go into town to gas up before I left, so I stopped by

86

that little diner to get something to eat. I overheard some people in there talking about you."

"About me? You must have misunderstood."

"Maybe," said Quinn. "They were talking about some woman who'd come up from New York to look at the Shepherd place."

Her surprise was all the confirmation Quinn needed.

"One of them said you never went back to your hotel last night. Why didn't you go back?"

"It's not really a hotel. More like a bed-and-breakfast. The woman who owns it locks the door at midnight. I probably could have gotten in, but my phone was dead and I didn't really want to wake everyone up pounding on the door. But my God, I haven't even been here twenty-four hours. How could anyone know...?" She was too incredulous to even finish the question, but Quinn looked almost amused.

"You've never lived in a small town, have you? Trust me, there are no secrets. Only things people pretend not to know."

The darkly cynical smirk on Quinn's face suggested she had some personal experience with that. Libby stared at her over the rim of her cup of coffee and wondered if she should even bother asking. Probably not, since Quinn hadn't even answered her original question yet. She was about to point that out when one possible, if improbable, answer dawned on her.

"Were you worried about me?"

Quinn froze, her hand hovering at the edge of Libby's plate where she'd been about to swipe one of the triangles of toast from Libby's breakfast. "What?"

"You were worried about me." She didn't bother making it a question this time. "That's why you came here. To check on me."

"I wasn't worried," said Quinn, apparently deciding she didn't want the toast after all. "I just figured you probably came here because—well, where else would you go?"

"I know why I'm here. I was just trying to figure out why *you're* here."

"I told you," began Quinn, but then apparently realized she

really hadn't told Libby anything. She dropped her scowl to the table. "I *wasn't* worried."

Libby couldn't have contained her smile if she tried, so she didn't bother. Several possible responses crossed her mind, but only one seemed truly appropriate.

"Well, thank you. For this, I mean," she added when Quinn looked up, indicating her breakfast. "Thanks to you, I feel almost human again. Now all I need is a hot bath and some clean clothes and I might even look human again."

"You look fine."

Quinn sounded so sincere she was almost tempted to believe her. "That's sweet. Complete bullshit, of course, but sweet."

Quinn tipped her head as if accepting a compliment. "One of my specialties. Sweet bullshit." Her raffish grin faded at the sound of car tires crunching over the gravel outside. "You expecting company?"

Libby pushed aside the curtain over the sink and saw a police cruiser pulling up in front of the house. He was climbing the steps to the porch by the time she got there.

"Good morning," she said, pushing the screen door open for him. He was tall, and filled out the crisp lines of his two-tone blue uniform with the kind of stocky build that always made her think of football players. His short, dark blond hair was neat enough to suggest he'd been to the barber as recently as this morning. "Is there something I can do for you, Officer?"

"Morning, ma'am. I'm looking for Libby Jackson."

"I'm Libby Jackson."

"Officer Bradley," he said, extending a hand that swallowed hers. "Welcome to Turtle Cove, Ms. Jackson."

"Thank you."

She realized Quinn had followed her out to the porch when she saw his gaze shift past her shoulder. He tipped his head in greeting. "Ma'am."

"Officer."

Quinn's tone sounded on the cool side, but maybe that was just a natural caution. Her own thought had been that someone must have called in a report of trespassers on the property, but since he obviously knew who she was, he probably knew why she was here.

"Don't tell me you drove all the way out here this morning just to welcome me to town," Libby said, bringing his attention back to her.

"No, ma'am." He pulled a small notepad from his shirt pocket. "We received a call from a friend of yours who was concerned that he hadn't been able to reach you." He consulted the notepad for the name written there. "A Mr. Galloway?"

"Brian?" she said, but her surprise evaporated almost immediately. Of course, Brian. She'd never called him yesterday after she got here. Those calls last night would have been from him, and God only knew how many had gone straight to voice mail after the phone's battery had died.

"He's pretty worried about you," said Bradley. "You might want to give him a call as soon as you get the chance."

"I know. I mean, I will. I was going to call him last night, but my cell phone wasn't working."

"So you haven't encountered any trouble, then? Mr. Galloway said he was concerned because you'd made the trip up here alone," he added with a casual glance in Quinn's direction.

"No, no trouble really," she said, making a point to smile because something told her Quinn wasn't.

"Any reason you didn't go back to Bernie's last night?"

"Bernie?" she said blankly.

"Sorry. Mrs. Garrison. You're staying at Cobbler's Inn, right?"

"Yes, but how did you—"

"Mr. Galloway said you'd come up here to talk to Mr. Latham, so I called him to see if he'd heard from you yet. He's the one who told me you were staying over at Bernie's place. She confirmed you'd checked in yesterday afternoon, but said you never showed back up after your meeting with Mr. Latham yesterday afternoon."

She stared at him, a bit dumbfounded. Last night in the cellar she'd been convinced she might not be found for days because no one knew where she was, only to learn this morning that if she stood here long enough, most of them would probably show up on her doorstep.

She realized Bradley was waiting for an explanation. "That's right. I just—well, it got to be later than I realized, and it seemed the simpler thing to just…stay here."

Bradley nodded, evidently satisfied with her explanation. His gaze drifted briefly toward Quinn's truck that was parked behind her car.

"You've been camping out here," he said. It wasn't a question and Quinn didn't answer. "Glad to see Buddy was able to get your truck back up and running."

Puzzled by Quinn's silence, she glanced over and felt her own smile stretching unnaturally to compensate for what she saw there. "Yes," she said, hoping to distract Bradley from the inexplicably hostile look Quinn was leveling at him. "It really was—"

"You keep track of all Buddy's customers?" said Quinn as if Libby hadn't been speaking.

"Small town," said Bradley, his amiable, we're-all-friends-here smile unfazed by Quinn's failure to return it. "Makes it kind of hard not to know what's going on." He turned his attention back to Libby. "I should probably get going, if you're sure everything's okay here."

"Yes. And thank you." She cast a quick glance over her shoulder as she followed Bradley to the door. She was worried that it might be too subtle to convey the warning she intended, but Quinn apparently got the hint because she stayed on the porch while Libby followed Bradley outside.

"I really am sorry you had to make the trip all the way out here," she told him.

"Don't be. To be honest, I was glad for the excuse to come out and meet you. Folks around here will be glad to know someone's looking after this place again."

The assumption caught her by surprise. "Actually, I haven't

decided what I'm going to do with the property. I only found out about it a few days ago, and—"

"Hey, no explanation necessary," Bradley assured her. "Sorry. Didn't mean to come across like a high-pressure salesman. But I hope you'll at least give it some thought. I know it's not New York, but we've got a nice little community here, and anyone Mark thought so highly of would certainly be welcome."

Libby was so used to thinking of him as simply "Shepherd" it took her a second to understand whom Bradley was referring to. "Thank you. I'll certainly keep that in mind. So, you knew— Mark, then, I take it?"

"Oh, sure. Most everyone around here knew him. You'd probably have a hard time finding someone who hasn't been out here at one time or another. At Christmas, he turned this place into one big winter wonderland. The kids loved it. Lights strung up on everything that stood still for it. He must have had, oh, I don't know, twenty or more Christmas trees set up in the house and on the porch. Every size imaginable," he said shaking his head. "You'd have to see it to believe it."

"Yes, I'm, uh, familiar with the Christmas trees. You know," she added on a whim, "I'm probably going to be in town for a few more days. If you happen to have some free time, maybe we could get together. I'd love to hear some more stories about him. If you don't mind, that is."

"Not at all," said Bradley, looking pleased. "If I'm not there, Cheryl will know how to reach me."

Bradley got in behind the wheel of the police cruiser and lowered the window. "Don't forget to call Mr. Galloway."

Libby nodded, waiting while he pulled out of the driveway. Turning back to the house, she saw the porch was empty.

She found Quinn in the kitchen, arms folded as she leaned against the sink, her back to the window.

"Well, wasn't he just Officer Friendly," Quinn said when she walked in.

"I thought he seemed nice." She kept her tone light, trying not to fuel Quinn's already bad mood.

"Yeah, and I bet he'd like to be a whole lot nicer." Quinn's expression insulting at best. "So you two are going to get together, huh?"

She hesitated, taken aback by the contempt on Quinn's face even more than the insinuation in her tone. "He knew Shepherd, so I thought it couldn't hurt to talk to him if he has time."

Quinn's response was a derisive snort. "Oh, I wouldn't worry about that. I'm sure he'll make time for you."

"Okay, why don't you just tell me what this is all about?" she demanded, feeling her own temper rising despite her best efforts to control it. "Because as much as I'd like to believe all of this hostility is directed at him, when you keep making comments like that I can't help feeling like some of it's splashing onto me." She wondered if the belligerent scowl Quinn gave her was supposed to be some kind of apology.

"I didn't like him."

"Trust me, that was pretty obvious. But *why*? He was only doing his job. Actually, I think driving all the way out here to check on me for a worried friend was even a little above and beyond."

"Wearing a badge doesn't make him a saint, Libby," said Quinn tersely.

"Who said anything about—" she began but then stopped, because Quinn had walked out, leaving her talking to a swinging door. Seconds later she heard the screen door slam shut.

After venting some of her frustration on the screen door as she shoved it out of her way, Quinn's long strides ate up the ground between the house and her truck. She found herself with one hand on the door handle before she'd cooled down enough to wonder what the hell she was doing. Leaving hadn't been on her mind as much as simply getting out of there before she said something *really* stupid or insulting. She knew she shouldn't be taking this out on Libby, but hadn't been able to stop herself. The way she'd been smiling at that asshole, like he was some kind of hero for delivering a freaking phone message. Couldn't she see that was just an excuse for him to come snooping around? Did she really believe he'd have come all the way out here if there wasn't something in it for him? *We're all friends here, my ass.* Maybe Libby was naive enough to buy into that lame Mayberry bullshit, but she was too familiar with his type to swallow it.

"I will not be made to look like a fool. Not by anyone and sure as hell not by the likes of you, little girl."

"Kind of late to be worried about that, isn't it?" She expected the slap and braced for it, but the sting of it left her eyes watering. She refused to wipe at them, worried only that he would think she was crying.

"Any other smart-mouth comments you feel the need to share?" he asked, indifferent to the hatred glaring back at him from eyes so like his own.

"Why don't you just let me go? You don't want me here anymore than I want to be here."

"Jesus Christ, you're not even old enough to drive yet. Just where the hell do you think you're going to go?" He paused as if waiting for an answer, but she said nothing. *"I know what happens to girls your age out on the street, and it ain't pretty. You'd be whoring before week's end and probably dead before the month was out."*

"Like you give a shit."

"I'm sick of your lip, little girl," he said jabbing a finger at her face. *"You're not half as tough as you seem to think you are. I'm not about to let you ruin what I've spent my life building here. No one's going to trust me to control what goes on in this town if I can't even control what goes on in my own house. Your days of running wild are over. From here on out, I'm going to know where you are every second of every day. If you don't show up at school, if you skip so much as a single class, I'll be getting a call and trust me, I will find you and God help your sorry ass when I do. If you don't show up in the cafeteria for lunch, I'm going to be notified. You're not going to able to take a piss without me knowing when and where and for how long. And whenever your ass isn't planted at that school, it'll be planted in this house, or your mother will be explaining to me why it's not. There is no place you can go where I won't*

have eyes watching you."

The memory, impossibly vivid even after all these years, brought with it an equally vivid echo of the helpless rage she'd felt. When she saw her reflection in the driver's side window, it was his eyes, black and cruelly arrogant, that she saw there. It wouldn't matter how many years or how many miles she put between them. The son of a bitch would always be too close for comfort. She slammed her fist against the tinted glass.

"You're going to break something doing that."

The quiet admonishment from only a few feet behind her had Quinn's throat closing over the little grunt of pain that had almost escaped. Ensnared in the memory, she hadn't even heard Libby come out of the house.

She made a conscious effort to relax her jaw before she spoke. "Car windows only break that easy in the movies." *Bones on the other hand...* She flexed her hand gingerly, careful to shield the gesture from Libby.

"It's not really the window I was worried about." Moving closer, Libby reached out as if to take her hand for a closer look, but she snatched it away.

"It's fine."

"If that's true, you're very lucky. Quinn why on earth would you—"

"Look, I know you've got stuff to do, so why don't I just clear out of your way." It was embarrassing enough that Libby had seen her lose control like that, she wasn't about to stick around for the lecture. She reached for the door handle hoping Libby would take the hint and move because she couldn't quite open the truck door with her standing there, but when Libby, after a brief hesitation, stepped back, she felt a perverse disappointment.

A grown woman wants to leave, you let her leave. Evidently she wasn't the only one who believed that.

"So you're really not going to tell me why you're pissed off." The frank disbelief in Libby's voice might have been enough to mask the underlying hurt, but there was nothing she could have done to keep it out of her eyes. It was her eyes that made Quinn hesitate, one foot already inside the truck.

"It's...not you," she said finally. "And I didn't have any right to take it out on you. I'm sorry."

"Then you're forgiven," Libby said, quietly and simply.

It wasn't that simple. She wanted to tell her it could never be that simple. But in the moment of silence while she was thinking about it Libby said, "You know, sometimes it really does help to talk about it. I've been told I'm a good listener. I mean, you know. If you need a friendly ear."

The fact that she was actually tempted was enough to make up her mind. "Thanks, but if you don't get to a phone pretty soon, it might be the National Guard that shows up next. Trust me, nothing I've got to say would be worth all that." For a second she thought Libby was going to argue the point, but when she only stuffed her hands in her pockets and stepped back from the truck, she had no excuse not to finish climbing in.

She closed the door and pulled her sunglasses down from the visor, slipping them on before she lowered the window.

"Well, Liberty Larue," she said, "I have to say it's been a pleasure."

Surprise, then disappointment, played over Libby's features. "So this is it? I was hoping I'd still have a chance to...I don't know. Buy you a cup of coffee or something. I owe you that much at least."

Quinn shook her head. "You don't owe me anything. If I hadn't come along—" She was about to say "Dudley Do Right," but caught herself just in time. "Someone else would have."

"But—"

She started the engine, effectively drowning out whatever Libby might have said. "Take care of yourself, Libby. And try to stay out of cellars, okay?" With one final grin and a brief wave, she put the truck in gear and pulled away.

Chapter Nine

When Libby arrived back at the inn, a couple was standing at the front desk talking to Mrs. Garrison. She saw the innkeeper's gaze slide past them, her smile faltering for a fraction of a second at Libby's disheveled appearance. Fortunately the woman's sense of propriety superseded her curiosity. She immediately returned her attention to her guests at hand, simultaneously cranking the professionally friendly smile up a notch with renewed purpose.

Libby moved quickly and quietly toward the stairs, already feeling better knowing a hot bath and a soft bed were close at hand.

She started water running in the tub before digging out the cell phone charger that was in her suitcase. While the tub filled, she dialed Brian's cell phone number, bypassing the office switchboard. He answered before the second ring.

"Where the *hell* have you been?" he demanded in lieu of hello.

"You called the *cops*?" she threw back at him.

"Oh, better I should wait a week and let your body be nice and ripe when they find it? You didn't call, you weren't answering your phone. I was worried sick."

"Well, you can stop worrying. I'm fine." Scanning the selection of travel-size bubble baths in the little basket on the vanity, Libby selected one, tucking the phone between her shoulder and ear while she twisted off the cap and poured the contents under the faucet. As the spicy sweet scent of freesia rose up on clouds of steam, she realized she was listening to nothing but dead air.

"Brian?" She tossed the empty bottle of bubble bath into the white wicker trash can next to the sink. "Are you there?"

"I'm here. I'm just waiting to hear what you think is a good reason for not calling until now."

Oh boy. She knew that tone only too well. While the tub grew frothy with bubbles, Libby gave him the highlights of the past twenty-four hours, unzipping her slacks as she did so and stepping out of them when they slid to the tiled floor. She managed to shake one arm free of her sleeve and then switched the phone to her other hand to free her other arm. Dropping the blouse on top of her slacks, she nudged the pile aside with her foot. By then the bubbles were cresting the edge of the tub and she turned off the water.

"Wait a minute," said Brian, interrupting her. "How did you finally get out of the cellar?"

Libby sighed. She'd deliberately skimmed over anything to do with Quinn, but doing so left holes in her story and she didn't have the energy to patch them right now. "I promise I'll give you all the gory details later, Brian, but right now I'm really, really tired."

There was a pause, and she knew he was listening for whatever she might not be telling him. "But you're okay?" he asked finally.

"I'm fine. Really," she assured him.

"All right. But I expect you to keep me posted."

"I will."

"Answering your phone when it rings would be a good start."

"I will."

"And it wouldn't kill you to—"

"Good*night*, Brian," said Libby, and hung up on his soft snort of laughter.

After leaving the lake house, Quinn drove, not paying much attention to time or direction until she saw a sign announcing the Maine state border just ahead. The surprise of it had her pulling over onto the narrow shoulder of the two-lane highway. For someone who'd recently spent a solid day of driving just to get out of Texas, being able to drive across most of one state and into another in just over an hour was a little amazing, but not so amazing that she couldn't do the math. Obviously if she could leave that fast, she could return as quickly.

Which doesn't matter because you're not going back.

If she told herself that enough times, maybe she'd listen. Seemed like all she'd been doing since she put her foot to the gas pedal this morning was thinking about turning around and then talking herself out of it. She couldn't seem to quit wondering what Libby might be doing now. Was she still at Shepherd's house or had she gone back to her hotel? Was she sleeping? Dreaming? And when Libby woke up, would she still be hoping to see her again? Or would she have figured out she'd be better off not to?

It annoyed her that she cared one way or the other. What did she know about Libby anyway, beside the fact that she had a soft spot for strays and an appetite no one would ever guess from looking at her? Eyes you could lose yourself in and a kiss that left you praying there was more where that came from. Except there wasn't going to be any more where that came from.

It was probably just as well. The last thing she needed was someone else to let down, and that's all that would have happened if she'd stuck around. Lately too much of what she'd thought was long behind her came flooding back with the least provocation. She didn't need a shrink to tell her why, but knowing why wasn't enough to prevent it from happening. And knowing why hadn't been enough to stop her from taking it out on someone whose only crime was having a soft spot for strays.

And that's all you are, she told herself. *Just one more stray she picked up on the side of the road.* But she could live with that. She'd only wanted to get out of there before saying or doing something to convince Libby she was a complete head case.

Kind of late to be worried about that, isn't it?

Quinn closed her eyes. "Shut up," she whispered to the familiar male voice sniggering in her head.

What's the matter, little girl? If you don't want me in your head, make me get out. Or maybe you can't. Maybe you're still not as tough as you think you are.

Quinn opened her eyes. "Fuck you, old man. You made sure I'd always be as tough as I needed to be."

Then what was she so afraid of?

Driving a hundred yards down the road, for starters, she decided, seeing as how she was still sitting here.

She glanced in the side mirror, checking the non-existent traffic with the intention of getting back onto the road, but still didn't move.

Because crossing that border ahead might be enough to trick herself into believing she'd made the decision to leave. And she knew leaving wasn't something she ever let herself change her mind about.

But maybe—just maybe—she wasn't ready to leave yet.

Libby was slapping at the nightstand before she was even awake, trying to find and silence the alarm clock she'd set to keep her from sleeping the entire day away. Six o'clock. She really hadn't expected she'd sleep that long. She fell back on the bed, luxuriating in the simple pleasure of waking up in a real bed with a real pillow under her head. *The little things you take for granted.*

She'd probably be taking it for granted again by tomorrow, but at the moment the memory of the backseat of her car was too fresh not to appreciate the differences. She stayed there in bed for a couple minutes, listening to the sounds of muffled voices and other signs of life coming from downstairs, but when the warm cocoon of covers threatened to lure her back to sleep, she made herself get up.

In the bathroom, she filled the small glass with cold water from the sink and drank it while studying her reflection in the mirror. She not only felt better, she looked better. Her hair was mussed from sleep, but the shadows under her eyes were gone. She was famished though, and since Quinn was not likely to show up here to surprise her with dinner, she'd have to go out and find her own.

It annoyed her that Quinn was on her mind so soon after waking, because now she couldn't quite shake the thought of her. Walking away last night hadn't exactly been easy, but she'd really only been walking away from her own hormones. Watching Quinn drive off this morning had been a bit harder.

That Quinn had been worried about her enough to go out of her way to check on her was touching. That she'd felt the need to disguise her concern with that ridiculous breakfast subterfuge made Libby smile even now. But you didn't try to punch out your own truck window without a good reason. Well, without *some* reason. Obviously there was something troubling her.

She selected clean jeans and a black turtleneck from her suitcase. Replaying the events of that morning in her mind while she dressed, she came to the same conclusion as she had earlier. Nothing about the officer's visit justified Quinn's reaction to him.

She sat down on the bed to pull on black ankle boots and decided there probably wasn't much point in wondering about what she'd never know the answer to.

Piano music greeted her as she stepped into the hall. Downstairs, someone was singing *My Wild Irish Rose* in a very respectable male tenor. At the bottom of the stairs, she glanced into the parlor where a group of maybe half a dozen people was gathered around an upright piano in the far corner. They broke into applause as the man at the keyboard finished the song and immediately offered up a lively bit of ragtime.

"He's very good, isn't he?"

She started slightly at the sound of Mrs. Garrison's voice coming from right behind her. "Why don't you come in and join us? I don't think you've had a chance to meet any of my other guests, have you?"

"No, not yet. I was just on my way out to get a bite to eat."

"Maybe when you get back, then," Mrs. Garrison suggested. "I think the Harrisons would like to meet you. That's Henry playing the piano. His wife, Joan, is the one in the green cardigan. They're interested in buying the inn."

"I didn't realize it was for sale."

"Oh, it's not." Mrs. Garrison seemed amused by the very notion. "No, my dream of one day opening this inn was what got me through my last seven years of teaching. I told them that I knew of some property out at the lake that might—and I did emphasize might—be going on the market soon. I would have introduced you this morning, but I thought it might be better to wait for a more opportune moment."

Libby couldn't help but smile at the woman's diplomacy. "I appreciate that." She glanced into the parlor where the entire group was singing *Bicycle Built for Two*. "I really haven't decided yet what I'm going to do with it, but I suppose it couldn't hurt to talk to them."

"They're going to be here through the weekend, so it doesn't need to be this evening. If you decide you'd like an introduction, just let me know."

On Main Street, the neon "Q" of Quimby's Diner caught her eye. The number of cars in the parking lot suggested it was a popular place, which meant the food was probably good.

She was walking up to the front door when someone came up beside her.

"Miss Jackson. How are you this evening?"

"Officer Bradley," she said, surprised.

"Call me Joe. We're not that formal around here, unless I'm writing you a speeding ticket."

"Joe, then. And please, call me Libby."

He smiled and glanced around, looking for Quinn, she supposed. "You by yourself tonight, Libby?"

"Afraid so."

"Well, in that case, why don't you join me? I hate eating alone."

Quimby's was a classic American diner. Long and narrow, with a dozen or so stools along a lunch counter and two rows of vinyl upholstered booths. Black, white and red dominated the color scheme with a heavy dose of chrome throughout, and the air was infused with the aroma of fresh brewed coffee.

Bradley helped himself to two menus and, ignoring the Please Wait to be Seated sign, led her toward a vacant booth, exchanging greetings with a few customers who spoke to him in passing.

"Thanks, Doreen," he said to the young waitress who appeared with a cup of coffee he hadn't yet ordered. She took Libby's drink order and said she'd be right back.

"I take it you're a regular here," said Libby, watching Bradley pour a cascade of sugar into his coffee.

"I try to make the circuit. You know, just for the sake of good PR. But this place is right across the street from the station, so it's pretty convenient."

"I hope all your days aren't this long," said Libby, remembering he'd shown up at Shepherd's place early that morning.

"Oh, I'm through for the day, but my wife's got a school board meeting tonight so I've been entrusted with handling my own supper. Can't say I'm too torn up about it. Janie's got us on some whatzit whozit diet. South Park. Laguna Beach." He shook his head. "All I know is it's been a month since there's been anything in the house worth eating." As if to illustrate the point, when Doreen returned he ordered a double cheeseburger with bacon, extra mayo, extra onions and a large order of fries.

Because she could feel her arteries hardening just listening to his order, she restrained herself and went with the turkey club, dry.

"So you're going to be staying out at the lake while you're here?" asked Bradley after the waitress left with their order.

The question caught her by surprise. It was something she

hadn't considered. "I'm not sure that would be appropriate."

"How's that? It's your place now, isn't it?"

"Well...yes. I suppose. But there's no electricity out there, and—"

"Oh, Darryl can fix that for you," he said, dismissing it as a concern. "I know he's had it turned on periodically when he's sent folks out there to do work on the place. It might just be a matter of flipping the breakers, but he could tell you that. Not that I'm trying to take business away from Bernie," he added.

"Not that I would ever tell her it was your idea," she assured him, smiling. "I don't know. It hadn't really crossed my mind. But I'll give Latham a call in the morning to find out about the electric." She'd planned to leave tomorrow because the room at the inn wasn't available after tonight. Even if she didn't stay, it wouldn't hurt to have some lights turned on.

Conversation slowed for a couple of minutes after the waitress returned with their dinner.

The sandwich wasn't bad, but what really captured her attention was the coleslaw. When asked what was in it, the waitress would only tell her that it was a "house secret."

"Pickled ginger," Bradley told her afterward.

She eyed him suspiciously. "How do you come to be privy to the house secret?"

"Perhaps you failed to notice the badge and the gun," suggested Bradley straight-faced, but cracked a smile when Libby laughed. "You might say I'm on the inside track here. My mother-in-law owns this place. And speak of the devil," he said, deliberately louder as the woman in question came up the aisle from behind Libby.

"How's my favorite son-in-law this evening?" She wore a threadbare navy sweatshirt over jeans folded up into cuffs. Her hair, heavily streaked with gray, hung in a thick braid down her back. "I was getting ready to leave when Doreen happened to mention you were here with some sexy younger woman," she said with a friendly if pointed smile in Libby's direction. "Thought maybe I'd better come investigate."

Bradley laughed. "Libby, this is Janie's mother, Sue Quimby. Sue, this is Libby Jackson. Libby's the one Mark left the lake house to," Bradley explained. "She's up here to look at the property."

"Is that a fact?" said Sue, looking at her with renewed interest. "Well, in that case, it's a pleasure to meet you, Libby." Sue lightly backhanded Bradley on the arm. "Squeeze over kid," she told him and slid onto the seat beside him.

"Joe was just telling me this is your restaurant."

"That's right. Almost twenty-two years now."

"The food's delicious. I especially like the coleslaw," she said, "but you'll be happy to know the waitress refused to divulge your secret ingredient."

"Oh, that's okay, I'm sure if Joe hasn't already coughed it up, he will as soon as I leave," said Sue with a knowing grin in her son-in-law's direction. "Besides, I got the recipe from Mark, so you'll probably find it in one of his cookbooks anyway. Speaking of which—" Sue's smile brightened even as Libby saw Joe wincing a little. "If you're of a mind to get rid of any of those recipe boxes of his, I hope you'll let me know. I'd make you a good offer."

"Sue," said Bradley with an admonishing glance in her direction. "Don't let her pressure you," he told Libby.

"I'm not trying to pressure her," said Sue, sounding indignant. "But if there's a chance she's going to get rid of them anyway, what's the harm in letting her know I'm interested? Not like I asked her to give them to me."

"Really, I haven't thought that far ahead." Not knowing either of them well enough to judge how seriously to take this little argument, she decided to preempt it to be on the safe side. "But I will certainly keep it in mind that you're interested."

"Thank you," said Sue. "See," she said, elbowing Bradley. "How hard was that?"

Doreen appeared to refill Bradley's coffee cup. "You staying, Sue? You want something to drink?"

"No, I really was headed out the door."

"It was nice meeting you," she said as Sue stood to leave. "And I promise not to do anything rash with any recipes I find until I talk to you first."

Bradley sipped his coffee, watching his mother-in-law over the top of the mug as she walked away. "Seriously," he said, returning his attention to Libby, "don't let her talk you into anything."

She smiled, a little bemused by the entire exchange. "We are just talking about some recipes, right?"

"No, we're talking about recipes Sue wants," he said, then chuckled. "She and Mark had this ongoing competition. Who could make the best apple pie, the best—I don't know, chicken salad. Anything. Everything. Part of that was trying to out-secret each other in the secret ingredient department. Evidently she was much more impressed by Mark's cooking than she ever let on to him if she's offering to pay you."

"Tell me about him," she requested.

Bradley hesitated. "What do you want to know?"

Libby shrugged. "Anything you want to tell me is going to be more than I know." Seeing the vague confusion on his face, she realized he was unaware of the situation. "I'm sorry. When you mentioned this morning you'd talked to Mr. Latham, I assumed he told you."

"Told me where to start looking for you, but that's all. Darryl's kind of a stickler for that attorney-client privilege thing."

"Oh. Right, of course," she said, chagrined. "Well, the abbreviated version is that I'd never heard of Mark Shepherd until I got a letter from Mr. Latham a few days ago, and I have absolutely no idea why he left his estate to me."

Bradley stared at her for a second. "You're serious."

She nodded. "I came up here expecting to find out it was all a big mistake. Since it isn't, I thought I might try to find out something about him." She paused. "This would be the part where you share entertaining and insightful anecdotes. You know, like the Christmas trees?"

"The Christmas trees." Seeing his gray eyes sharpen, she couldn't help but think it was the police officer in him looking at her. "How would you know about—"

"He kept them in the cellar. I happened to find them last

night." She smiled at his still dubious expression. "Hey, if you're having a hard time believing it, imagine how I feel."

"I'm not sure I can," he admitted, but evidently had decided she was telling him the truth. He was thoughtfully silent for a few seconds. "He was a nice guy. I know that probably sounds like faint praise, but he was. I don't think I ever heard him say an angry word to or about anyone. Don't get me wrong, the man lived like a hermit. But not one of those crotchety old farts you see sometimes. I think he was just one of those people who appreciated solitude."

"A hermit?" She was surprised by the characterization. "I was under the impression he'd rented out the cottages until just a few years ago."

"Oh, yeah, he had the rentals, so there were always folks up there in the summer and into the fall. But that was just business. And a few times a year he'd do something out there that'd get quite a few people from town turning out. The Christmas tree forest was one. He'd have hot chocolate on hand for the kids. Doughnuts, cookies, whatever. And then for the Fourth of July there was a big barbecue picnic that drew quite a crowd. I think that's where the whole competition thing between him and Sue started. But the rest of the time he was pretty much by himself out there. And I'm assuming he liked it well enough that way, since he didn't do anything to change it."

"So he'd always lived out there by himself then?"

Bradley nodded. "Well, I say that, but let me think. Seems like there was another fellow staying out there for a while, but he disappeared not too long after the cabins went up. He might've been someone Mark hired on to help him build those."

"He built those?"

"Yeah, it used to be just the house out there."

"This other guy, does he still live around here?"

"No, I haven't seen him in a good fifteen years or more. I don't think he was from around here to begin with."

"So then there wasn't anyone you were expecting him to leave everything to?"

Bradley shook his head. "Never really thought about it. Some, maybe, after he had the stroke and it became obvious he wasn't going to be able to come back to it. I imagine a lot of people were wondering by then, especially after that first Christmas when the trees didn't go up. But I doubt any of them would have come out and asked. Not really anyone else's business for one thing, but mainly because you're too busy trying to maintain this...false optimism. You know. You're going to get through this. Do what the doctors tell you and you'll be home in no time. That sort of thing. It's not like you're going to go in there and say, you know Mark, you could go any day now. You given any thought to what's going to happen to the place after you're gone?"

"Can you think of anyone he might have talked to about it?"

He looked doubtful, but took another moment to think about it. "I suppose anything's possible, but if he did, I don't know who it would have been. Like I said, he was on pretty good terms with everybody, as far as I knew. But if I had to pick one person I thought he was especially close to..." He shook his head. "I know he used to spend time over at Father Joel's."

"Father as in—priest?"

"Yeah, but I don't mean that he spent time at the Church. I don't know for sure that he attended church around here anywhere. But he and Father Joel used to play chess every now and again. You could try talking to him. And I know Mark and Rhonda were friendly. Rhonda Flynn, she's one of waitresses here," he explained.

"Hey, Doreen," he called out, spotting her behind the counter. "Rhonda's not working tonight is she?" She couldn't hear what Doreen said, but the answer must have been no because Joe said, "She'll be here in the morning. She might know something, but..." He hesitated and she could see him changing his mind. "I don't know. If she knew anything, she'd probably have told Sue by now and one way or another I'd have heard about it. But you could try talking to her."

"Thanks, I might do that." She leaned back in her seat

when Doreen returned to clear their dishes. "I'll take the ticket whenever you've got it ready," Libby told her. "My treat," she added to Bradley, to pre-empt any argument.

"Sorry," said Doreen. "Sue said this was on the house. Said to tell you welcome to town."

"Oh, I couldn't," Libby protested. "Tell her I appreciate it, but—"

"And she said if you argued with that, I should tell you to consider it a down payment on the recipes. Or a bribe," she added, smiling. "Whichever you're the most comfortable with."

Doreen winked at Bradley, who only laughed and said, "But no pressure."

After leaving the diner, she'd planned to return to the inn. Maybe take advantage of that tub once more and hope that hot water and bubbles would ensure another six or eight hours of blissfully sound sleep. She didn't remember making a conscious decision to drive right past the inn and just keep going, but thirty minutes later she was back at the lake and pulling in to an empty campsite.

The low beam of the headlights created a distorted shadow of herself that stretched out in front of her as she walked over to the abandoned fire pit. She tapped one of the stones with the toe of her boot, her gaze settling on the tire tracks still visible in the dirt where Quinn's truck had been parked the night before.

Overhead, the sky was a panorama of flickering stars. She tilted her face toward them, remembering how as a little girl she used to lie out in the backyard at night, staring up at the stars and imagining another girl on one of those far-off worlds, lying in her own yard staring back and imagining Libby.

She kicked the stone again, harder this time, and shoved her hands in her coat pockets. If she hadn't expected to find her here, why was she disappointed? Maybe expected was the wrong word. She really hadn't expected Quinn would still be here. But she'd hoped.

Something moved in the undergrowth nearby. Another

rustling sound had her backing up a step, but helped her narrow down the direction of the movement in time to see a familiar black and white shape emerge at the edge of the trees.

"PJ!" She went down on one knee, expecting him to come right over, but he only stared at her.

"Hey, fella. It's me." She made a little clapping come-here gesture. When she realized he had no intention of coming closer, she stood and put her hands back in her pockets.

"Sorry I don't have anything to feed you," she said, knowing that's probably what had brought him back here. "Quinn took all the good stuff with her." She suspected Quinn would have been receiving a nightly visit from him for as long as she'd stayed here.

He turned suddenly and disappeared back into the shadows. She wondered, too late, whether he'd expected her to follow him, but quickly dismissed the idea. Quinn said he'd been very insistent when he wanted her to follow him, so whatever he was up to tonight, he didn't seem to require any assistance.

She stood there for another minute, but the woods remained silent. Eventually the wind picked up, sending her back to her car to return to the inn.

Chapter Ten

The next morning Libby called Latham and found out that Bradley had been correct. Electricity at the house was simply a matter of flipping the main breaker.

"You're on a well out there, so you'll have water too, once you kick the electric back on. And you might find it a little cold in the evenings. I believe there's an oil furnace out there, but I wouldn't recommend turning it on unless you have someone check it out first. I'm not even sure there's any fuel left in it."

"I'm sure I'll be fine," Libby assured him.

"There's still a bit of paperwork to be done, so stop by my office before you leave town. Oh, and one other thing." She could hear papers shuffling in the background. "I was going through his file again and it looks like he did prepare a list of a few items he wanted distributed, but it was contingent upon your approval."

"My approval?"

"If there's anything on the list that you want, he wanted you to keep it."

"I think whatever's on there should be given to whomever he intended. It's not as though I have a sentimental attachment to anything."

"Either way, it's completely up to you."

Libby was less curious about what items were on the list than she was about the people he'd named. If there was the slightest chance she still might be able to learn something from anyone in this town, the people Shepherd considered personal friends would probably be a good place to start. She asked if she could pick up a copy of the list before she headed out to the lake and Latham said he would have it waiting for her.

After a quick breakfast downstairs, she checked out of the inn and then stopped by Latham's to pick up the list. She arrived at the lake house shortly before eleven and found the breaker box at the back of the garage before letting herself into the house.

She supposed locating the items on Shepherd's list would be as good a place as any to start. She dug the envelope Latham had given her out of her bag. It contained two sheets of paper, both in what she assumed was Shepherd's own handwriting. An unexpected chill gathered at the back of her neck when she started reading.

Libby, if these items are of no use or interest to you, I'd appreciate it if you'd see to it that the following folks get them. If there's anything here that you'd prefer to hold onto, please do so, with my blessing.

Mark Shepherd

His use of her name was more than that. Obviously he'd known her name—he'd left everything to her, hadn't he? Still, to see it used with such…casual familiarity. A familiarity that seemed at odds with the way he'd signed his own name, and was a little unsettling.

She turned her attention back to the list.

Father Joel Moore—My hand-carved chess set and the four-leaf clover paperweight (Don't know if it'll help, but God knows it can't hurt).

Beckett Langstrom—My luggage, and some advice. Just go—I promise you won't regret it.

Rhonda Flynn—My Give the Lady What She Wants / *Lena Horne.*

Sue Quimby—My red three-ring binder of recipes and my apron that says "I'd tell you the recipe but then I'd have to kill you."

The last bequest put a smile on her face. She'd planned to give her the recipes anyway, but Sue would probably appreciate knowing he'd intended for her to have them.

The only other thing on there was a request that his books be donated to two libraries. History, art and any reference books to the high school; the rest to the public library.

Most of the items shouldn't be too hard to locate, like the books. The luggage would probably be in a closet. Or maybe the attic. Since she was already in the kitchen, Libby decided to start there and found the recipe binder and the apron in short order.

Sue's obvious enthusiasm for the recipes had tweaked her curiosity enough to spend a few minutes flipping through the contents of the binder. Pages of notebook paper were filled with what Libby now recognized as Shepherd's handwriting. She couldn't claim to understand what the fuss was all about. One cup of this, two tablespoons of that. Lots of things to be beaten and whipped. Others chopped, diced or thinly sliced. Why would anyone want to go through all that trouble when they could just pick up the phone and order in? Of course, that wasn't really an option up here, she reminded herself, and realized that if she was going to stay out here, she'd need to make a trip back into town to pick up a few things at the grocery store.

She went in search of Father Moore's paperweight and eventually found it among the curios scattered throughout the living room. The chess set was there too. Two more items checked off the list.

She found the luggage in his bedroom closet. Since she was there, she spent some time rummaging through the little cubbyholes and drawers of the roll top desk. It felt intrusive, but it also seemed like the most logical place for him to have left any kind of clue about his motives for leaving everything to her. There seemed to be everything but a clue. Notes and postcards from guests telling him how much they'd enjoyed their visits. Two address books, one containing what looked like local addresses and the other evidently with the addresses of guests who'd stayed with him numerous times. She found receipts and warranty information for what she imagined must be every electrical appliance that was now or had ever been in the house. The usual stubs from phone and utility bills. Visa statements that didn't reveal anything more interesting than how much he'd spent on heating oil the winter before last. Bank statements for accounts she knew didn't exist anymore. A lot of nothing.

Maybe there was nothing to find. Even if he'd intended to leave something, maybe he'd never gotten around to it. He couldn't have anticipated his stroke, and she knew from experience it was human nature to assume you had all the time in the world to do—well, whatever was on your list of things to do.

She carried the luggage out to join the other items she'd left on the dining room table. All that remained was Rhonda's album and the books.

Shepherd's music collection proved a bit distracting even after she located the album she was looking for. He had dozens of vinyl recordings in addition to CDs. Big Band. Jazz. Rock. Heavy on the sixties, she noted. The Doors. Otis Redding. Some early Rolling Stones. The Moody Blues. Some stuff she'd never heard of, she realized, frowning at an Electric Prunes record.

No reason she couldn't entertain herself with a little music while she worked. The novelty of having a record player at her disposal—one with a stacking arm, no less—sent her back to Shepherd's collection of vinyl. Moments later, the first of three records dropped to the turntable.

She stood in the middle of the living room, surveying the packed bookshelves. This would be a lot easier if they were all going to a single library. It crossed her mind, briefly, that he'd left her an easy out. If she didn't want to get rid of them, she didn't have to. It wouldn't raise any eyebrows if she just gave them all to the public library either, but that would be tantamount to ignoring what amounted to his final requests, something she wouldn't be comfortable doing.

The easiest thing would probably be to pull out what there

was the least of and then box the rest. That meant separating the books intended for the high school. Over the next hour, Mel Torme and Nat King Cole kept her company while she went through Shepherd's bookcases shelf-by-self, removing the volumes that would go to the school and stacking them on the coffee table.

By the time the third record dropped, she'd gone through all the shelves she could reach and was thinking seriously about calling it a day. Maybe head into town in search of a late lunch or early dinner. But then the speakers crackled back to life with Etta James's voice in all its imperfect vinyl glory.

No way she could quit on Etta James's watch, so she brought a chair in from the kitchen and went to work on the upper shelves. While it wasn't exactly step class, she told herself that climbing up and down from the chair was bound to be doing her butt some kind of good.

Spotting the name "Picasso" along the edge of a book on a top shelf, she climbed up onto the chair to pull it out. She blew at the dust that had settled over the top of the pages and realized that was a mistake just before she sneezed.

"Gesundheit."

Startled, Libby had to grab at the edge of a shelf to catch her balance.

"The door was open," said Quinn. "I knocked. Figured you just couldn't hear over the music, but thought I'd better come in to check. You know, just to be on the safe side," she added with a tentative grin.

Libby wanted to say something, but her mouth was suddenly dry. She told herself it was almost falling that had her heart thudding and not merely the sight of Quinn suddenly standing there looking...good. Really good. The collar and sleeves of a long-sleeved black T-shirt peeked out from under the blue plaid flannel shirt tucked into black jeans. God, she felt like such a cliché, but she couldn't help it. There was just something about a butch in flannel. Her fingers, itching to touch, tightened on the book in her hands.

114

When she didn't say anything, Quinn's grin faded. "I see you got the power turned on."

"Seemed like a good idea if I don't want to get stuck in the dark again," said Libby, finding her voice as she hopped down from the chair. She watched Quinn pick up one of the record jackets lying next to the stereo. She appeared to give it only a brief glance before she set it back down, her gaze returning to Libby.

A little guilty for being caught staring, Libby tried to cover it by bending to set the book she was still holding with the others on the coffee table.

You weren't staring, she told herself. *You were looking. You're allowed to look.* Quinn was standing right here, after all. It would be rude not to look at her. Not to mention nearly impossible, she decided, finding her eyes drawn back to her once again in spite of herself.

"I thought you were leaving yesterday," she said casually, trying to make it sound less like the question it really was.

"Yeah, well…" This time it was Quinn who looked away. "Turns out I may have a little unfinished business here after all." Quinn picked up the same record jacket she'd had in her hand only a couple of seconds earlier only to once again set it down without having really looked at it.

"Oh?"

"Yeah, it's—well, nothing really. I mean, just, you know just…"

"Business," supplied Libby.

"Right." Once again Quinn's hand moved toward the record jacket, but this time to tap out an awkward, hasty rhythm that had nothing to do with the music that was playing.

Was she nervous? Libby was unexpectedly delighted and on the verge of being a little flattered by it before it occurred to her what the one thing might be to make a woman like Quinn nervous. After all, that was the last thing she'd said to Quinn before she drove away, wasn't it? Sometimes it helps to talk about it. Whatever had been bothering her earlier, maybe she'd decided a friendly ear might help after all. If she didn't decide to run off again, that is. She looked like she was on the verge of flight right now.

The situation seemed to call for something to drink. It was always easier to bare your soul when you had something to occupy your hands. Unfortunately she didn't have any coffee, and it was too early in the day for liquor—not that she had any of that either. Which left only…

"Water?"

"Excuse me?"

"I meant, can I offer you something to drink? I have…um, water."

In contrast to the incredible lameness of her offer, Quinn's acceptance was unexpectedly enthusiastic. "Water would be good."

Some poured over my head would probably be even better, Quinn thought, staring after Libby as she walked toward the kitchen and wondering how it was possible for anyone to look that sexy in a pair of khakis. And what the hell was up with that shirt? Unlike the businesslike silk blouse Libby had been wearing the last time, this one was made out of some kind of stretchy brown fabric that molded to every curve, hugging her breasts and making them look so, well…*there*. How could anyone expect her not to look?

Hoping for something to distract herself with, Quinn picked up a book from the pile on the end table, but the sound of running water from the kitchen had her picturing Libby standing at the sink, a mental vision that quickly segued into an impromptu fantasy…

Coming up from behind Libby at the sink, she'd gently brush aside her hair and kiss the back of her neck, slowly making her way over to that sensitive spot she'd found before, that little dip just near the curve of Libby's shoulder. Then she'd reach for the hem of Libby's shirt to draw it up over her head. She'd unfasten her bra, slipping the straps down from her shoulders so she could reach around and fill her hands with the soft weight of Libby's breasts. She could feel Libby's nipples tighten beneath her fingers, hear her breathless little moan. When she couldn't resist the temptation any longer, she'd turn and lift her so that Libby was sitting on the counter. Then, standing between her legs, she'd bow her head to pull one of those perfect, taut, rosy buds into her mouth. Libby's fingers would curve against the back of her head, holding Quinn to her breast while she rolled Libby's nipple with her tongue, sucked at it, and then—

"Is that something you're interested in?"

The proximity of Libby's voice startled her back to the moment. "What?"

"That book," said Libby with a nod toward the book in Quinn's hand. *A Thematic Study of Tribal Arts.* Looking at it, she saw the cover art she'd evidently appeared so interested in was very obviously a phallic symbol.

"If it's something you'd like to—"

"No," said Quinn quickly, putting the book down. "No, I was just, uh…" She took the glass Libby offered and drank half of it before pausing for breath. Libby was watching her, looking a little startled. "Guess I was thirstier than I realized."

Libby's only response was a polite smile before taking a much more lady like sip from her own glass. She watched Libby's tongue flick over the moisture clinging to her pale, soft lips and wanted to swallow her whole. When she saw Libby's cheeks flush a delicate pink, she realized too much of what she was feeling must be showing on her face.

She couldn't do this.

She was a dyke, for Christ's sake. She didn't want to be friends with women, she wanted to sleep with them. Touch them. Taste them. And all the conversation in the world wasn't going to change that. At best it would be foreplay. Ordinarily that would be fine. She was a big fan of foreplay. She just didn't care to be the only one getting worked up.

She drained the rest of her water and set the glass down on the end table.

"I have to go."

"But—you just got here," protested Libby, confirming that

she had, in fact, said it out loud.

"I know." For a moment, silence hung on those words like a hook while Libby stared at her and she tried to think of something to say that wouldn't leave her looking like more of an idiot than she already did. No words came to mind. She cleared her throat. "Really I just came by to, uh…well…"

"What? Make sure I hadn't gotten myself stuck in the cellar again?" said Libby with a self-deprecating little chuckle that made it clear she was joking.

"Uh…yeah," she said, and watched Libby's eyebrows lift briefly in surprise. Okay, so it was a little insulting as reasons went, but it was also as good as anything she was likely to come up with, because at the moment the only idea she seemed capable of coming up with was kissing her until neither of them could see straight.

"But you didn't," she added quickly. "Which is good. And obviously you're not going to, which is—well, even better, right? So you just keep doing whatever it is you were doing and I'll just—show myself out." Screw not looking like an idiot. If she left looking like an idiot, surely that would be enough to talk herself out of ever coming back.

She'd almost made it to the hallway before Libby's voice trailed after her.

"It must be so difficult for you."

It was the unexpected and completely sincere sound of sympathy in Libby's voice that had her looking back, certain she'd misheard her. "What?"

Libby had settled a hip against the back of the couch. "This superhero fantasy you have going." She took a sip of water before continuing, eyeing her over the top of the glass. "I mean, really, how many women can there be, stuck in cellars just waiting to be rescued? And I don't think any of us are getting tied to railroad tracks anymore. I can only imagine how frustrating that must be for someone like you," she said, brown eyes going soft with pity. "Not knowing what to do with a woman who doesn't need… saving."

Against her better judgment, she turned back into the room. "I'll admit I've got a few shortcomings. But not knowing what to do with a woman..." The suggestion was enough to make her smile. "That's never been one of them."

Libby's look of polite skepticism was so well-played she couldn't help taking it as a challenge. The sensible part of her brain was urging her to turn and keep on walking, but that tiny voice of reason was silenced by the part of her already so turned on it was willing to seize any excuse to linger. "Take you for instance."

Libby's eyebrows popped up as if to say, *Who, me?* "Sorry," she said, not looking very apologetic. "No damsel in distress here."

"Maybe saving you isn't what I had in mind."

She moved closer, her eyes deliberately tracing the curves her hands had previously traveled, reminding her what she'd felt, what she'd wanted to make Libby feel. When her gaze drifted back up to Libby's face, the amber eyes had lost all of their skepticism and most of their focus, suggesting that Libby had been doing a little remembering of her own.

She took the glass from Libby's hand and, without taking her eyes from Libby's, set it down on the end table.

"Maybe," she murmured, pulling Libby against her, "there's something I've been wanting to do ever since I walked in here."

Sliding an arm behind Libby's back she held her close—close enough to feel her ribs straining to control each shallow breath. Slowly, she lowered her head, letting her gaze linger on those perfect, pale pink lips already parting in anticipation. Libby's eyes drifted shut. Their lips were only a shared breath apart…

"Gotcha."

Libby's eyes flew open again, looking confused and vaguely disoriented for a moment before she realized they were moving in a slow circle to the music coming from the stereo. Her face a little flushed, Libby offered up a wry smile. "I suppose you think you're pretty clever."

"Hey, you gotta be clever to be a superhero," she said, unable to resist. "You don't think they let just anyone into the club, do you?"

"You asked for that, you know," Libby told her with a good-humored glower.

She smiled hopefully. "Does that mean you're going to give me everything I ask for?"

"Oh yeah, live in that fantasy," said Libby, but she was smiling too.

"Can't blame a gal for trying." A moment later she was pleasantly surprised when Libby moved closer to rest her head on her shoulder. She doubted—despite Etta's suggestion in the background—that her lonely days were over, but her afternoon had certainly taken a turn for the better. Maybe there was something to this dancing business after all.

Almost as if reading her mind, Libby said, "Don't take this the wrong way, but you didn't strike me as the dancing type."

"It's been a while," she admitted. "My mother taught me when I was a kid. Sunday evenings she'd haul out her forty-fives and drag me into the living room."

As seemed to be so often the case lately, every memory she dredged up inevitably brought others with it. Sunday nights with the forty-fives had stopped shortly after the first time she'd tried to run away. She remembered thinking at the time what a joke that was, that her mother actually believed that was any kind of punishment considering what her father was capable of dishing out. Now, for the first time, she found herself wondering whether the person being punished was her mother. Was it possible her father had tried to blame her for their dyke daughter? Surely not. Not even he could be that ignorant, that *warped*, that—

"Your dad wasn't much for dancing, I take it?"

"Not especially." The tension she managed to keep out of her voice took up residence in her neck and shoulders and brought with it the now familiar urge to get out, to get away—from here, from him. But then she felt Libby's fingers gently stroking the space between her shoulder blades. Whether it was calculated to soothe or merely an absent gesture with a very pleasant side effect, she didn't know.

The song had ended. Quinn kept her arm around Libby in anticipation of another song, but then she recognized the tediously rhythmic sound of a record that had reached its end. She relaxed her hold on Libby, but didn't quite release her. "So back to what you were saying earlier," she began conversationally. "Something about me not knowing what to do with a woman…?"

She allowed the playful push to free Libby from the loose circle of her arms.

"I thought we agreed you had that coming," said Libby.

"I'm pretty sure I haven't agreed to much of anything," she pointed out, smiling because she couldn't help it.

Libby smiled too, but it was fading at the edges. When she walked back to the stereo, Quinn hoped it was to put on another record, but she began putting them back in their respective jackets. The time for dancing, it seemed, was over.

Well, that was understandable. Obviously she'd shown up when Libby was in the middle of… She noted the gaps on the bookshelves and the short stacks scattered around on the floor and coffee table.

"So, uh, what's up with the books?" she asked, frowning a bit at the rather obvious, if primitive, cover art of her earlier selection. "Just a little light afternoon reading?"

"Oh, they're not for me," Libby said absently as she put the last of the records to order. "He wanted his books to go to the library."

"He being this Shepherd guy?"

Libby nodded. She turned to survey the room, looking a little beleaguered. "I'm going to need boxes."

"We can get boxes." She'd intended only to dispel some of the stress she'd detected in Libby's voice by suggesting that obtaining a few boxes would not be that big a problem. It was only when she registered the mild surprise on Libby's face that she realized the cooperation implied by her comment. "So, uh, how many do you think you'll need?" She looked at the books scattered about and estimated two or three should be sufficient.

"I have no idea."

She noticed then that Libby wasn't looking at the books stacked about the room, but the still nearly filled shelves.

"How many of these are you donating, anyway?"

"All of them."

All of them? She made an effort to pull her eyebrows back down. "Oh, yeah. We're going to need boxes." She hadn't meant to be funny, but Libby snickered anyway. "So what was this guy," she asked, noticing many of the books Libby had already pulled seemed to have a common theme. "Some kind of art teacher?"

"I don't know. Earlier I was wondering if maybe he'd painted some of these," Libby said, with a nod to the paintings hung around the room. "A lot of them seem to be signed by the same person, but it's really more a scrawl than a signature, and not anything that looks like Mark or Shepherd. But from all these books," she said, picking one up, "you'd think he had some connection to art. Teaching, painting—something."

"So what was he then?"

"I told you I—" Libby's slightly exasperated look dissolved in mid-sentence and she shook her head apologetically. "Sorry. Of course you don't know. But that's kind of why I'm here, because I don't know either." She grinned at the look on Quinn's face. "And that made all the sense in the world, didn't it?" She dropped the book back onto the stack. "Come on. I'm ready to get out of here for a bit. Why don't we take a walk and I'll tell you all about it."

Walking along the path that wound through the trees and past the cabins, Libby relayed the reasons for her visit to Turtle Cove and how she'd hoped the trip here might jog some forgotten memories.

"I can remember staying in one of these cottages," she said as they approached the first one, "because I remember thinking when I grew up I wanted to live in a house just like it. My very own cozy little dollhouse," she mused, looking, Quinn thought, just a bit wistful. "That didn't happen, by the way. Turns out there's a shortage of these in New York," she added, angling her head toward Quinn's with an air of confidentiality. "But that was the one and only time we came up here. My mother..." Libby paused. "Well, she's not really the roughing it type."

Roughing it? Quinn eyed the buildings in question. The cabins—Libby called them cottages, but that wasn't a word that sat comfortably in Quinn's vocabulary—were small, but by no means shacks. If the place had been up and running, she might have been tempted to rent one of them herself.

She tried to imagine what it would have been like to come here for a family vacation. Her family had never taken a vacation together. She remembered her mother taking her to El Paso a couple of times where they'd stayed with a grandmother who never seemed happy to see them. There had been visits with some aunts and a few cousins. She didn't think that qualified as a vacation. Her father's traveling usually was done solo or maybe with a couple buddies for a week or two around hunting season when they'd head up to Oklahoma or Colorado. Although he inevitably returned home empty-handed, it didn't occur to her until years later to suspect those trips might have been for something other than hunting.

Shaking off the unwelcome train of thought, she brought herself back to the moment. "So how many of these things are there?" she asked as they continued walking.

"I don't know. This is the first time I've had a chance to walk down here." They'd passed three so far and another was coming up ahead, each one a tiny mirror image of Shepherd's own house with its weathered shingle siding and faded white trim. Each of them sported a tiny covered front porch large enough for a couple chairs—maybe three, if you didn't mind one of them blocking the door.

The path forked off, one way continuing along the curving inlet of the lake, the other leading away from the lake and farther into the woods where yet another cottage was nestled back in the trees. She was surprised but pleased when Libby steered them down that path by hooking an arm through hers.

"I'm sure it's all spelled out somewhere in Latham's files,"

Libby said, "but we didn't get that far. He just kind of tossed the keys at me and said come take a look around. I did get the impression he might have a buyer if I decide to sell. And actually there's a couple in town who may be interested."

"Is that what you're going to do? Sell it?"

"Probably. Maybe. I don't know." They'd reached the cottage at the end of the path and Libby sat down on the porch steps. "I haven't quite wrapped my brain around the idea that it's mine, so I can't bring myself to think about what to do with it."

Quinn walked around the side of the porch to peek through one of the screened windows. There wasn't much to see from this angle, just the edge of a counter and a set of bunk beds against the far wall.

A bright spot of color was creeping along the worn white of the window ledge. Quinn put her finger in its path and the ladybug obliged her by crawling onto her hand. She watched it exploring the new terrain for a couple seconds and then started to tap it off back to the windowsill, but on impulse changed her mind. She carried it over to where Libby was still sitting on the steps, staring through the trees toward the water.

"Close your eyes and hold out your hand."

Humoring her with a look, Libby closed her eyes and held her hand out, palm up. Quinn turned her hand over and then gently tapped the ladybug onto the back of Libby's hand. "Okay. Look."

"Oh!" exclaimed Libby softly, her eyes lighting up. She brought her hand up to her face, angling it to keep the small insect in view. "I haven't seen one of these in ages. They're supposed to be good luck, aren't they?" Libby appeared too caught up in studying the tiny creature to really expect an answer, so she didn't offer one. Watching her, she had no trouble imagining the child Libby had probably been, fascinated by every flower, bug and pinecone.

Whether ladybugs were good luck or not, she couldn't help feeling that hers had improved dramatically, if only for a little while.

"Come on." Quinn stood up, suddenly in a much better mood than she had any right to be in. She held out a hand to Libby. "Let's find out how many of these little dollhouses you have."

Smiling, Libby reached for her hand and together they continued down the path.

By the time they were finished, they'd counted eight cottages, six close to the lake and two set farther back in the woods. Five were a simple two-room design with one space dedicated to a kitchenette and eating area and another larger space for sleeping. The other three were slightly bigger, with the bedroom space divided into two separate rooms. Each cottage had a tiny bathroom with a claustrophobic shower. Functional, nothing fancy.

All of them were in need of re-staining, fresh paint and other minor repairs—replacing a screen or cracked window, fixing a loose step here or there—and as Latham had warned, several showed evidence of mice or other furry vermin. On the whole, though, they seemed to be in pretty good shape. It didn't take Quinn long to figure out Libby was in love with them as much now as when she'd been a child, especially once she started speculating about what kind of plants would look good in the narrow space on either side of the porch and how cute this one would look with some window boxes.

"You could always put a white picket fence around it and call it the honeymoon suite," she suggested, not entirely serious, but Libby's hand tightened on hers with an enthusiastic little squeeze.

"I love it! Listen to you, with the ideas. Keep that up and I won't be able to part with it. I'll have to move in myself."

"You don't expect me to believe you'd give up your fancy New York penthouse for one of these," she teased.

Libby rolled her eyes. "I don't really see the whole penthouse thing happening in my lifetime."

"That doesn't answer the question."

Libby gave her a patient smile. "Well, if those were really my only choices...Yeah, probably. My family was pretty well-off.

Not penthouse fancy, but I can't say I grew up wanting for much of anything." She paused. "I don't know that we were that much happier because of it."

Chapter Eleven

After exploring the cottages, Libby suggested they run into town to get something to eat and try to find some boxes. They ended up going to Quimby's so that Libby could drop off the items she had for Sue. It was still early for most people to be thinking about supper, so there were only a handful of cars in the parking lot. As they walked up the steps to the diner, someone called Libby's name. Across the street, Officer Bradley raised one arm in greeting before he got into his cruiser. Smiling, Libby waved back.

"My, my," murmured Quinn. "In town only a couple days and already so popular." When Libby shot her an admonishing glance, she held up her hands in a gesture of mock surrender. Reaching around Libby, she opened the door and followed her into the diner.

"Well, look who the cat dragged in."

Caught off guard by the greeting, Quinn hesitated. It took her a second to locate the source of the loudly familiar voice. Rhonda was refilling napkin dispensers behind the counter. "Have to say you're looking a sight better than you were the other day."

"Uh...thanks," said Quinn uncertainly, mindful of the handful of customers in the diner who looked up to see who Rhonda was addressing. She wasn't sure, but thought she heard a softly murmured "My, my" coming from Libby's direction, but when she glanced over at her, Libby's bright smile was focused entirely on the woman behind the counter.

"Don't stand on ceremony," instructed Rhonda, oblivious to Quinn's discomfort. "Grab a menu and a seat and I'll be with you in a sec. You girls know what you want to drink?"

They each ordered a soft drink. Quinn pulled two menus from the table by the door and then led Libby to a booth and slid in opposite her.

Rhonda brought their drinks and pulled two sets of silverware rolled in red cloth napkins from a pocket in her apron and set them down on table. "Hope you know what you're getting into, hanging around with Trouble, here," she told Libby.

Quinn, without even bothering to look up from her menu, said, "She doesn't have a clue and I'd like to keep it that way if you don't mind."

"Oh, I don't know about that. She looks like a pretty smart cookie to me," Rhonda said with a wink for Libby. "Now what can I get you girls today?"

"I take it you've been eating here," said Libby after Rhonda collected the menus and headed toward the kitchen.

"I stopped here for breakfast the other day—this is where I got that omelet—but that was it. I can't believe she even remembered me," she said, thinking how packed the place had been that morning.

"Oh, I'm sure a lot of women have found you quite memorable."

She was sure that little smile was intended to provoke rather than reassure. Fortunately she was spared the chance to dig herself into a hole when Rhonda returned with a basket of dinner rolls.

"Excuse me," said Libby.

For one horrified second, she thought Libby was actually going to invite Rhonda into that conversation, but all that came out of Libby's mouth was, "Is Sue here, by any chance?"

"You just missed her," said Rhonda, looking at Libby like she was trying to figure out if maybe she should recognize her. "She had to make a run over to Bryantville. She'll be back, but it'll be a while."

"Oh," said Libby, clearly disappointed. "Well, when she gets back," she said, pulling a loose-leaf binder from her bag along with what appeared to be a folded up apron, "would you tell her Libby was here and left these for her?"

"*You're* Libby?" A broad smile broke out over Rhonda's face. "I sure am glad for the chance to meet you. And I know Sue's going to be sorry she wasn't here. Especially if that's what I think it is," Rhonda added, eyeing the red binder. "You know..." She glanced around as if to make sure there was no one within earshot. "She's already planning on how she's going to sweet talk you out of those. Might be fun to let her try. Just to see what she comes up with."

Libby smiled at the conspiratorial gleam in the woman's eyes. "You're probably right," she admitted, "but it's not really me giving them to her. He intended for her to have them." Libby glanced at the name tag pinned to Rhonda's shirt. "Your name was on the list too. There's a record. Lena Horne."

Rhonda laid a hand against her chest. "*Give the Lady What She Wants*? I love that record.

"Joe mentioned that you worked here. I should have thought to bring it with me."

"It's not like I'm going anywhere," said Rhonda, dismissing Libby's apology with a don't-worry-about-it wave. The chime sounded over the entrance. "No rest for the wicked," she declared, and went to seat the new customers.

"So *you're* Libby," Quinn said, cheerfully mimicking Rhonda's enthusiastic greeting once the waitress was out of earshot. She grinned at Libby's exasperated expression. "Seriously, you have to tell me how you managed to become so popular in only two days."

"Do not start," Libby warned her, with a slightly embarrassed

129

flush that took any sting out of the reprimand.

She contrived to look disappointed. "I understand. You're probably sworn to secrecy by the Popular Girls Union or something."

"Hey, you're no one to talk about keeping secrets," said Libby.

"Excuse me?"

"You know all about me," Libby said, "and I barely know anything about you. Only that your name is Quinn and you're from Nevada. License plate," she said when Quinn lifted her eyebrows. "And that you like to camp. Which I assume means you're here on some sort of vacation?"

"You could say that."

The little sigh Libby puffed out suggested her dissatisfaction with that answer. "I could say anything. The point is for you to tell me. Look, I'm not trying to delve into your psyche, but come on. You did get to second base. I think the least you could do is tell me your last name."

Okay, she had a point. "Barnett," she said, and then added, "but I'm pretty sure that was only first base," she added and discovered it was impossible to talk about it without thinking about it.

"Over the bra is first base," said Libby. "Under the bra, definitely second base."

Okay, fine, think about it if you have to, but you will keep your eyes up front and center like the good little Girl Scout you never were.

"So, Quinn Barnett is it?"

"Yup."

"Middle name?"

"Yup." She didn't pretend to misunderstand Libby's look, but all she said was, "No point in telling you what you're never going to use anyway."

"Oh, come on," Libby wheedled. "I told you mine." But she wasn't budging on this one.

Fine, Libby said with her eyes. "So what do you do out in Nevada, Quinn who-won't-tell-me-her-middle-name Barnett?"

130

"Oh, you know. This and that. Sometimes the other thing," she said just to tweak, but then relented. "For the past couple of years I've been working as a cook at a truck stop outside of Reno."

"What's that like?"

"Hot and hectic," she said, moving her drink aside to make room for the plates Rhonda brought over. As soon as the waitress left again, Libby jumped back into interrogation mode.

"So brothers? Sisters? Mom? Dad?"

"Hey, don't I get a turn at this?" she said, a little more impatiently than she'd intended.

For a moment she thought Libby was going to argue, but then she seemed to relent. "Okay, your turn." She smiled. "Ask me anything."

Libby's agreeability was a little disconcerting. "This is a trick, right?"

"Is that your question?"

"No, but I know how this works. I'll ask you something and you'll answer, but then you'll ask me something and expect me to answer just because you did."

Libby regarded her with a mild look. "Where I come from, that's called conversation. Does the term paranoid personality disorder mean anything to you?"

"Is that your question?"

"No," said Libby. She paused to eye Quinn over a forkful of mashed potatoes. "But I'm reserving the right to come back to it."

"Fine."

"Fine," Libby mimicked, eyes smiling.

"So who's this Brian person?" She hadn't intended to just spit it out like that but blamed Libby for throwing her off her rhythm even though she hadn't established one yet.

"Brian," repeated Libby, looking surprised.

"Isn't that his name? The one who called looking for you."

"He's a friend. He worries about me."

"Just a friend?"

"Well, no, we work together, too. That's how we met actually."

"But he's not like your, uh, boyfriend or anything like that?"

"Brian? No." The suggestion shocked a little laugh out of her. "I'm not really his type."

"What type would that be?"

"Male," she said simply. "Brian's gay."

Oh? "Oh."

"Not that that really matters," she said dismissively, "since I am too, but you knew that already." Libby started to take a drink but then hesitated, offering Quinn a slightly concerned look over the top of the glass. "You *did* know that, right?"

"Well—yeah. I mean, you know, I'd pretty much, uh…yeah." Despite her nearly flawless confirmation, Libby's eyes widened a little with disbelief.

"You *didn't* know?" Libby sent a quick, cautious glance toward the empty booths alongside theirs before leaning in over the table. "How could you *not* know?"

"Well, okay, since you asked, I *did* know. Or at least I was pretty damn sure. But then after all that I-can't-do-this business the other night—"

"What?" interrupted Libby, looking baffled.

"When you threw me out at second base, remember?" She couldn't help thinking it was almost worth it, just to see Libby's cheeks turning bright pink like that.

"That wasn't because I'm straight," Libby hissed. "That was because I…look, all I meant was I don't have sex on a first date. Not that that even qualified as a date," she added. "But—that's all I meant." Libby buried her face in her hands. "I can't believe we're having this conversation in a…a diner."

"You started it," muttered Quinn.

They were still eating lunch when a young boy of about eight or nine came in with a handful of flyers. He spoke to Rhonda for a few seconds, then gave her one of the flyers and left.

"Hey Frank," Rhonda called through the pass-through to the

kitchen. "Charlie's labradoodle ran off again. I told him we'd put a sign up for him." An unintelligible acknowledgment drifted up from the back.

"Labradoodle?" said Quinn.

"You know. Labrador-poodle mix? Labradoodle."

"In other words, a mutt." Quinn made a face. "What'd they do, use a ladder?"

"I'm pretty sure it was a standard poodle," said Libby, laughing. "And actually, they're not considered mutts. They're 'designer dogs.' You know, like the schnoodle. Schnauzer-poodle mix," she explained. "Or the yorkipoo. A yorkie and a poodle. The cockapoo—"

"Let me guess. A cross between a cockatiel and a poodle," she said, with enough of a smirk to let Libby know she was kidding. "Sounds to me like poodles are getting all the action. I wonder if our friend PJ knows about this?"

Libby glanced up from the green bean she was pushing around on her plate. "I saw him last night."

"Oh yeah? So he's okay, then." She hadn't really doubted that he was, but remembered how upset Libby had been when he disappeared.

"Oh, he's fine. Didn't want anything to do with me though. Probably because I didn't have anything for him to eat."

"I'm telling you, he's just a little con artist," said Quinn, amused that Libby actually looked a little wounded by the snub. "It's all about what's in it for him. Free ride. Free meal. The occasional hook-up with a hot little poodle," she added, hoping to make Libby laugh because she liked the little lines it etched at the corners of her eyes. Forty years from now those lines would be permanently etched, and she'd be even more beautiful when she laughed than she was today.

"You're probably right," admitted Libby.

"I know I'm right. Canine, bovine, human, doesn't matter," she assured her. "Males are all the same."

"Just heartache waiting to happen, aren't they?" said Rhonda, coming in at the end of Quinn's comment when she returned to see if they needed anything else. "Trick is, you've got to let them know right off the bat there's some stuff you're just not willing to put up with," she said, slicing the air with her hand. "I'm telling you, if women put the same effort into training their husbands as they do training their dogs, the world would be a better place."

"Actually," said Libby, trading an amused look with Quinn, "it was a dog we were talking about. A stray I picked up on the way into town."

"Say, it wasn't a big curly guy, was it?" said Rhonda. "Chocolate brown? About yea-high—"

"Trust me," Quinn interrupted. "This guy's no labradoodle. PJ's more of a—"

"PJ?" Rhonda brightened. "That was my dog's name. Well, really he was Mark's dog," she said, with a glance toward Libby. "I took him in when Mark went into the nursing home."

"Is he missing?" said Libby. "Maybe—"

"No, he died earlier this year. Right before Mark, in fact. I came home from work one night and found him curled up on his little pillow. I thought he was sleeping, but..." She shook her head. "I didn't know how I was going to break it to Mark, but as it turned out I never had too. He passed on the next day himself." Rhonda's normally cheerful smile took on a sad light. "I like to think he somehow knew what was coming and went on ahead so there'd be a familiar face waiting for Mark on the other side." Her brief sigh suggested she was still comforted by the thought.

"After he died, I thought about getting another dog, but," she shrugged. "I knew I'd always be comparing him to PJ and that didn't seem fair, you know? Not that he was anything special. Just a little Heinz 57. Had these bushy white eyebrows that made him look like a grumpy old man," she said, illustrating with a scowl that Quinn thought looked more like a pouty Shirley Temple impersonation.

"Sweet disposition though. And smart like there was no tomorrow. I remember Mark telling me once about this family that had been staying out there whose little girl had wandered off. She was just a little thing, all of five or six maybe. Mark said everyone was panicking because for whatever reason, they thought she'd drowned. The mother's hysterical, of course. The father's demanding someone be called to dredge the lake. And in the middle of all the commotion here comes PJ leading her out of the woods. I guess she'd started out picking up pinecones or something—you know how kids are—and just gotten lost. She told them PJ came and found her and she just followed him out. I'm telling you, he was one smart little dog.

"Be right with you, Sam," Rhonda called back to a man sitting at the counter who was apparently ready to order. "Speaking of grumpy old men," she muttered, then winked at Libby. Tearing the ticket from her order pad, Rhonda set it down on the table. "Oh, hold your horses, you old coot," she said, heading back to the front. "You got no place better to be and we both know it."

After leaving the diner, they stopped at what seemed to be the town's only grocery store. Quinn volunteered to see what she could round up in the way of boxes while Libby did her shopping. By the time they met up at the front of the store, there was a thick gray cast to the sky, and by the time the groceries were bagged a full-scale downpour was well underway.

They waited for a couple of minutes under the narrow awning along the front of the store, but there was nothing to suggest the rain was going to let up any time soon. Behind them, the store's automatic door slid open and an elderly woman with thinning white hair exited the store with her single sack of groceries. As she walked without hesitation into the downpour, Quinn thought she heard her muttering something about sugar.

"What did she say?" she asked when Libby giggled.

"She said, 'What are you, made of sugar?' It means—"

"I *know* what it means," she said, glaring after the old woman, but Libby only laughed again.

"Come on, she's right. You ready to make a run for it?"

"I'm game if you are." She had to set a six-pack of diet soda on the sidewalk and juggle the plastic sacks she'd insisted on carrying in order to fish her keys from her pocket. The headlights on the truck flashed as she unlocked the doors with the remote.

"Race you," said Libby, dashing out into the rain when she bent to retrieve the soda.

"Why don't you let me get the gas," said Libby when Quinn turned into the gas station a couple minutes later.

"And why would I do that?" asked Quinn with a look that clearly said she wouldn't.

"Seeing me stand out in the rain might make you feel better about losing the race."

"I didn't lose the race. You cheated. Besides," Quinn added as she pulled up to the pumps and the drumming sound of rain on the roof stopped, "the pumps are covered, so you standing out there would hardly make up for anything now, would it? So *I* will pump the gas, and you, little miss cheater," she said, getting out of the truck, "can sit here and stew in your own guilty juices."

She started to close the door and then poked her head back in, a good-humored glint in her eye. "But I'm sure if you really wanted to, you *could* think of a way to make it up to me." Her grinning face disappeared behind the rain-blurred glass.

Libby leaned back against the seat, her heart beating with a nervous thrill of anticipation she hadn't felt in a long time. Biting her lip to control the slightly giddy smile that wanted to break out, she reached up to brush at the wet hair clinging to her cheek, groaning as she suddenly realized what a mess she must be. Some women managed to look very sexy with wet hair, but she always felt her own style fell more into the drowned rat category.

She lowered the visor looking for a mirror and a small piece of paper drifted down to the floorboard. When she reached down to pick it up, she saw that it was an obituary.

Helena J. Barnett, beloved wife and mother, died in her home Thursday. She is survived by her husband, former Flat Rock Chief of Police Robert Barnett, and daughter Quinn Barnett. In lieu of flowers, the family is requesting donations be made to the National Alzheimer's Association.

The name of the funeral home and information regarding services followed. She assumed the picture was not a recent one because the woman didn't appear to be much older than Quinn was now. It made it easy to see the resemblance. Her mother had the same dark hair, but wore hers long and loose over her shoulders. Same narrow jaw, same stubborn chin. The smile was different though, and didn't seem to reach her eyes. She almost looked a little sad.

Libby looked at the date again and realized with some shock that it was less than two weeks ago. She was so distracted she didn't notice Quinn had finished with the gas until the driver's door opened.

"So did you think of—" Stopped by the look on Libby's face, Quinn broke off, her eyes dropping to the newspaper clipping in Libby's hand and then to the visor.

"I was looking for a mirror," said Libby, hating the faint sound of guilt she heard in her own voice, as if she'd been caught snooping, although the look on Quinn's face hadn't been anything as pointed as accusation.

"You found one," said Quinn after a beat of silence, gesturing briefly toward the underside of the visor. She climbed into the truck, started the engine and shifted into drive without looking at Libby again.

"Quinn, I'm so sorry." Her natural inclination was to touch her, just a hand on her arm meant to comfort, but Quinn's body language wasn't inviting such familiarity.

"Don't be. If I didn't want it found, I should have put it someplace where it wouldn't be."

"I meant I'm sorry about your mother," she said, although she didn't believe Quinn had misunderstood that. She saw Quinn take a breath, but hold it for a beat as if gathering herself.

"Thanks."

"Do you—"

"I'd rather not talk about it, if you don't mind," said Quinn, her eyes never leaving the road. Although her tone was mild, her stiff-necked posture gave the words an edge her voice lacked.

"All right." No longer concerned with what her hair looked like, Libby lifted the visor and tucked the small piece of newspaper behind it. "But if you—"

"I said I don't want to talk about it." Her tone wasn't as mild as before.

She nodded mutely and turned her own gaze out the passenger window. The delicious thrill she'd been feeling only minutes earlier was gone as if it had never been, replaced by an uncomfortable silence. She watched the edge of town slip past through a veil of rain, then laid her head back against the headrest and closed her eyes.

It took more concentration than it should have for Quinn to keep her face passive, her hands light on the wheel instead of in a tension-filled grip. She didn't want Libby to think she was angry with her, but it was probably too late to be worried about that. If she was angry with anyone right now, it was herself. Why had she put that in the visor? Why not in her wallet or in the glove compartment or any of a dozen places she could think of where Libby wouldn't have found it? It had been a stupid thing to do. Careless.

Okay, get a grip, Barnett, she told herself, deliberately relaxing her fingers one more time. *It's just an obituary. It was published in a freaking newspaper for Christ's sake and it's probably on the goddamn Internet by now if anyone cared to look for it.*

Her eyes drifted toward the rearview mirror, less concerned with checking the non-existent traffic behind her than the woman sitting next to her. Without doing anything as obvious as adjusting the mirror, she could only see part of Libby's face at the edge of the reflection. With her head back, eyes closed, she might have been sleeping, except for a slight tension to her expression and the faintest line between her eyebrows that sleep probably would have erased. She wasn't sleeping.

It crossed her mind that she should apologize, but apologies had never been her strong suit. And what would she be apologizing for? It wasn't like she'd bitten Libby's head off. All she said was she didn't want to talk about it. She had a right not to want to talk it about, didn't she? She tried to work up a little righteous indignation, but wasn't able to summon enough to distract her from the truth. She'd overreacted—not much, but enough to turn it into a thing. A thing that probably wouldn't go away unless they talked about it, which was what she hadn't wanted to do in the first place because she doubted Libby would understand, and she'd just come off looking like an even bigger jerk than she already did.

Neither of them spoke the rest of the way to the lake house. She tried to tell herself it was for the best, but was more than a little relieved when they finally reached the turnoff to the lake. It was only after she pulled in next to Libby's car and cut the engine that she realized she didn't know what to do next. Raindrops were rapidly obscuring the view through the windshield, and their arrhythmic hammering only emphasized the silence inside the truck. Was she supposed to have sense enough to leave without being asked? Or would Libby want the pleasure of telling her to get lost? She sat there, the lead ball in her gut now cushioned in a thick coat of dread. But no one moved and no doors were slammed.

"I hadn't talked to her in almost six years," she said finally, her voice little more than a whisper. She wasn't sure Libby had heard her over the sound of rain drumming on the roof, but when she worked herself up to look, she found Libby watching her, quietly waiting.

"I left that house the day I turned eighteen and never looked back. I hadn't seen her since then. Not once in more than fifteen years."

She thought Libby might say something. But she just laid her hand over Quinn's where it rested on the stick shift, and waited.

It all came pouring out of her then. How her mother had spent her life kowtowing to the whims and wishes of the overbearing son of a bitch she called husband. How even after the Alzheimer's had gotten bad, she'd refused to send him to a nursing facility, and continued to care for him at home long after his doctor thought it was wise, simply because *he* said he didn't want to go. Everyone seemed to think that was a sign of her devotion to the man, but she knew it was only because her mother was so used to taking his orders she didn't know how not to do it.

No one had even come looking for her until she failed to bring him for a scheduled doctor's appointment and wasn't answering the phone. After three days they'd sent Adult Protective Services over to check not on her, but on her father. He'd been fine—happily oblivious to everything except some Jerry Springer-inspired talk show on the television. The sound of running water had led them to the bathroom where her mother lay, fully clothed and dead on the bathroom floor.

The coroner's theory was that she'd slipped in water on the floor and hit her head on the side of the sink. An accident, they said, even though bruises on her body suggested other recent episodes of violence. An unfortunate side effect of the disease, they said. Unable to express their frustration with limitations imposed by the disease, patients often responded with violent outbursts toward their caretakers. That's why they'd urged her to place him in a home, they said.

"Like it was all *her* fault." She didn't recognize the noise that bubbled up from her throat. It was supposed to be a laugh, but it came out sounding humorless and just a little desperate. Libby's hand tightened around hers.

The whole time she'd been growing up, she'd never understood why her mother took it from him, day after day. Why couldn't they leave, just the two of them? Go someplace he'd never find them. She wondered now where exactly she thought her mother was supposed to have gone.

But *she* could have given her mother a place to go. She could have gone back and *made* her leave him. She should have at least tried.

"Why don't you come inside with me," Libby suggested quietly. "You don't have to talk anymore, not if you don't feel like it. I'll just make some coffee and we can…sit on the porch and listen to the rain."

What was it about that face, those eyes, Quinn wondered, that appeased her personal demons with just a look? Or a touch, she thought, looking down at Libby's hand over hers. She turned her hand to entwine her fingers with Libby's.

"I'm sorry." Funny how easy that was to say when she simply meant it and didn't waste time analyzing why.

"That's all right," said Libby, not quite hiding her disappointment.

"No." Quinn's hand tightened on Libby's. "I'm sorry for reacting the way I did. Before."

"There was nothing wrong with the way you reacted, Quinn," Libby told her. "And really, if you'd rather be alone... I'll understand. But," she hesitated, her gaze dropping to where Quinn's hand was still wrapped around hers, "I'd be lying if I said I wasn't hoping you'd stay."

It was a couple long seconds before Libby looked up again, but she waited because she wanted Libby to see her face and know how much she meant it when she said, "I'd like to stay."

Chapter Twelve

In the kitchen, Libby turned on the light over the sink to offset the early darkness brought on by the storm. She found a couple of kitchen towels and tossed one to Quinn, using the other to wipe off her own face and arms.

"Why don't you change into something dry," she suggested, making a cursory pass over her hair to stop the cold trickles that were running down her neck. She planned to do the same herself, as soon as she put away the few things that needed to be refrigerated. Even as she opened her mouth to ask what that look was for, she realized that all of Quinn's clothes would be in her truck. "I'm sure I have something you can put on," she said, trying to think what that might be.

"That's okay. I was thinking about going back out anyway to see if there's any firewood left in that bin by the garage," she explained. "Then—" she paused when a loud crack of thunder rattled the windows, "—if we happen to lose power, we'll already have a little light going."

Less than thirty minutes later, the damp chill was receding in the face of a crackling fire and the sound of Billie Holiday playing softly in the background. Libby thought Holiday, familiar and comfortable, seemed a safe choice. Just something to soften the mood without being overly romantic. After what had transpired on the ride back here, she didn't want Quinn to think she was trying to stage some big seduction scene.

Not that there was much chance of that, she knew, now snug in the navy sweatpants she almost hadn't packed and a loose-fitting flannel shirt with the sleeves rolled up. It wasn't exactly an outfit that screamed romance.

Quinn had replaced her own wet clothes with drier versions of the same—jeans and a long-sleeved black T-shirt that fit across her shoulders with distracting snugness—and left her boots off to reveal shockingly bright fuchsia socks. It was the socks Libby found herself staring at and trying not to smile as Quinn added another chunk of wood to the fire.

Retrieving her mug of coffee, Quinn sat down on the sofa, propping her bright pink feet on the coffee table. Neither of them had said much since they'd come inside. She'd deliberately given Quinn a little space, worried that she'd regret opening up like she had, or that she'd feel the need to escape again. But watching her now, staring into the fire, she looked almost…content.

"I've never understood why anyone would want a house without a fireplace," Quinn said.

"You have one?"

"No, but if I ever settle down enough to buy a house it will."

"When I drove over here the first time I was imagining him here by himself in the winter. You know, with the lake frozen over. All the summer tourists gone. Just him and a bunch of empty cabins. It seemed like it would be so lonely." She paused, enjoying the warmth radiating from the stoneware mug she cradled between her palms. "But maybe it wasn't so bad. I'm starting to see where it might be pretty cozy." She was aware of Quinn watching her over the rim of her mug.

"You don't live alone, I take it," Quinn said.

"No, I do."

"But you don't like it?"

"I don't mind my own company, if that's what you mean."

But living alone in a city of millions and living alone a million miles from nowhere—those were two different things.

Quinn's lips quirked in a restrained smile. "But if you were home right now, I bet you wouldn't be sitting around by yourself tonight, listening to sad music and staring at a fire."

"Not unless my building was burning down. I don't have a fireplace either." She smiled when Quinn chuckled. She was about to argue that this was not sad music when she paused long enough to actually listen to the lyrics. She managed not to groan audibly. *I guess there's a reason they call it the blues.*

"Sorry about the music." How many more ways would she find to screw up before the day was over? "I was—going for a mood, I guess."

"Suicidal?" queried Quinn brightly.

"*No.*" Unable to summon the indignation she was reaching for, she tried to mask her gaffe with humor. "If I'd wanted something really depressing," she said archly, "I'd have gone with country."

"You know what you get if you play a country song backward?"

"You get your girl back, your job back, your dog back, your house—"

"Heard that one, huh?" said Quinn, rubbing the end of her nose to hide a sheepish grin.

Outside, another crack of thunder echoed overhead and they both waited a little expectantly as the lights on the end tables flickered and then steadied.

"Refill?" She held out her hand for Quinn's empty cup. "Better drink it while it's hot. And if you want to put something else on, feel free," she said over her shoulder as she headed into the kitchen. "You won't hurt my—feelings," she finished when the music cut off before she'd even reached the coffeemaker.

Quinn was still standing by the stereo when she returned to the living room and set the mugs down on the coffee table. "Can't decide?"

"Actually," Quinn said, turning as the speakers came to life with a gentle swell of strings, "I was waiting for you."

144

Even before Etta James sang the first note, she'd recognized the music. It was the song that had been playing when they'd danced earlier this afternoon.

Quinn held out a hand. "What do you say? Once more for old time's sake?"

"I don't know," she hedged, finding she needed a second to absorb the unexpectedly sweet surprise. "Have we known each other long enough to qualify for old times?"

Quinn favored her with a mildly exasperated look. "This song's over in about three minutes. You gonna spend it giving me grief or are you gonna dance with me?"

Smiling, she allowed herself to be gathered into Quinn's arms. *Once more for old time's sake.* Trying not to dwell on the fact that that sounded more like an ending than any kind of beginning, she concentrated instead on committing every detail to memory. The warmth of Quinn's body, solid and firm against hers. The reassuring feel of Quinn's shoulder beneath her cheek. The slightly possessive feel of Quinn's arm at her back. She'd almost forgotten what this was like, the simple pleasure of being held by someone who wanted you in their arms. She pulled the moment in around her, wearing it like a cloak, warm and protected from the storm outside.

"I'm glad you decided to stay," she said. She wasn't sure how to feel about the warm puff of laughter that moved across her hair in response. "Why is that funny?"

"It's not," Quinn said quickly. "It's just that when you said that…well, I was thinking I was glad you asked me to stay. I didn't exactly come here on an invitation."

Libby raised her head to look at her. "Why did you come back?" For a moment she thought Quinn might not answer.

"Because I couldn't stop thinking about you," Quinn said simply. "Wondering what you were doing just about every minute from the moment I drove away. Wondering how many smiles you had that I hadn't seen yet. Like that one." She traced an index finger over the curve of Libby's cheek before pulling her close again. "Because I couldn't stop remembering what it felt like to hold you and how much I wanted to hold you again. And," she added, "because I decided even if you were straight, any woman who could kiss another woman the way you did was probably a closet case anyway."

Libby snorted out a little laugh. "And what, you thought you had the key to help me escape that particular closet, is that it?"

"Well, you know, what with my superhero gig and all," said Quinn, but the quiet laughter in her eyes faded quickly. The music was still playing, but they'd stopped dancing. "I only wish I could say my motives were that pure."

"I don't." Encouraged to see Quinn temporarily struck silent, she took advantage of the moment to lean forward and press her lips to Quinn's for a long, slow kiss. "I'm sure your impure motives are much more interesting."

"Libby—" She silenced the note of caution she heard in Quinn's voice with another kiss, and then another. Not to devour, but to taste. No hungry, probing tongue, no desperately clutching hands. Just soft, slow, lingering kisses that demanded nothing but offered everything. The windblown sheets of rain sweeping against the windows, the rumble of thunder outside, even the music faded from her awareness as a heat that had nothing to do with the logs burning in the fireplace welled up inside her. Every nerve in her body was wanting more, begging for more. But as much as she wanted more, she wanted this, and she knew that once they moved beyond this moment, it would be gone forever.

Her body protested when Quinn's fingers closed around her arms to move her back a step. "Libby, you really don't—"

"*Yes*, I really do. I'm not a closet case, Quinn. I know what I am and what I want."

"But you don't know *me*. And I don't want to hurt you."

Then don't, her heart wanted to plead, but she silenced it. She wasn't going to ask for promises she didn't believe in anymore.

"I just don't want you to do something you're going to regret later."

"I'm not," she assured her. "I'm not," she said again, but

Quinn only shook her head, unconvinced.

"But how do you—"

"Because I trust you," she said. "What's changed is that I trust you. Trust that if you're here with me, it's because you want to be. Here. With *me*. That I'm not just—convenient. Someone you happened to stumble across, right place, right time. *That's* what's changed."

She closed the space between them to take Quinn's face in her hands. "So be with me," she said, her voice dropping to a whisper. She brushed her lips across Quinn's. "Be with me tonight."

She stared into Quinn's eyes for a long moment, and when it became clear that Quinn had no argument left, she took a step back, wondering briefly where was the nervousness she thought she would be feeling as she lifted her hands and began unbuttoning her shirt.

Even when Quinn reached for her, the flutter of anticipation in her belly had nothing to do with nerves and everything to do with how badly she wanted this woman standing in front of her. When Quinn's fingers closed over hers and drew her hands down to her sides, the only worry she felt was that Quinn really had changed her mind.

"Let me do that."

Maybe she did have a few nerves left, she decided, when Quinn reached for the parted V of her shirt.

Quinn unfastened two buttons before dropping her gaze to watch her handiwork. She parted Libby's shirt, revealing the shimmer of pale green satin covering Libby's breasts, her nipples a hard outline against the sheer fabric. She stroked her fingertips over the exposed curve of flesh before reaching for the drawstring of Libby's pants. Sliding her thumbs into the waistband she drew them down and found matching green covering Libby's hips as the sweatpants slipped to the floor.

She stood there for a long moment, the air heavy in her lungs as her gaze traveled up the line of Libby's legs to the curve of her hips and soft swell of her stomach, over her full breasts, nipples straining against the green satin.

"If you don't touch me soon, Libby said when their eyes met, "or let me touch you..."

"Oh, I definitely plan on touching you." She swung Libby off her feet, ignoring Libby's startled gasp of protest and the sweatpants that came with her, dangling from one foot as she carried Libby down the hall. She turned sideways to slip through the door to the bedroom, depositing Libby on the bed with less ceremony than she might have liked so she could snatch at the stubborn sweatpants and finally fling them away.

Rising up on one elbow, Libby watched her pull her shirt over her head and toss it aside. When Libby scooted toward the edge of the bed, presumably with some thought of getting her out of the rest of her clothes, she stopped her with a strategically placed knee, then pushed her back onto the bed, claiming her mouth with a kiss that, unlike Libby's slow torture, was neither gentle nor teasing.

Libby's arms wrapped around her shoulders, trying to pull her closer still as the world dissolved into a heated tangle of limbs and hungry mouths. Fingers, distracted by the very skin they were trying to expose, fumbled blindly with buttons and zippers.

Bracing one leg on the floor, she grasped Libby by the hips to haul her to the edge of the bed. She dropped to her knees, sliding her cheek across the smooth satin Libby still wore at her hips and filling her lungs with Libby's scent. She kissed her through the thin fabric that was already damp and felt her own desire spilling between her legs when with a desperate sound, Libby arched against her mouth.

"Oh, God," Libby's voice was strained, her fingers trembling as they slid into Quinn's hair. "Please."

The harsh whisper of Libby's plea threatened to dissolve what was left of her control. Because she didn't want to be gentle, she forced herself to be as she removed the last barrier between them.

When Libby cried out at the first tentative flick of her tongue, she thought she would come herself, incited only by the sounds of Libby's pleasure. Every moan seemed to send a shocking pulse of heat vibrating through her. As Libby's body gave itself over to the hungry ministrations of her mouth, she allowed her hands to journey over the contours of Libby's thighs and the slope of her hips. She slid her palms over Libby's stomach, committing to memory every curve of flesh and the way Libby's body lifted on a gasp of pleasure and melted on a sigh.

Too soon Libby's breathless sounds of need gave way to harsher moans until with a final cry of release Libby arched against her, her thighs tightening around Quinn's shoulders before she finally fell back gasping and limp.

Her own heart pounding, she rested the side of her face against Libby's stomach, her fingers absently playing over whatever skin was within reach. After a moment, she felt one of Libby's hands on her head, steadier now as it stroked her hair.

"Come here," Libby whispered. She turned her face to kiss Libby's stomach. "Come here," Libby said again, her fingers tugging weakly at her shoulders. "I want to feel you on top of me."

She rose up, her hands trailing down Libby's thighs as she stood as if she was unwilling to lose the physical connection. When Libby opened her arms she covered Libby's body with her own and, burying her face in the curve of Libby's neck, listend to the reassuring rhythm of Libby's heartbeat as it slowed. She felt like she should say something—wanted to say something—but couldn't seem to find any words.

When she started to roll off, certain that Libby couldn't really be comfortable being squished into the mattress like this, Libby's arms tightened around her as if to hold her there.

"And just where do you think you're going?"

So instead of rolling off her, she used her weight to roll with her so that she was now on her back with Libby on top of her. She smiled at the startled eyes now staring down into hers.

"Pretty smooth move, Barnett," Libby murmured, then leaned in for a kiss. "Looks like you've got me right where I want

149

you." She rose up on her knees to straddle Quinn's hips, looking impossibly sexy in that ridiculous flannel shirt over her barely-there green bra.

Looking even sexier without it, she decided when Libby slipped the shirt off and let it fall to the floor behind her. She all but stopped breathing when Libby reached behind her back to unhook the clasp of her bra.

She pushed herself up so that she was sitting on the edge of the bed with Libby still straddling her lap. With both hands, she swept Libby's hair back and kissed her, sliding her hands down to pull the straps from Libby's shoulders. She just looked at her for a long moment until Libby took one of her hands and brought it to her breast, pressing herself into Quinn's touch and reminding her she wasn't taking anything Libby didn't want to give.

Libby leaned closer to kiss her again and slipped a finger under the band of the sports bra she had never gotten around to removing. She raised her arms and let Libby draw it up over her head.

Libby smiled, stroking her hands across her bare shoulders and arms and caressing her breasts. "You're so beautiful," she whispered, and pulled her closer.

Somehow they'd ended up with their heads at the foot of the bed. Quinn was on her back again with Libby's upper body draped awkwardly across her stomach, one of Libby's hands resting limply between Quinn's legs. At some point the temperature had prompted one of them to pull the bedspread up for some kind of cover. It was hard to say how much time had passed. They'd at turns drifted into moments of blissful, exhausted unconsciousness interrupted only when one woke and with restless hands and mouth teased the other's body awake and began the whole thing over again. Libby was surfacing again now, her fingers coming to life before she did as if recognizing where they'd left off.

Quinn reached down and clamped a hand around her wrist. "I can't," she said on a barely audible groan. "Please don't make me."

Her eyes still closed, Libby smiled, speculating with her fingers. "*Could* I make you?"

"Oh God, probably," she admitted. "But you might kill me in the process." She yanked Libby's hand away and tucked it firmly around her waist. "No means no."

"But you didn't *say* no," Libby pouted, pushing herself up on one elbow to look down at her.

"I'm saying it now. God, how can you still be moving? You're a fucking machine."

Libby's eyebrow twitched. "Is that supposed to be some kind of weird compliment?"

She laughed weakly, wondering what muscle could possibly have been abused enough to make even that hurt. "If I could move, I'd give you a compliment."

"Now *that*," murmured Libby, leaning down to place a gentle kiss at the corner of her mouth, "was definitely a compliment."

Libby snuggled in against her shoulder and they lay there without talking for a couple of long minutes before her own light sigh broke the silence. "Where the hell did you come from, Liberty Larue Jackson?"

There was a pause. "From the sound of your voice...I'm going to go with left field for two hundred, Alex." The truth of that earned a weak chuckle. "If it makes you feel any better," Libby added, "I wasn't expecting you, either. But isn't that when they say it happens?" The fingers that had been absently stroking the sensitive skin at the inside of her elbow stilled suddenly.

She wasn't oblivious to the meaning implied by Libby's words, but a sudden tension in the body that had been relaxing against hers only a moment before told her it was more than Libby had intended to say.

"Quinn, I didn't..."

"What happened to trusting me?" she said, but without any sting of accusation.

"I do."

"Then why are you trying to suck words back in?"

For a moment she thought Libby might try to deny it, but all

151

she said was, "I don't want you to feel...uncomfortable."

"Too late for that." She shifted onto her side, brushing back Libby's hair so she could trail her fingers over the curves of Libby's cheek. "Ever since I met you I've been feeling one thing or another. Some comfortable. Some...not so much."

Libby's gaze dropped for a moment, and when she looked up again her solemn intensity of a moment ago had been replaced by a look of such tenderness that being on the receiving end had her heart clenching inside her chest.

"Make love to me again," Libby whispered. And she willingly complied.

Chapter Thirteen

When Quinn stepped out onto the screened-in porch the next morning, there was a bite in the air that had her hurrying to close the door quietly behind her. She pulled her jacket on before going outside, coffee mug in hand.

The dull thud of her boot heels against the weathered boards of the dock was the only sound interrupting the still morning. A wash of pale, white light was easing up from behind the trees on the east side of the lake, bleaching the last of the stars from the sky. She let the steam from her coffee warm her face before taking a long sip, scanning the lake for signs of life.

What day was it anyway? Sunday? Monday? A little unnerving how quickly one could lose track when there was no particular reason to remember. Too bad she couldn't forget everything that easily, she thought, and then froze with the coffee cup raised to her lips as it occurred to her that for a little while at least she'd pretty much done exactly that.

She waited for a sense of guilt to settle over her, and didn't know whether to be relieved or bothered when it didn't happen.

Any other day that might have been enough to leave her wondering whether she was capable of feeling anything at all, but whatever doubts she might have entertained about that were put to rest when she heard the porch door swing shut. She turned to see Libby walking toward her wearing a smile that lit up the morning much more effectively than the slow climbing sun.

When was the last time anyone looked at her like that? Like they were actually happy to see her because...well, just because. She was used to seeing polite, sometimes even friendly smiles of the people she worked with. The calculated if not unwelcome smiles of women who were hoping to have sex with her. But no one who looked at her quite like Libby did. No one who could make her feel—

"It's got to be either cold or empty."

She had been so wrapped up in her own thoughts she hadn't even noticed Libby was carrying two steaming mugs. She glanced in her cup and then drained the last mouthful of cold coffee.

"Both." She bent to set the empty cup down on the dock and took the one Libby offered, simultaneously leaning in to steal a kiss. "Good morning."

"Good morning," said Libby, eyes sparkling. "I'm not interrupting, am I?"

"What would you be interrupting?"

"I don't know. You looked like you might be doing some serious thinking out here."

Quinn made a face, dismissing the idea. "Way too early for serious thinking. But I didn't want to wake you, and it was too nice a morning to stay inside." She took a sip of coffee, and then made a little toasting gesture with the mug. "Much better. Thanks."

Libby took a step closer so that they were standing side by side at the end of the dock. "Looks like it's going to be an early fall," she said, looking across the water.

Quinn followed her gaze to where the blossoming daylight illuminated a few spots of yellow amid the green high on the hills.

"Have you ever seen the fall foliage up here?" Libby asked. "It's really something."

"I've seen pictures," said Quinn, scanning the distant trees and spotting more scattered patches of color. "When I was a kid, my mother had this book of poetry." She paused abruptly, a little disconcerted to realize her guard had dropped so around Libby that she was talking about this without having to decide first if it was something she necessarily wanted to share.

She took a moment, willing into focus the fuzzy memory of sitting on her mother's lap with the book open in front of them. "It was a big book," she remembered. "I don't know if it was all Robert Frost, but I know some of them were. And there was a picture—a photograph—with each poem. They were all pictures of New England. You know, the rocky coast of Maine, covered bridges, winding roads. Sometimes she'd read the poems to me, but most of the time we'd just sit there and look at the pictures. The ones that showed the leaves changing...those were her favorite."

She drifted into another moment of reflective silence, seeing her mother again, her fingertips caressing the pictures as if she expected to find something there other than the glossy smoothness of the page.

"I asked her once why the leaves changed color like that. Living in West Texas I'd never seen anything like that before. She told me it was because the leaves were getting ready to die for the winter and wanted to give the trees something happy to remember them by."

"I like that," murmured Libby, reaching out to link her hand with Quinn's. "That's sweet."

"It's stupid," she muttered, embarrassed, and felt an admonishing tug on her hand.

"It's not stupid. I think it was a lovely answer to give a child. And there's a wonderful symmetry there because, in a way, she made them something happy for you to remember her by."

"I suppose," she admitted reluctantly. She stared into her coffee cup, debating with herself. "That's why I'm here," she said finally. "She used to talk about coming up here someday, to see it for herself." Her gaze drifted back toward the trees. "As far as I know, she never made it. So I...I brought her ashes up here. I thought I'd wait for the leaves to change and then find a nice spot to scatter them."

Libby was silent for a moment, and then nodded, a slow smile warming her eyes. "I think she'd like that."

"Do you?" She'd been starting to doubt herself lately. It wasn't a feeling she was accustomed to.

"I think it would make her happy that you remembered something that meant so much to her. To both of you."

"Yeah," she said after a moment, looking back toward the trees and wondering now what had become of the book. "Yeah, I guess it did." She released a breath. "Anyway, that's why I'm here. I should have realized when I headed up here I'd be getting here too early, but..." She let the thought trail off with a little one shoulder shrug, grateful to be distracted by a movement along the trees at the edge of her vision.

"Look who's back." She gestured with her chin. "Over there."

"PJ," said Libby, surprised. Then louder, calling out to him, "Hey! PJ." She whistled.

"Apparently he has more important matters to attend to," she said dryly when the dog barely paused to glance in their direction before continuing down the path away from them.

"Evidently," said Libby, watching him trot away in the opposite direction. "Where do you suppose he's going?"

"Your guess is as good as mine." She finished her coffee and then glanced at Libby who was still staring at where PJ had disappeared from view. "Why, you thinking about following him?" she asked, trying to understand the look of consternation on Libby's face.

"Hmm?" murmured Libby distractedly, and then turned to find Quinn watching her. "Oh," she said, belatedly catching the question. "No," she said, the furrows in her brow suggesting it was a silly idea. "No, I've got too much to do today to waste time chasing after him."

She was reminded that Libby did have an agenda of her own up here. "Guess I ought to get those boxes out of the truck for you. You going to try and get those books delivered today?"

"I thought I'd get them boxed up, but it would take a dozen trips to deliver them with my car. I could probably manage the few that are going to the school, but I think I'll call and see if the library at least can't send a truck out for the rest.

"Actually I was thinking I might go into town today and visit with a couple of the people he left things to, just to see if they might be able to tell me anything. And the lawyer said there's more paperwork to sign, so I'll need to pay him another visit before I leave."

Before I leave. The not so subtle reminder of the inevitable set the coffee churning in Quinn's stomach.

Libby sipped what had to be now cold coffee. "So, uh, what do you have on your agenda for today?"

She hesitated, wondering if that was a polite way of suggesting it was time for her to be moving along. Since Libby had stuff she needed to accomplish on a schedule that was a lot less flexible than her own, she probably didn't need her hanging around and being a distraction, which is all she'd be doing if she stayed. Not that it wasn't a tempting thought. In fact, she'd started thinking of possible distractions the moment she'd woken up and found Libby still sleeping next to her, looking so soft and tousled and… touchable. She'd spent several long minutes watching her sleep while thinking of the numerous ways with which she might wake her, but in the end decided she looked too peaceful to disturb after only the few hours sleep they'd had, so she'd come outside hoping the morning's chill would cool her off.

She let her gaze drift back toward the hills on the other side of the lake. "So how long do you think, now that it's started?" During the pause that followed her question, it occurred to her she might have confused Libby with the detour in their conversation, but apparently Libby figured it out.

"Hard to say. To be honest, I never really paid that much attention. You know—well, no, I guess you wouldn't, but when you're a kid, it seems like you just wake up one morning and there it is. I know it depends on the weather. You get a lot of clear days, cold nights..." She eyed the landscape more narrowly. "It'll probably move along pretty fast now that it's started. But until it's full blown…a couple weeks maybe?"

"That long?" Quinn embarrassed herself by saying it out loud. Two weeks wasn't much time in the greater scheme of things. But now that she was beginning to feel like she might have a good reason for getting on with her life, two weeks sounded like an eternity. "What about up north?"

"This *is* up north," said Libby patiently, and then laughed at the deliberately bland look Quinn aimed at her.

"I meant farther north. Doesn't it, you know, start up and work its way down?"

"Pretty much. But I really don't think you'd see much difference unless you're talking about heading into Canada. Or Maine maybe."

Maine, huh? She thought about that for a minute. Why not? She knew from her drive yesterday she could be there in about an hour. Plenty of time to drive in, have a look around. Maybe it wasn't a bad idea. Get out of Libby's hair for a while, and if she was lucky…

She felt the twinge of guilt she'd avoided earlier. *Not that I'm in a hurry to get rid of you, Mom, but it* is *what we came up here for.* Reminding herself of that helped and she nodded. "Okay. Good idea. Thanks."

Libby looked confused. "What's a good idea?"

"Going to Maine," she said.

"I didn't say—" Libby broke off. "You're going to Maine—now?"

"Well, you've got stuff you need to get done so I thought I'd—"

"But I really—"

"—head up there and see if I can't find a nice spot for Mom." Libby's smile seemed flustered. "What, is that a bad idea?" Then she remembered the books. "Oh, hey, I'll still help you with the books," she assured her. Libby probably thought she was a jerk, offering to help and then bailing on her.

158

"No," said Libby quickly. "I didn't mean—don't worry about the books. There's no hurry on that." Whatever she thought she'd seen on Libby's face a moment before was gone now, replaced by a gently supportive smile. "No, you go on and do what you need to do. I don't think it's a bad idea at all."

"Are you sure? Because—"

"I'm positive. I just thought..." She rolled her eyes, an obviously self-deprecating gesture to discount whatever she'd been about to say. "Sorry, my mind's all over the place. You know, things to do, people to see," she said, jokingly. "But maybe when you—" Libby stopped abruptly.

She waited. "When I what?"

"Oh, I was just going to say... That is, I was wondering if you...um…"

Her puzzlement vanished into understanding. "Are you trying to ask me if I'm coming back?"

"Something like that."

She smiled, amused by Libby's obvious reluctance to admit the truth. "Hold this, would you?" She passed her still half-full coffee cup to Libby and then, taking her face in her hands, kissed her, savoring the already familiar taste of Libby's mouth laced with the darker flavor of coffee. She felt Libby lean closer, then utter a frustrated little sound at the back of her throat when she realized both of her hands were already occupied.

She'd planned only to tease. To offer just enough, remind Libby of just enough, to ensure that Libby would want her to come back. She understood it was a two-edged sword when she felt her own body remembering and took a half step closer, angling Libby's head back as she deepened the kiss to fuel a hunger that her mouth couldn't satisfy and her body wouldn't forget.

When she finally raised her head, Libby's brown eyes had gone a shade darker, but it was hard to feel smug about that when she was pretty sure Libby was seeing a similar change in hers.

She figured it should have been enough to make the answer obvious, but asked anyway.

"What do *you* think?"

Libby managed to keep the disappointment off her face until Quinn drove away, because—well, for one thing, that goodbye kiss hadn't left a lot of room for disappointment. But really, what could she say? While she would have gladly put off anything she was about to be doing for a chance to spend the day here with Quinn, there was no way to suggest she put her plans for her mother on hold without sounding completely callous. *And it would have sounded completely callous because it would have* been *completely callous*, she told herself sternly.

It's not that she was unsympathetic for what Quinn was going through. In fact, she'd been very tempted to suggest that she could go with her. It seemed a little harsh to let her go off to do this by herself, but at the same time she couldn't be sure it wasn't something best tended to by Quinn alone. Then, when she'd factored in her own reluctance to see Quinn drive away, she'd decided her motives were probably more selfish than not and so hadn't even made the offer.

Now she was cursing the part of her heart that had turned to lead watching Quinn's car disappear around the curve of the driveway, and the dark angel at her shoulder whispering *She's not coming back.*

She told herself she was just feeling edgy from having woken alone in that silent, empty house and, for a few painful moments, thinking that Quinn had simply—left. Then she'd found the scrawled note by the mug left sitting next to the coffeemaker. *Come find me when you wake up. I'll be down by the lake.*

The note was neatly folded in her pocket. She'd felt ridiculous for it at the time, but was glad for it being there now.

Quinn said she'd be back, and she would be. That didn't mean there wouldn't be goodbyes later, but she'd deal with that...later.

She drove into Turtle Cove with Beckett Langstrom's luggage in the trunk and Father Joel's chess set and paperweight on the seat next to her. Her first stop was the public library where the librarian, Mrs. Carmichael—a woman Libby was sure had to be approaching eighty—was thrilled with news of the donation. She assured Libby that it would be no problem to find someone with a pickup truck to send out to the house, and said the two young people who volunteered at the library would also help Libby pack the books. She insisted on thanking Libby with a tour of the small library and her refresher lesson on the Dewey Decimal system left Libby feeling like she was in grade school all over again.

She got Beckett Langstrom's telephone number from directory assistance. Mrs. Langstrom answered the phone, and told Libby that her husband had died only a few weeks before.

She offered her condolences and, even though the timing of this had been beyond her control, a heartfelt apology for not having been here sooner to relay Shepherd's words.

"Now don't you worry about that for a minute," Mrs. Langstrom told her. "It wasn't anything he hadn't told Beck a dozen times over before he died. And if gloating's not a sin in Heaven, you can be sure he's having a fine time with I told you so."

"I told you so?"

"My husband hadn't talked to his brother in almost fourteen years," Mrs. Langstrom told her. "Just one of those family squabbles that got out of hand. Mark had been after Beck for ages to mend fences before it was too late, but Beck wouldn't listen. But Beck was a stubborn old poop, and he'd be the first to admit it. And Roger, his brother, why he was just as bad, if not worse. But when Mark died…well, I think that got to him. And not a minute too soon. We'd only been back from Pensacola—that's where Roger lives—a week to the day before Beck died. A heart attack…"

"Mrs. Langstrom, I'm so sorry," she said, hearing the woman tearing up talking about it.

It was a moment before Mrs. Langstrom gathered herself to speak again. "Roger and Sherry came up for the funeral. They've asked me to spend the winter with them. I wasn't going to do it, but I decided it might be good to get away from here for a while. In fact, if you'd called tomorrow you would have missed me."

She told Mrs. Langstrom again that she was sorry for her loss. She'd already decided she wasn't going to bother the woman with any more questions about Shepherd, but found out it wouldn't have done any good when Mrs. Langstrom said, "I'm sorry, dear, you might have already told me, but I missed it. How is it again that you knew Mark?"

"Oh, he, uh…he was an old family friend."

"Well, I'm sorry for your loss, too, dear. He was a sweet man."

She mistook Father Moore for a yard man at first. At a glance, the man in fraying jeans and Notre Dame sweatshirt raking leaves in the yard in front of St. Cyril's didn't look old enough to be a priest, although on closer inspection he was probably closer to thirty than twenty.

He paused in his work to watch her approach up the walkway, his hands resting on top of the rake handle and a light breeze ruffling his unruly chestnut hair. "Good morning," he greeted her with an easy smile.

"Good morning," she said, idly speculating how many girls had fallen for this one just because of his dimples alone. "I'm looking for Father Moore."

"You found him."

It was probably because of Shepherd's age that she'd expected the man he'd played chess with to be older as well. The slight surprise struck her silent for a moment. "Sorry, I was expecting someone…"

"Taller?" he joked, drawing her attention to the fact that he was barely taller than her own five-seven.

"Older."

He surprised her with another grin. "Points for saying that." His gaze shifted to the box in her hands. "What do you have there? And do you need help with it?" he asked, lowering the rake to the ground.

"Oh, it's not heavy. But it is for you," she said as he reached out to take it from her. "It's something Mark Shepherd wanted you to have."

He looked into the open box. "Mark," he said, with a look she couldn't quite decipher.

"He left a message," she told him. "*Hope it helps; God knows it can't hurt.* I assume he was talking about the, uh, four-leaf clover." She hoped that wasn't somehow disrespectful. She'd been raised Episcopalian, and wasn't sure about the sensibilities of Roman Catholic priests.

He raised his eyes from the contents of the box to give her a vaguely appraising look. "You must be Libby."

She felt a flicker of excitement. "He mentioned me?"

"No," he said, sounding oddly apologetic about it. "After Mass yesterday, Joe Bradley mentioned you might be coming by to talk with me. He explained a little about your situation."

"Oh." She didn't try to hide her disappointment. "And I'm pretty sure from the look on your face that you don't know anything either."

His lips compressed in a smile of regret. "I'm afraid not." He indicated the rectory steps with a tilt of his head. "Sit with me for a bit," he said, his tone somewhere between a request and a command.

When they sat down, he pulled a pack of cigarettes and a lighter from his jeans pocket. "Do you mind?" he asked, lighting one after she shook her head. "Yeah, I know," he said, acknowledging the surprise she'd tried to keep from her face. "But everyone should have at least one vice. And smoking helps keep me away from the rocky road. Ice cream," he clarified. "My real vice."

"I've always been more of a fudge ripple girl myself," she said, her smile acknowledging his efforts to put her at ease. "Joe tells me you and Shepherd used to get together to play chess."

"Shepherd, huh?" He looked amused. "You really didn't know him, did you?"

"How did you two meet, if you don't mind my asking? Joe

163

said he didn't go to church here."

"No, he did not. Said he respected me too much to come and listen to me preach." He laughed at that, clearly not offended. "My first year here some parishioners dragged me out to the Fourth of July bash out at the lake. He saw me admiring his board and asked me if I played. That was maybe four years ago." He reached into the box at his feet and pulled out one of the game pieces. A bishop, she noticed, and wondered if that had been a conscious choice.

"Did he ever talk about his family at all?"

"Not really. I gathered there was some falling out at some point, but he never talked about the specifics and I got the impression that was a lifetime ago for him. He didn't make an issue of it, but I could tell it…influenced him. That was one of the few things I ever saw him display any real impatience for. People—families—subdividing themselves because of petty little differences." He set the game piece back in the box. "So what about you. Not even a theory? That must be incredibly frustrating."

She told him briefly about Brian's idea that Shepherd might have been a friend of her stepfather. He admitted he'd never heard Shepherd mention anyone by that name before, but told her that didn't necessarily mean anything.

They talked for a few minutes more before she excused herself saying she still had a couple items to drop off. "I'll pray for your peace of mind," he told her. "Come back anytime you like."

She didn't realize how much of the morning was behind her until she saw the number of cars in the diner's parking lot. She went in anyway, intending to simply drop off Rhonda's record and leave, but Rhonda insisted she'd never hear the end of it if she let her run off without letting Sue know she was there. A moment later, Sue popped her head out long enough to insist she sit down and have something to eat until she could escape from the kitchen for a proper thank you. She disappeared again in the middle of Libby's insistence that no thanks were necessary.

Looking up from a tray of glasses she was scooping ice into, Rhonda gave her an amused *Told you so* look. "So where's Trouble today?"

"She had some errands to run," she said, surprisingly touched by the inquiry. "She'll be back later though."

"Well, why don't you grab yourself a seat before they're all taken? I'll find you in a minute."

Eventually the kitchen slowed enough to allow Sue to come out and sit with her. While they were chatting, Bradley came in for a late lunch with his wife, and Sue waved them over. At some point even Rhonda found a few minutes to join them, after which the conversation seemed to take on a life of its own, even drawing in a young couple eating at the adjacent booth when reminiscing about Shepherd led to tales of youthful exploits out at the lake.

It was odd to find herself feeling so at home among people she hadn't even known a few days ago. Odder still, how the shared laughter over stories she had no part in left her feeling not like an outsider, but almost like she belonged. Or could belong. As if the door was open and all she had to do was...step through.

She didn't need anyone telling her what a crazy thought that was. She already belonged somewhere. She didn't need anyone telling her that either, but she spent a good deal of the drive back to the lake house reminding herself of that anyway. She had her own friends with their own stories. Stories she was a part of. She had a career. A life. And it wasn't here. She still wasn't sure what *here* was at this point. Here was still a puzzle. A mystery. She'd come here looking for answers, not choices.

Of course she hadn't come here looking for Quinn either, but that didn't stop her from wishing Quinn were here now. She didn't realize how much she'd been hoping to see her truck waiting in the driveway until she pulled in and it wasn't there. It was silly to be disappointed. In all likelihood, Quinn wouldn't be back for hours. Too much time to spend simply waiting, she told herself, automatically shouldering the stubborn front door with the little nudge it needed to open.

While she couldn't claim to be comfortable with the idea

that this place belonged to her now, she was feeling a little less like an intruder, which made it easier to appreciate the cozy niche Shepherd had created for himself.

She lingered in front of a painting in the living room that had caught her eye the first time she'd seen it. One of the watercolors Shepherd seemed to have a penchant for, this one held a gently unfocused image of autumn. Despite the fiery blur of reds, burnt oranges and bold yellows against a pale blue sky, there was nothing even remotely warm about it. Maybe it was the lingering shadows beneath the trees or the darkly rippling water visible at the lower edge of the picture. Whatever the source of the chill, she knew if she could step into that painting she'd better have her coat along.

If she hung it in her bedroom, she decided, lifting the frame down from the wall, it would be the perfect excuse to buy that expensive comforter she'd been lusting after, the one with the jacquard pattern woven in coppery threads against a shimmering russet fabric. She could call it a planned decorating strategy and there'd be no reason to resist. She added a few throw pillows and some candles to the vision, fleshing out her own little romantic retreat, and wondered if she'd be able to finesse all of it before Quinn saw her bedroom for the first time.

She heaved a mental sigh as she leaned the painting against the wall. The point of staying busy was to keep her mind off Quinn, not create romantic little scenarios for her to star in.

At some point she'd need to make a decision about what to do with all of this, but in the meantime, it wouldn't hurt to pick out a few things to take back to her apartment. The colorful pattern of what looked like a Moroccan accent rug would probably haunt her if she didn't take it home. A couple of those vintage cookie jars in the kitchen just screamed Brian's name, and would probably go a long way toward smoothing the feathers that were sure to be ruffled when he learned how long it had taken her to tell him about Quinn. The thought brought her back to the subject she was trying to avoid.

Her annoyance with herself lingered as she roamed

through the house, trailing her fingers along rows of books and occasionally picking up one of the figurines and other keepsakes that Shepherd had scattered about, only to put it down again.

Hadn't she already given herself this lecture? She hadn't asked for any promises and suspected Quinn didn't want any. And given the way Quinn felt about New York, she wouldn't be stopping by because she "just happened to be in the neighborhood." That made the odds of seeing her again after they left Turtle Cove depressingly slim. But it was hard to suddenly be feeling so much and not imagine the possibility of more, even though she knew she couldn't realistically expect Quinn to abandon her own life to do what? Move to New York?

Why not? argued the small voice inside her head. *Isn't that what you did?*

That was different. She'd been younger. Not settled in anywhere. She would have traveled to the moon if necessary to be with Amanda. She felt pretty stupid for it now, but at the time heading to New York hadn't seemed like that much of a sacrifice because she'd been in love.

And Quinn wasn't in love with her.

You're not in love with her either, she told herself, a little desperately. *You can't be in love with someone you've only known a few days.* As much as she led with her heart, she wasn't naive enough to confuse sex with love, but she also knew she never would have slept with Quinn in the first place if it hadn't meant something to her. If she hadn't felt on some level the possibility that it could become more.

Yeah, well. Could be, should be, *isn't,* as her mother used to say. She set a brightly painted porcelain butterfly back on the shelf with enough force to have her flinching afterward, but was relieved to see no damage done.

God, she hated it when she was reduced to quoting her mother.

Quinn's not in love with you. You're not in love with her.

But you could be, argued the little voice that she was trying very hard not to listen to.

Maybe so. But what was the good of one person in love, unless you were in the business of depressing love songs?

You know what you get if you play a country song backward?

She bit her lip, trying to control the smile that broke free at the memory. Oh, Quinn felt something, she was sure of that. She'd been too sweet, too tender, for this to be just about sex. Too worried about her doing something she didn't want to do.

The only thing she was worried about is that you'd do exactly what you're doing. Trying to make it mean more than it did.

Finding herself already thinking about it in the past tense sent a little arrow of pain straight to her heart. How did Brian do it, she wondered. How did anyone do it? Sleep with someone, allow yourself to be that open, that vulnerable, and still keep them at a distance emotionally? Even if someone could tell her how to do it, did she really want to be that kind of person? She didn't think so. But not being able to turn off that part of herself meant living with the consequences.

Quinn had been driving for longer than she'd intended, lured on by slightly more colorful hilltops that always seemed to be just ahead. But the roads were slow and the hills that seemed to be "just ahead" were inevitably a little farther than they appeared, and traveling toward them continued to take her farther off the beaten path than might have been wise.

When she discovered a narrow and rutted dirt road that looked like it would take her in the right direction, she turned onto it without much thought other than *Thank God for four-wheel drive.* After bouncing along on it for fifteen minutes or so, she'd quit paying any attention to the scenery and began to wonder how far she might have to drive until she found a place at least wide enough to turn the truck around. A few bone jarring miles later, curiosity was edging toward concern. She'd stopped the truck and was weighing the odds of successfully backing out when a silver flash caught her eye through the trees.

She lowered her window and was starting to think she'd imagined it when she saw it again. Sunlight, glinting off water.

She got out of the truck and stood motionless, listening past the rustling leaves for the sound before she headed into the woods. About thirty feet back from the road, water poured from a cleft in the rocky hillside, spilling into the stream below where it created a sparkling froth before it moved on, swirling around moss-covered stones and tumbling over submerged rocks.

The sunlight, falling through the branches overhead, shimmered on the water and painted an abstract of shifting light and shadow across the ground. The woods here were already bright with patches of yellow and orange. In a couple weeks, maybe even less, they would probably be on fire with color—a page straight out of her mother's book. But the odds of returning to this very spot in a couple of weeks, or even a couple of days... She wasn't sure she'd be able to find it again and it was too perfect a spot to pass up. Besides, her mother might enjoy watching the work in progress after all those years of seeing only pictures of the finished product.

She returned to the truck to get the simple white box that had been her traveling companion for the past few weeks. The weight of it always managed to surprise her a little. She'd expected a box of ashes to weigh next to nothing, but it was heavy enough to remind her that what she was carrying had not so long ago been a living, breathing person and, once upon a time, before that, her mother.

Quinn walked back to the waterfall holding the box and was suddenly unsure how to proceed. The moment seemed to call for some sort of ceremony, but the idea of standing here talking to herself felt a little silly. Then again, maybe it wasn't herself she should be talking to.

"I think you'll like it here," she said finally. "At least I hope you will. It's the sort of place you always said you wanted to see. I'm just sorry you had to wait until...well, until now." Easing the lid from the box, she opened the plastic liner that held her mother's ashes.

"I want you to know I don't blame you. Not for any of it. I mean that. I used to, when I was younger. But I know now it wasn't fair, expecting you to protect me when you didn't even know how to protect yourself. And I want you to know...I'm okay. I mean, yeah, I can be a real asshole sometimes. But I've never tried to hurt anyone. Not deliberately, just for the meanness of it. That's the truth. And I hope...well, I hope wherever you are now, you're happy."

Taking a deep breath, she opened the bag of ashes and tipped it, scattering her mother's remains on a final journey over the water and across the breeze.

"Goodbye, Mom."

Chapter Fourteen

Eventually Libby was able to concentrate enough on the task at hand to finish collecting a few small items to take back to her apartment. On impulse, she selected another painting, this one of an overgrown and rambling flower garden. Although Harry's flowerbeds had never been allowed such disarray, the vibrant colors reminded her of him nonetheless and she thought her mother might enjoy it.

As for the rest, there must be someone in the area who handled estate sales. It was already hard for her to imagine this place stripped of everything Shepherd had put into it to make it a home. Maybe it would make more sense to sell it furnished.

The thought brought her up short. Had she already decided to sell it then? The more she thought about it, the more she knew it was the only practical option. After all, she did well to get away once a year for a long weekend. What did she need with some lake house? Lakeside retreats in New Hampshire were for rich lawyers from Boston.

It was probably the darkness gathering outside the windows, she thought, that had her noticing the chill more than before. It might be time for some coffee and maybe a fire. She decided to tackle the fireplace first.

Quinn had made it look easy, but it didn't take her long to figure out there was a certain amount of talent involved in laying a fire. She knew her eventual success was due to luck and tenacity more than any real skill, but that did nothing to diminish the surge of pride she experienced when the logs finally flared to life.

Feeling just a bit butch, she stood back to admire her work. Mentally rehearsing her own version of Tom Hanks' *I have made fire!* speech, she retrieved her cell phone to call Brian, but then heard a strangely familiar bark coming from the front of the house. Setting her phone down on the coffee table, she went to investigate.

"I suppose you expect me to just let you in," she said to PJ who was sitting on the other side of the screen door. She didn't need a canine interpreter to understand the single quick bark she got in response. When she pushed open the door, he trotted past her into the house without a backward glance.

Wondering just where he thought he was marching off to, she followed him into the living room to find him already stretched out in front of the fireplace, his furry little body settling with a satisfied sigh that suggested he didn't plan to move any time soon.

It must have been the smell of the wood that caught his attention. She couldn't argue with a good idea, especially when she had pretty much the same one herself. She was going to get that coffee started and then spend a little time curled up in front of a fire with some coffee and a good book. There was bound to be something on these shelves she could distract herself with enough to pretend she wasn't really just waiting.

"God*damn* it!" Quinn slammed the hood down. "Shit!" She kicked the tire closest to her because she needed to kick something but still had enough presence of mind to know she didn't want to put a dent in the side of her truck. It'd just be one more thing she'd have to fix before she sold the—kicking the tire again— "goddamn fucking piece of shit! *Shit!*"

She paced a few steps away from the truck, raking her fingers through her hair. Taking a deep breath, she stared down the road she'd just traveled and then up ahead. Not that anyone could see more than three hundred feet in either direction, between all the freaking trees and the freaking turns and the freaking—

She felt herself winding up for another go at the tire and released the breath she was holding. It could have been worse, she reminded herself. She could have broken down back on that ruined road to the waterfall. This road at least looked pretty well maintained, so it must get some kind of use. Although aside from the two motorcycles she'd passed, she couldn't remember the last vehicle she'd seen, and the motorcycles had been almost an hour ago.

On the bright side, she'd already been headed back before the truck shuddered to a stop, so she was at least headed in the right direction and not even deeper into nowhere. Aside from that, she didn't really have a clue as to where she was in the greater scheme of things, or how far she was from where she wanted to be. Only one thing seemed certain. She had some walking to do.

She left the flashers blinking even though she doubted anyone would come along to see them. Shoving a couple extra batteries for the flashlight into her pocket, she locked the truck and started walking.

Libby had sipped her way through half a pot of coffee and the first few chapters of a Stephen King novel before she finally gave up. King's tale hit the ground running, but it hadn't been enough to distract her from the passing of time. Not much point in pretending otherwise, with no one here to fool but herself.

She'd expected Quinn to be back by now. Surely she would have turned around when it got dark, if not before. You couldn't see anything after that, what would be the point in continuing? She settled another log onto the fire—as much as it took to get it started she wasn't going to let it go out now—then carried her empty mug into the kitchen.

Pushing aside the curtain over the sink, she looked out with some small, vain hope of seeing headlights coming down the drive. She was greeted only by her own reflection and the thought written too plainly on her face that if Quinn hadn't bothered to turn back before it got dark...

A sound coming from the hallway caught her ear. "Damn it, PJ," she complained under her breath. "What kind of trouble are you getting yourself into now?" She poked her head into the living room to confirm that he was no longer asleep by the fire, and then followed the intermittent scraping sound down the hall toward Shepherd's bedroom.

"PJ," she said again, wanting only to get him out of here and close the door. "Come on, get out of there. I'm not kidding." A small shuffling sound came from under the bed. Sighing, she went down on one knee to peer underneath.

"What *is* it with you and this..." Her voice trailed off when she saw not PJ, but a small brown valise beneath the bed. It moved slightly and the brass fittings at the corners scraped against the wood floor—evidently the source of the noise she'd heard. PJ's face peeked around from behind it.

"What have you found there?" she wondered aloud, reaching under the bed to pull out the old suitcase.

In the living room, she tugged an armchair closer to the fire and sat down with the case in her lap. Her first impression was of papers. She shuffled through them. Letters. Postcards. Some loose photographs. Greeting cards still in their envelopes. Newspaper clippings. Ticket stubs from a Boston Pops performance twenty-five years ago and other mementos of a similar nature.

She turned her attention to two small leather books and was disappointed to discover that they were sketchbooks, not journals. The pages were filled with odd bits of this and that, drawn by an obviously immature hand, but one that showed promise. Simple inanimate objects progressed to small animals. Cats. Squirrels. Birds. Simple stuff. The second book contained more of the same, but showed a growing confidence as he turned

174

his attention to the human form and started filling pages with eyes, noses, hands—hands had given him a bit of trouble, she noticed absently, flipping through several pages of awkward but progressively better attempts. Closer to the back she found some sketches of human torsos. Mostly male, though not all. And some were really quite good, including one headless figure that might have been Michelangelo's *David* except she was pretty sure Michelangelo's version was not quite so...well-endowed.

Setting the sketchbooks aside, she picked up a couple of the postcards at random. One showed the outside of a rather majestic looking hotel. Across the top it said *Bellagio Grand Hotel* Italy. The only message was "Missing you." The picture on the other one was identified as *Venice Vendramin Calgeri Palace.* That one said, "Forget Paris—Venice is the most romantic city in the world." Both of them were signed only "B."

She opened a handful of greeting cards and discovered they were mostly sympathy cards. She put those aside to flip through a few of the photos, not really expecting to recognize anyone familiar, but one caught her eye.

It must have been taken when Harry brought them up here, she decided, squinting slightly at a much younger version of herself standing at the end of the dock in a bathing suit and sporting a pair of inflatable water wings. She turned it over. — *Libby 5 yr.* was written in pencil on the back.

She pushed aside the papers in the case to find more photographs and found another of her happily putting the finishing touches on a rather unimaginative sand castle. Sticking out of the sand next to her was the little blue plastic sand pail she'd evidently used to create the lopsided structure. The same one she remembered using to wash turtles down the slide. Written on the back again was *Libby 5 yr.* and beneath that, *Future architect?* and a smiley face.

A vague disquiet settled over her, somehow made worse by the presence of the smiley face. It was all harmless enough, she told herself. Granted, it seemed a little odd that someone she didn't know would have kept pictures of her like this, but that's all they were—pictures, and pretty innocuous ones at that. And if he had no family of his own, which he apparently didn't, and if he and Harry had been good friends, which they apparently were... maybe it wasn't all that odd that he'd keep pictures of his buddy's kid. Certainly not any more odd than leaving his entire estate to that same kid, she reminded herself.

She began looking through the contents of the case in earnest, not really sure what she was looking for until familiar handwriting on an envelope caught her attention. It was a letter addressed from Harry to Shepherd. Comforted by the sight of Harry's familiar handwriting, she slipped the single sheet of stationery out from the envelope.

Dear Mark,

Thank you again for agreeing to help me with this. I know things may be a little awkward at first, but I'm hopeful that if we can just sit down and talk face-to-face we'll be able to come to an amicable resolution. Family is a precious commodity, and I agree that it's important for Libby to have a chance to know hers. Please believe me when I say I have only her best interests at heart.

We'll drive up on the 18th and should arrive before noon.

Looking forward to meeting you,
Harry Peerman

The fact that the paper kept moving made it difficult to read the words and it took her a moment to connect the problem to her own trembling hand.

Looking forward to meeting you.

Contrary to Brian's theory, one that she'd become very attached to, Harry hadn't known Shepherd and they hadn't been old friends. They hadn't been any kind of friends.

Family is a precious commodity, and I agree that it's important for Libby to have a chance to know hers. Her eyes zoomed in on the

176

words that seemed to grow bigger on the page as she stared at them.

I agree that it's important for Libby to have a chance to know hers.

She didn't want to let her brain make the next leap, but was incapable of stopping it.

Mark Shepherd was her father.

Chapter Fifteen

Dawn found Libby still in the chair, staring blindly at a fire long burned to ash. The suitcase was on the floor, its contents scattered across her lap and at her feet. She'd looked at each and every paper and photograph in it, desperate to find something that would convince her she was wrong.

There hadn't been much more to discover. More pictures, mostly of people she didn't know but a few more of her that all appeared to have been taken while they were up here. There was another letter from Harry to Shepherd apologizing for something her mother had apparently said and suggesting they wait for things to "calm down a bit" and then maybe try again. And she'd found a letter and what appeared to be a card that Shepherd had evidently mailed to her mother. Both envelopes were still neatly sealed and "Return to Sender" was written boldly across the front in her mother's handwriting.

She'd sat holding them for a long while, struggling with her need to know the truth and an equally intense desire to throw the letters, the pictures, the valise—all of it—into the fire. But she'd waited too long, and when there hadn't been enough of a flame left to destroy the truth, she'd slid her finger under the edge of the flap of the envelope postmarked about seven years ago. It held a single sheet of paper.

Madeline –

I understand you have many reasons for not wanting to speak with me, so I will not attempt to call you again. But I hope that after you've had some time to think about what I said, you'll see that this is not about me, or you. It's about what's only fair for Libby.

I hope to hear from you, but if I do not, I'll simply do what I feel is right.

Mark

The date on the other envelope was more recent—the month after Harry died, so she wasn't entirely surprised to see yet another sympathy card. Her gaze slid past the pre-printed expression of condolence printed inside to what Shepherd had written beneath it.

Harry was a fine man, and I grieve with you for his loss.
With deepest sympathy,
Mark Shepherd

She wasn't sure how long she'd sat there, but her eyes burned with exhaustion and a painful ball of bottled-up emotion seemed to be permanently lodged in her throat.

They'd lied to her. All of them. Even Harry, which probably hurt most of all. She'd trusted Harry. *Loved* him. And even he'd lied to her. His tender and seemingly heartfelt pledge of a father's love all those years ago, a memory that had long been a comfort for her, now carried the sting of a slap in the face. Tears welled up and although her exhausted eyes should have welcomed the relief, she refused to let them fall.

Had there been signs? Snippets of conversation she'd overheard but had chosen to misunderstand? Or forget? Times when, in hindsight, she should have been able to see her mother or Harry had been trying to tell her something, but couldn't? Almost too tired to think, she stumbled down foggy trails of memory trying to find some way not to blame them for keeping this from her.

Because Harry had been part of the deception, she tried to tell herself that if they'd lied to her, they must have believed it was in her best interest that she not know. Of course that would be easier to accept if Shepherd—if her *father*—had been some kind of monster. Some psychopath they thought they needed to protect her from. Obviously that wasn't the case if they'd brought her up here to meet him.

She'd come up here looking for answers only to find even more questions—ones she'd never anticipated. All she wanted now was the whole truth, even though she was pretty sure she wasn't going to like it.

She wasn't consciously aware of making a plan, but by the time she'd gathered up the scattered contents of the case and tucked it all back inside, she knew what she was going to do. Her mother was due back this evening and she intended to be waiting for her when she arrived home. That would mean leaving here earlier than she'd planned, but hopefully Quinn would understand why she...

Her eyes were drawn to the pale glow of morning seeping in around the edges of the curtains. She had no idea what time it was, but that didn't really matter. It was morning and Quinn wasn't back. Wasn't coming back.

Had she decided it would be easier this way? No emotional goodbyes. No pathetic attempts to turn what they'd had into something it was never meant to be. Or maybe she'd never intended to come back, and thought she'd been doing her a favor, giving her a few more hours to believe in fairy tales. Even start spinning one of her own.

What did it even matter? Gone was gone. Who cared about the why of it? Gone was gone and dead was dead and leaving— leaving seemed to be the easy way out for everyone but her. Well, she was sick of it. Sick of people taking the easy way out and just *leaving*. First her father, then Harry. Amanda. Her mother might still be alive, but she'd left emotionally years ago. And now Quinn...

The sharp ball of ache in her throat expanded until she thought she wouldn't be able to breathe past it. In spite of a sudden urge to lie down on the floor, or maybe because of it, she started to climb to her feet, but when her hand closed on the handle of the suitcase, a sudden spike of anger had her flinging it across the room. It clipped the edge of an end table, the lamp sitting on it teetering for a second before it fell. When the ceramic base crashed against the hardwood floor, she felt something inside her breaking with it and sinking back to her knees, she finally let her tears flow.

Chapter Sixteen

As much as she'd needed it, Libby had known she'd never be able to quiet her mind enough in that house to get any kind of sleep. She wasn't sure if the hurry with which she'd packed and left was born of desperation to confront her mother or just a desperate need to get the hell out of there. Whatever the reason, it hadn't occurred to her until she was halfway to Hartford that she could have at least taken the time to clean up and get herself together before she left Turtle Cove. Fortunately, she'd have time to clean up at her mother's and hopefully get her head together before Madeline arrived home.

She let herself in the back door to the kitchen and stood there taking in the unnatural stillness and slightly stale air of a house that had been closed up for over a week. She dropped the keys onto the breakfast bar just to hear them clink against the tile.

It had been months since she'd been here. Nothing had changed. That didn't surprise her. Nothing ever really changed here. Same white walls. Same bland beige carpet. Same drapes in tasteful shades of taupe. She walked through the formal dining room no one ever ate in and past the formal living room no one ever sat in to reach what Madeline referred to as the den. Harry had always called it the family room, even though he was really the only one who'd spent time in there.

She had carried only one item in from the car and she set it down in this room, in the center of the couch. The fact that Madeline had not changed anything in here was a bit of a surprise and something of a comfort. Harry's black leather recliner was still angled toward the wide-screen television. On top of the bookshelf, an ice bucket still sat on a tray with a crystal decanter and four matching rocks glasses. The decanter was almost half full. Libby removed the stopper to breathe in the scent of Harry's favorite scotch. She poured a bit in one of the glasses and then set the bottle back on the tray.

The humidor that she had given Harry for Christmas several years ago sat on the coffee table. She set the glass of scotch down next to it and raised the lid, surprised all over again to find it still held several of Harry's favorite cigars. Madeline wouldn't let Harry smoke cigarettes in the house and even his cigars never left this room. Libby would have expected these to be long gone from here. She picked one up, rolling it between her fingers before lifting it to inhale the familiar aroma.

She knew she should go upstairs and shower. Find something clean to put on and get herself presentable while she figured out exactly what she was going to say when her mother got home. But there was plenty of time, she thought, sitting down in Harry's recliner, and it wouldn't hurt to sit here and let herself relax for a minute or two in the room that was as close as she would ever again be to him.

It still hurt to think of the part he'd played in the lie for all those years, but there was no way she could stay angry with him. The man had been the source of the happiest memories of her childhood. Even the summers at Nana Peerman's house wouldn't have existed if Harry hadn't been part of her life. Whatever else he may have been a part of, he'd given her far more than he'd ever taken away. That was her last conscious thought before Harry's cigar dropped from her fingers.

Chapter Seventeen

"Oh, for the love of God." Seeing the blue lights flashing behind her, Quinn took her foot off the gas and pulled over to the shoulder. The day she'd thought couldn't possibly get any worse slipped another notch when she saw the man who was getting out of the police car behind her.

She lowered her window, making a conscious effort to wipe any trace of annoyance from her face before she turned to look at him, her license and registration at the ready.

"Officer Bradley. We meet again," she said without enthusiasm.

"Ms. Barnett." Bradley took the proffered items without looking at them. "And where might you be headed in such a hurry?"

Had she been speeding? She didn't think so, but then again she couldn't remember the last time she'd actually looked at the speedometer to be sure. "Sorry, officer. Was I speeding?"

"How about you answer my question first."

"If you must know, I'm going back Libby's place."

Bradley looked at her. "And why would you be going there?"

What the hell kind of question was that? Wary of being baited by a possibly homophobic cop, she struggled to curb her temper. Libby seemed to like this guy, but she could still see "Potential Asshole" written all over him.

"Look, if you're going to write me a ticket, can you just do it already and—"

"I don't ask questions just to hear the sound of my own voice." A voice, she noticed, that had lost much of the conversational quality it held a moment ago. His eyes were unblinking on hers.

"Because she's expecting me, not that it's any of your damn business."

"I don't think so. You want to try again?"

"Hey, you seem to like making trips out there. Feel free to follow me and you can ask her yourself."

"She's not there."

"You know that for a fact, do you?" she said, telling herself he'd probably run into Libby in town earlier, or seen her filling up at the gas station.

"She left this morning."

She left? Town? She was too surprised to keep some of it from showing.

"I heard she was pretty upset when she took off. You wouldn't happen know anything about that, would you?"

"No," said Quinn carefully, not sure whether to believe him.

He glanced down at her license and registration, tapping them against his open palm. "So when's the last time you saw her?"

"Yesterday morning." She turned her gaze toward the road ahead. "Who told you she was upset?"

"She talked to one of the waitresses over at the diner before she left."

"Rhonda?" she said, looking back at him.

His gray eyes regarded her with a different kind of interest. "How do you know Rhonda?"

"I didn't say I know her," she said carefully, "but we've met. Did she say why? Rhonda, I mean. Did she say what was wrong?"

"Just that Libby came in early this morning and seemed to be pretty worked up about something." Bradley turned at the sound of an approaching car and apparently recognizing the vehicle or the driver, lifted a hand in casual greeting before turning his attention back to Quinn. "Said something about leaving a dog locked up in the house. She wanted Rhonda to go let him out for her. You know anything about a dog?"

"She was probably talking about PJ."

"PJ?" said Bradley. "Mark had a dog named PJ."

"Yeah." When Bradley's eyebrows bounced up, she said, "I mean—obviously he's not the *same* one. But Rhonda told us about Shepherd's dog and we kind of figured he fathered this one. Little black and white terrier mix." Bradley nodded at the description. "He seems to hang out around the lake," she continued. "Libby was kind of fond of him."

"Enough to let him into the house?"

"Oh, yeah. Definitely."

Bradley nodded. "Well, Rhonda went out there. Said she looked high and low and there wasn't any dog in the house."

She made a face to suggest that it wasn't anything to worry over. "Libby probably let him out and forgot." Or maybe he let himself out. It wouldn't be the first time.

"Rhonda called me because she was worried something might have gone on out there. Said there was a broken lamp on the floor in the living room and a bunch of books pulled off the shelves. Some stuff stacked up by the door. Artwork. A few dust catchers. Nothing of much value, really."

"I know Libby was boxing up books the other day to donate to the library," she told him. "I don't know about any lamp..." What he'd said suddenly sank in. "You think somebody broke in?" she asked, suddenly worried.

"I went out there and had a look around. I couldn't find any sign of forced entry, and it didn't look like the alarm system had been tampered with."

"There's an alarm system?"

"Just one of those wireless systems. I talked Mark into

letting me put it in when he went into the nursing home. Just a noisemaker really, but it seemed to do the trick. There's never been any trouble out there to speak of." *Until now* seemed to hang in the air, unspoken.

She thought about that for a second or two. She hadn't known about any alarm system, but if Libby had expected her back last night, maybe she'd left it off. She might have even left the door unlocked. But that wouldn't explain the broken lamp, or why Libby had left it there. And not why she'd taken off without telling anyone what had happened.

"So you really don't know what went on out there?" said Bradley, who was still watching her, but not quite as keenly as before.

"No, I told you I—" She stopped, finally realizing what he'd been fishing for. "I *wasn't* there last night. I left yesterday morning and drove over to Maine. I'd intended to come back last night, but my truck broke down. I had to walk all over hell's half acre just to find someone to tow it and couldn't get it looked at until this morning. I've got the receipt from the tow truck if you need to check it out."

She didn't offer the receipt from the mechanic's shop because when he'd turned the key, the truck had started immediately. She'd been prepared for some disparaging comment about women drivers, but when the driver of the tow truck piped up with the fact that it wouldn't start for him the night before, the mechanic had just shrugged and said, "Works now."

"I don't think that'll be necessary." Bradley stared down the road in the general direction of the lake as though he could see the house from here. "Maybe the dog knocked it over. Animals used to being outside can get a little rambunctious."

"Maybe, but..." She shook her head. "I can't see Libby leaving it all over the floor like that."

"Hard for me to say. I really don't know her."

I guess I don't either, she thought.

"Well, when you hear from her, would you let me know?" Bradley handed her back her license and registration. "Better yet, ask her to give me a call. I'd like to make sure nothing happened out there that needs looking into."

"Sure," she said, knowing she wouldn't be hearing from her because Libby had no way of contacting her. And she had no way of contacting Libby. She couldn't help wondering if that was any part of the message meant to be conveyed by Libby's sudden departure. Don't call me and I won't call you.

"What the *hell* did you do to that girl?" demanded Rhonda, barreling out from behind the counter the moment she saw Quinn step through the door.

Quinn took an involuntary step back. "What are you talking about? I didn't do anything."

"Well, *some*body sure as hell did. Poor thing looked like she'd about cried her eyes inside out."

She flinched a little at the imagery. "Uh, maybe we could take this outside," she suggested, mindful that almost every eye in the place was now aimed at them, curious to know what had set Rhonda's tail on fire.

"That'd be just fine with me, young lady."

"*Jesus*, Rhonda." She was a little alarmed by what she saw in the older woman's eyes. "I'm not looking to fight you. I just—" She lowered her voice for all the good it would do "Do we really have to talk about this in here?"

When Rhonda swung her gaze in their direction, curious eyes all suddenly found something more interesting to be looking at. "LeAnn," Rhonda called out, "take care of my tables for a minute, would you?" She gathered in Quinn with a heated glance. "This won't take long."

"Well?" Rhonda demanded before the door had even closed behind them. "What do you have to say that you didn't want anyone else to hear?"

"Rhonda, what the hell are you climbing up my ass for?"

"Because she was fine when she was here yesterday afternoon, laughing and happy as a lark. And this morning she looked like... like..." Rhonda broke off and jabbed one ruby red fingernail in her direction. "There's only two things I know of that can make a woman cry like that and—"

"For Christ's sake," Quinn interrupted, "I wasn't even *here* yesterday. I went over to Maine for the day and my truck broke down on the way back. I didn't hit town until about thirty minutes ago. That cop, Bradley. He told me what happened. That's why I'm here. He said you're the only one who saw her before she left."

"As far as I know." Rhonda stared at her, obviously weighing her story. "So...how was she the last time you talked to her?"

"She was *fine*. Had a list a mile long of stuff she wanted to get done, but nothing she seemed stressed over. I think she was headed over to talk to that lawyer again when I left. Said something about some more paperwork and—"

"I meant how was she last night," Rhonda interrupted impatiently. When Quinn only stared blankly, Rhonda said, "You called her, didn't you?" The answer, written plainly on Quinn's face, sent her off again. "You didn't even *call*? What did you think, little psychic fairies were going to let her know your truck broke down, but you were fine?"

"How was I supposed to call her?" she demanded. "I don't have a cell phone and by the time I got to a phone—there's no phone connected at the house. Libby's got a cell phone, but I don't know the number."

"Well, then you should've called me! I would've—"

"Rhonda, I don't even *know* you," she said, pointing out the obvious. "You really think I'm going to call you to run out there in the middle of the night? Besides," she added grudgingly, "the diner closed at ten and I couldn't get your number from Information either. I couldn't remember your last name."

"It's Flynn," said Rhonda, her ill temper visibly fading. "So you did try."

"Hell, I even tried to get a hold of Officer Bradley to ask him to go out there to let her know what was going on, but some the-Turtle-Cove-Police-Department-is-not-a-messenger-service *bitch* was on duty—"

"Cheryl," surmised Rhonda under her breath.

"—and said—well, it doesn't matter what she said. But yeah. I tried." She pressed the heel of her hand to her forehead, certain her brain was about to come exploding out any moment. "You don't really think she took off just because I didn't make it back?" she said, still having a hard time believing that. "Is that what she said?"

"Not exactly. Okay, no." Rhonda admitted, then recounted pretty much the same story Bradley had told Quinn earlier. "She looked god-awful. I tried to get her to sit down and have some coffee, something to eat. She just shoved the keys into my hand and made me promise to go get the dog out of the house. But I could tell she'd been crying and I just assumed..." She glanced away guiltily. "I suppose I should've known better. But that's the first thing that popped into my senile old brain." She smoothed her hands over her brief apron nervously before offering an apologetic look to Quinn. "Sorry."

She dismissed Rhonda's apology with a tired gesture. "Don't worry about it. You barely know me, why wouldn't you think..." She stopped, digesting the truly sympathetic look in Rhonda's eyes. "Rhonda, you barely know either of us. How did you—I mean, why would you...?"

"I may just be an old woman living in some pissant town in New Hampshire," Rhonda told her, looking insulted, "but I do know a thing or two about the ways of the world, young lady. We get Showtime up here too, you know," she said, smiling briefly when she succeeded in getting a choked laugh from Quinn. "You know, you don't look so hot yourself right now. Why don't you come in and let me fix you something. My treat."

Quinn shook her head, thinking about all those people inside the diner who'd probably had their eyes glued to the scene playing out in the parking lot for the past ten minutes. Just because they couldn't hear wouldn't keep them from speculating and she wasn't in the mood to try to ignore all those prying eyes right now. "Thanks Rhonda, but I don't think so."

"Well, take something with you, at least. Or tell me where

you're staying and I'll bring something to you later."

"I think I'm just going to hit the road," she said, making her decision on the spot. "There's no reason for me to stick around here."

"Of course there is. If she comes back and you're not here—"

"She's not coming back," she said with quiet certainty.

"You don't know that. Look, I've still got the keys," she said, pulling a key ring with a half dozen or more keys from her pocket. "Why don't you take this and go back to Mark's place and wait for her there."

"I can't do that," she protested when Rhonda tried to give her the key.

"Sure you can. Look, she made me responsible for the place when she left the key with me. What if someone did try to break in last night? I'll be worried sick wondering if they'll come back."

She wasn't buying that for a second. "You don't really think someone broke in. Bradley said he couldn't find any sign—"

"The point is we don't know *what* happened, now do we? And until we do, someone needs to be keeping an eye on the place. Someone who could scare away an intruder, not an old woman like me."

She snorted, wondering if Rhonda really believed that hesitant, slightly downcast look made her look frail and helpless. "Rhonda, you're about the scariest old woman I know."

The waitress's grin was nothing short of wicked. "If you want me to take that as a compliment, you'll do what I'm telling you."

They stared at each other for several long seconds before Quinn said, "*Fine*. But if she's pissed when she finds out, *you're* taking the fall."

"Deal," said Rhonda, clearly willing to risk it. She held out the ring of keys.

Quinn rolled her eyes, but took it.

"Libby, what on *earth*—"

Libby's eyes flew open as if from a bad dream to find her mother standing in the doorway.

"What are you doing here? Are you all right? You look...you look—" Because Madeline couldn't seem to find an appropriate word, she returned to her original question. "What are you doing here?"

"Good to see you too, Mother." So much for being altogether presentable. She glanced around, but with the drapes closed it was impossible to know the time. "What time is it? Did you just get back?"

"A few minutes ago." Her mother's gaze fell on the framed floral landscape sitting on the couch. "What is that?"

"A gift, Mother. It made me think of Harry when I first saw it. I thought you might enjoy it."

"It's...very nice." Libby couldn't quite tell if it was surprise or suspicion underlying her expression when Madeline looked back at her. "You came here just to bring me this?"

"Not exactly. Did you enjoy your cruise, Mom?"

"Yes, actually I did. Did you get my postcard?"

"No, but I haven't been home to check my mail."

"Is there some problem with your apartment?" Her mother's brief look of concern transitioned rapidly to exasperation. "Libby, I really wish you'd—"

"I've been in New Hampshire." She paused, wanting to be sure she had her mother's full attention. "The cutest little town, actually. Turtle Cove. You've probably never heard of it."

Madeline's expression was so carefully neutral that Libby had the passing thought that with a poker face like that, her mother's talents were being wasted playing bridge.

"As a matter of fact, I have. You've been there before yourself, although I'm not surprised you don't remember, you were so young at the time." Madeline crossed the room to straighten the decanter that Libby had apparently left slightly askew on the tray. When she saw the stopper lying next to it, she turned back toward Libby and noticed the near empty glass sitting on the coffee table. "Have you been drinking?"

"No, I—"

"Libby, the glass is empty."

"That's because I didn't put that much in it to begin with. I wanted to—I just like the smell of it. It's like this room," she said, looking at it again. "It helps me to remember him."

"Libby." Madeline hissed her name like a mild reprimand. "You make it sound as though your father was a lush."

"That's not what I meant and you know it." Then, almost as an afterthought, "And Harry *wasn't* my father." She wasn't surprised to see her mother appear taken aback by her statement. While it was true, she'd never acknowledged it quite so blatantly before.

"I know he wasn't your biological father," she said carefully. "But he was the only father you ever knew and I don't think you—"

"And whose fault was that, Mother?" she said, cutting her off.

"What?"

"Whose fault is it that I never knew my biological father?"

"It's certainly not mine," her mother snapped. She'd expected to see possibly guilt on her mother's face, but not this thinly veiled anger. "What is this all about, Libby?"

"It's about me finally knowing the truth."

"The truth? You've known your whole life that Harry wasn't your father."

"You let me think my father was dead."

"Your father *is* dead."

"I know! He died three *months* ago."

"He died twenty *years* ago," countered her mother hotly.

"Stop *lying*, Mother. Mark Shepherd died three *months* ago."

"Mark Shepherd? Mark Shepherd was not your father." Her mother even managed to look appalled by the idea.

"Mother, will you stop? I know the truth. I found the letters and I—"

"Letters? What letters?"

"Letters Harry wrote to him. Letters Shepherd wrote to you after we went up there. A card he sent not even two years ago, after Harry died. Maybe you don't remember writing 'Return to

Sender' on them and sending them back, but he kept them. He kept them and I've read them and—"

"Young lady," said her mother with an icy tone Libby hadn't heard since she was a teenager, "if I didn't open them I obviously can't claim to know what they said, but I am quite certain there was *nothing* in there to insinuate that that man was your father."

Libby might have found it easier to argue the point if her mother's gaze hadn't been quite so level, her tone quite so adamant. "Well, if he wasn't my father, then who was he?" she challenged. For a moment she really didn't think her mother was going to answer her.

"He was your father's lover."

As soon as Quinn walked in, she saw the painting that Bradley had mentioned leaning against the wall, along with what appeared to be a small rug rolled up and a box containing a butt-ugly and ancient-looking cookie jar that appeared to be a pig in a dress, and a few—what had Bradley called them?—dust catchers. As good a name as any, she supposed, squatting down next to the box. They definitely didn't look like anything a would-be burglar would have selected. Even with her seriously limited knowledge of such things, she'd seen several items in the house she was sure would be worth more than the odd little collection gathered here. No, more likely Libby had planned to take these with her, making the obvious question why didn't she?

In the living room she found the pieces of the broken lamp still on the floor along with a decorative glass dish that had survived the fall. The few books Libby had already pulled from the shelves were in two boxes stacked in one corner. Nothing else seemed to be out of place.

She was sweeping the remnants of the lamp into a dustpan when she was startled by a jarringly cheerful tune that seemed to erupt out of nowhere. Her ears tracked the source to the cell phone she hadn't noticed sitting on the coffee table. She snatched it up, flipping it open. "Libby?"

"No-o-o," said a cautiously amused male voice after a beat. "I was hoping to find her on that end of the phone."

Idiot! Quinn berated herself. *Why the hell would she be calling her own phone?*

"She's, uh, not here right now. If you want to leave a message—or better idea, why don't you call back and I'll just let it go to voice mail."

There was another slight pause. "We could do that."

"Great, I'll just—"

"Or," he continued brightly before she could disconnect, "Here's a crazy thought. You and I could have a little chat."

Quinn's eyebrows shot up. "Excuse me?"

"Don't worry. We'll start with something easy. Like—who are you?"

Libby stared at her mother dumbly for a moment. "He was… what?"

"His lover," repeated her mother contemptuously. "His homosexual male lover. Is that what you wanted to hear? Are you happy now?"

She wasn't anything, except stunned. "My father…was gay?" She needed to sit down for this. She dropped onto the couch and watched her mother pick up the glass on the coffee table to swallow the scotch that was in it before pouring another inch from the decanter.

"I would have thought Shepherd would have told you all about this."

"He's *dead*, Mother," she reminded her. "He didn't tell me *any*thing, he just left me…everything. Why would he do that?"

"Why?" Madeline scoffed. "I can think of a dozen reasons. Try a guilty conscience for one."

"Guilty about what?" She knew that was the wrong question—or rather, exactly the right one—when her mother's eyes flashed.

"He stole my husband—*your* father—and you don't think he had anything to feel guilty about?"

Her mother's point was a little lost in the bigger truth here, that even if Shepherd wasn't her father, the man who was had not died before she was even born as she'd been told. He'd died only—what had she said? Twenty years ago? She would have been seven. Old enough to have known him, and to have remembered him, if she'd been given a chance.

Had she been given a chance?

"Why did we go up there?" she asked suddenly. "If you hated him so much, why did you go up there and take me with you?"

Her mother didn't say anything as she carried her glass over to Harry's recliner and sat down. Either the shock was wearing off or the scotch was taking hold, because she seemed to be calming down.

"Harry thought if Robert saw us—the three of us—as a family, that he might agree to sign away his parental rights so that Harry could adopt you."

"Harry…wanted to adopt me?"

Her mother looked at her with so much sadness she felt horrible for having shouted at her moments before. "Libby, he loved you so much. It broke his heart that he couldn't adopt you. He was convinced that if Robert saw us all together it would make him see reason. Of course, he realized later letting him see you at all had been a mistake. It was as if seeing you, meeting you, made you real for him. And then when you wandered off, he—"

"What do you mean, I wandered off?"

"You were right outside the cabin door one moment, and then the next—gone. I couldn't find you anywhere. I admit, I panicked. I just knew you'd gone into the lake, looking for more of those damn *turtles* you were so crazy about once Robert showed you how to catch them."

"That was—him?" She didn't know what to call him. "Biological father" made her feel like a science experiment, but calling him Robert didn't feel natural, and "Dad" was just plain wrong.

"I think Harry was trying to get divers sent out when suddenly there you were, strolling out of the woods with that damn dog. Filthy with pine sap and God knows what else, but happy as you please. You'd just been off chasing pinecones or something. I swear you tried to bring half that place home in your pockets," she said, shaking her head with a vexed look.

"Dog?" She could barely get the words past her throat, but her mother didn't seem to notice. "What dog?"

"Oh, just some stray that had been hanging around there," said Madeline dismissively. "You claimed you'd been lost and that he'd found you and led you out of there, but I'm sure you'd followed him in to begin with. But that's when Robert turned into a real son of a bitch. Started accusing me of being an unfit mother. He threatened to sue for custody, to take you away from me. From *me*," she said, outraged. "As if any court would have turned you over to those two—"

Her mother didn't finish her comment, swallowing her words instead with another sip from the glass in her hand. But it wasn't hard for her to imagine what might have been on the tip of her tongue.

And it also wasn't hard to understand, now, her mother's antipathy toward Libby's own life as a lesbian. It had to be the bitterest of ironies to view a daughter who embraced the same life that had taken her own husband from her. Libby looked at her, for the first time, with compassion.

Chapter Eighteen

"So did he try to get custody of you?" asked Brian.

Libby had been catching him up on the events of the past few days while squeezing in a quick workout at the gym over the lunch hour. So far he'd listened to her story with surprisingly few interruptions.

"No. Maybe Harry or Shepherd talked him out of it. Or maybe he just he didn't want me after all," she said, with a careless laugh to show she really didn't care. And she didn't. Not so very much anyway. Whatever little hurt there might have been was more than made up for by the knowledge that Harry had wanted to adopt her and not just because she'd asked him to.

"I don't think the man knew *what* he wanted," said Brian, surprising her with his slightly pissed tone. "Why did he marry your mother in the first place?"

"Apparently he stood to inherit a sizeable trust fund, but only if he was married before he turned thirty. Sounds like someone already suspected he might not be the, uh, marrying kind." She paused in the middle of a lat pull and blew at the hair clinging to her damp forehead. "How many is this?"

"Sixteen."

She raised and released the bar. "Stop me at ten on the next set, would you? I can't talk and count at the same time."

"You should probably add more weight, then," Brian said as she reached for the water bottle sitting on the floor by her feet. "That looked like it was way too easy for you."

"Easy for you to say." Not that she was complaining really. It felt good to work up a little sweat and the physical aches and pains she'd likely be feeling tomorrow might help take her mind off some of the mental ones she'd been obsessing over the past couple of days. Besides, this was the first chance she'd had to talk to Brian since she got back yesterday and she was grateful he didn't mind her horning in on his workout time. She took a long pull of water.

"So did your mom know?"

"About the trust fund? Yeah. Not about the preconditions though." She reached up to begin her next set, making a face when she noticed the extra weight Brian had added.

"She said she began to suspect he was having an affair right after she found out she was pregnant. The usual signs, I guess. Too many late night hours at work, being away from the office when she called. She said when she confronted him, he actually tried to pacify her with the fact that it wasn't another woman. Can you imagine? He insisted he intended to honor his 'obligations' and that he had no intention of divorcing her. So, instead, she divorced him. By then he'd already received his trust fund, so she ended up with a nice settlement out of it."

She might have received more if she'd at least threatened to go public with the truth, but her mother had been too humiliated to want anyone else to know. It was after the divorce that she'd moved from Boston to Hartford where she'd met Harry. Madeline hadn't even told Harry the truth at first. It wasn't until after they were married and Harry had brought up the matter of adopting her that her mother had been forced to tell him the truth.

At a signal from Brian she finished her set and released the bar. Because they were running short on time, she gave him an abbreviated version of the rest of the story, which was painfully thin on detail.

Madeline had met her father when he was a curator of an art gallery in Boston. Even then he'd been spinning the fantasy of some idyllic existence in rural New England or upstate New York—a quiet life where he would be inspired by nature and could dedicate himself to his own art instead of promoting other people's. She assumed it was a dream Shepherd was agreeable to, because after the divorce her father had purchased the property in Turtle Cove.

Shepherd, who'd been some thirteen years older than her father, had apparently taken easily to the quiet life, but it didn't sound like it had suited her father for more than small doses at a time. In between he'd traveled, his itineraries evidenced by the postcards she'd found, as well as the eclectic jumble of keepsakes that she now suspected were souvenirs from his travels, brought home either for his own enjoyment or possibly as gifts for Shepherd.

She suspected, although she'd never know for sure, that adding on the cabins had been Shepherd's idea. Maybe he'd been able to live out some dream of his own in the role of hospitable host, and so honestly didn't mind staying behind while his young lover escaped the monotony of closeted, small-town life by traveling the world and taking long weekend trips back to his old stomping grounds in Boston. According to her mother, it had been on one such trip to Boston that he'd been stabbed after leaving a gay bar. Madeline seemed to believe it was just a mugging gone bad, and maybe it had been. No one had ever been arrested for it.

Her father's Will had left everything to Shepherd, which she chose to believe was a sign that he really did love the man. Shepherd apparently had felt that at least some of it should have come to her mother, but she had refused his offer. So instead he'd just left everything to Libby in his own Will.

"Think that was what he meant in his letter, when he said he'd just do what he thought was right?"

Brian's question surprised her because she thought he'd

stopped paying attention. For the past couple of minutes his gaze had repeatedly left her to watch something or someone in the mirrored wall behind them.

"I suppose so. But it would have been nice if he'd left me, I don't know—a letter or something, explaining it all."

Brian puffed out a little snort of amusement. "I want to see *you* try to explain all this in a letter to someone you don't know. His gaze returned again to the mirror. "Who is that?" he asked, directing her attention behind him with a discreet tip of his head.

She glanced past him to see a dark-haired Amazon of a woman making her way in their direction. She was wearing yoga pants and a black sports bra that appeared strained to its functional limits. It wasn't anyone she recognized.

"I have no idea," she said, wondering what Brian's interest in her was.

"Well you're probably going to have a chance to find out. She's been watching you for at least the past ten minutes. Seriously," he said, catching her skeptical look. "I noticed a while ago, but didn't want to say anything because I was afraid you'd get that deer in the headlights look."

"I don't get a—" she shot him a glance. "Is that supposed to be some kind of boob joke?"

"Please," said Brian, looking offended. "The mind of the gay male does not lend itself to boob jokes, as you so quaintly put it. Although that certainly tells me where *your* mind is." His eyes returned to the mirror. "Forget the boobs. Get a load of those arms. I bet she could bench press you without even breaking a sweat." He grinned. "I think you can probably take it from here," he said. Then, in a voice loud enough to be overheard, "I'm going to grab some lunch, then, and I'll see you back at the office."

"Brian, you don't need to—" But he was already gone with the brunette so smoothly moving in to take his place it might have been choreographed.

"Mind if I work in?" The woman's easygoing smile might have left room for doubt about her intentions if not for the fact machines identical to this one were vacant on either side.

Wow. Brian was right. She realized she'd been caught staring when the woman reached up to grip the ends of the towel hanging around her neck, a rather obvious move designed to flex the muscles in her well-developed arms ever so slightly.

"Uh—actually I just finished," she said, reaching for her water bottle and the towel lying next to it. She started to leave and then remembered gym etiquette required her to wipe down the seat before moving on. "Just let me—" She stopped, backing up a step when the brunette moved closer.

"That's okay." The woman's smile shifted effortlessly from casual to calculating. "I like it sweaty."

You're not a deer, she assured herself as she started backing away. *You're not a deer. You're just—not interested.*

"Okay, then. Well, uh—have a good workout," she said too brightly, mentally kicking herself until she could get back to the office and kick Brian.

As it turned out, she didn't have to go that far because he was standing at the water fountain outside the locker rooms. He didn't look surprised to see her. If anything, he looked like he'd been waiting for her.

"Why did you take off like that!" she hissed, swatting at him with the towel.

"Don't even try to tell me I was wrong about her. I know a troll when I see one."

"You weren't wrong. Not about her, anyway. But I'm off the market, remember?"

"Off the market? And when exactly did you make *that* decision?"

"I didn't mean off the market as in *off* the market," she said, backpedaling. "I'm just—you know. Not *in* the market. Not for—well, you know I'm not into...that I don't *do* casual..."

"Sex, Libby," Brian said with a trace of real impatience. "The word is *sex*. What, you won't do it and now you can't even say it?"

"I can say it! Sex! There? Satisfied? Sex, sex, *sex!*" she hissed, gaining the attention of a petite blonde who happened out of the locker room right at that moment and gave Libby a not-so-subtle once-over in passing.

Brian eyes tracked the exchange with no small interest. "Why the hell do you come here at the crack of dawn every day," he asked quizzically, "when noon is obviously lesbian happy hour? Oh, that's right. You're off the market."

"I'm just not interested, okay?" she snapped, frustrated with this entire conversation. The truth was, her feelings for Quinn were still close enough to the surface she couldn't even think about jumping into anything else, serious or casual. But she hadn't told him about Quinn yet and given the way it had turned out, she wasn't sure she wanted to.

Brian looked at her for a long moment. "You're really not, are you? I don't know, babe," he said with an exaggerated look. "Girlfriend had some serious muscle going on."

Without thinking, she made an ambivalent sound and said, "I've seen better."

"Do tell," said Brian with interest.

Stalling, Libby bent down for a drink from the fountain despite the bottle of water still in her hand. When she raised her head, her own sweaty image in the mirror over the fountain provided a convenient, if not the smoothest, segue. "Besides, how is anyone supposed to feel like flirting when they look like *this*?" she said, shoving back the damp strands of hair that had escaped her ponytail and clung to her sweaty face. "I'm all sweaty, stinky—"

"I bet she likes it sweaty," said Brian with an impudent little smirk.

She turned on him, eyes wide. "Oh my God, you could hear that from *here*?"

"Hear wha—" began Brian and then snorted. "Jesus, she really was a troll. You're right. You can do better. As skanked up as you are, you're still the belle of the ball, babe."

"Great," she said, rolling her eyes. "I get to be belle of the sweaty, skanky ball."

"Hey, best you can be is belle of the ball you're at, right? Come on, we need to shower and get back to—" He broke off when she grabbed onto his arm.

"Belle of the ball you're at..." she murmured, eyes darting back and forth as if looking at something Brian couldn't see.

"Belle of the ball you're *at*." Grabbing his head between her hands she went up on her tiptoes to yank him into a quick, hard kiss. "Brian Galloway, I love you!"

"Should've known," muttered Sports Bra coming around the corner on the way to the locker room, but Libby spared her barely a glance.

"Hurry up and shower," she told Brian. "We need to get back to the office."

"Wait a second, aren't you going to tell me—" But she left him talking to the door of women's locker door as it swung shut.

Chapter Nineteen

Midway through the presentation of her idea of an ad campaign for Lady Belle Cosmetics, Kevin was already shaking his head.

"Libby, I really don't—"

"And I'm thinking we should use real women, not professional models. Show them in grocery stores, picking up kids at day care, running to the cleaners. Whatever. Because it's not about looking glamorous. It's more like something they take the time for because it makes them feel—presentable. That's the audience I want to aim at. The ones who tune out during the glitzy commercials for high gloss lipstick that lasts twelve hours because, hell, her husband hasn't taken her out dancing till midnight since they were dating. These days she's asleep before ten o'clock most nights because she's got to have breakfast ready for him at six and the kids packed up for school by seven. Who cares about glamour!"

"Libby, selling makeup is all about making women *want* the glamour. Making them believe if they wear that lipstick, if their lashes look that long, maybe their husband *will* take them out dancing until midnight."

"Kevin, please." Libby wasn't so much leaning over his desk as she was holding onto the edge to stop herself from climbing over it. "I know there's something here. Just give us a little time to work it out and—"

"I'm sorry, but there isn't any time to give you. We're meeting with Elizabeth Belle—" he glanced at his watch, "—just over an hour from now." He seemed to derive some small measure of satisfaction from watching her face fall. "As I said, no time."

"An hour's an hour," said Libby, despite the sound of hope crashing in her ears.

"Precisely."

"Kevin," said Brian, his calm voice in stark contrast to Libby's slightly desperate one. "What do we have to lose? If Belle loves your presentation, great. Fantastic. We don't even mention Libby's idea and the first round of drinks is on me. But if she doesn't—would it be so bad to have a Plan B?"

"In case you've forgotten, this presentation *is* Plan B."

"Plan *C*, then," interjected Libby. She took a breath, gathering herself. "Kevin, please. I know this sounds rough—it *is* rough—but it could be good. I can *feel* it."

"I'm sorry, Libby," said Kevin, not sounding sorry at all. "If you'd thought of this a week ago..." He shook his head. "If it makes you feel any better, I doubt Belle would go for it anyway. As much as I appreciate your enthusiasm, it seems fairly obvious you don't understand our target audience here. Perhaps your talents are better suited to plying the soy milk and granola crowd. Now if you'll both excuse me, I have a meeting to get ready for."

"I don't know where you got your self-control from." Brian's carefully played illusion of calm had vanished as soon as they left Kevin's office. "He made that soy milk crack and you never even blinked. And where the hell does he get off—"

"It's okay, Brian," said Libby, silencing him with a distracted pat on the arm. "Don't worry about it."

"Oh, I get it. If they crash and burn with this, in the back of his mind he'll always be wondering whether he shouldn't have let

206

you run with it. Personally, I prefer my revenge to be a little less cerebral, but—"

Libby was shaking her head. "There's no *if* about it. They *are* going to crash and burn. Come on," she said grabbing onto his arm and pulling him with her down the hall. "We don't have a lot of time."

At precisely two thirty-seven, feeling a little sick to his stomach, Brian used his desk phone to dial his own cell phone number. "Papa Bear to Baby Bear. Come in Baby Bear. Who's your daddy? Over."

"Brian, will you quit screwing around!" Libby's voice was an impatient hiss in his ear. In the background he could make out the slightly muted sounds of foot traffic in the lobby downstairs.

"Spoilsport. Belle's leaving."

"Already?"

"Hey, things move fast when they're going downhill."

"Is anyone getting in the elevator with her?"

"From the look on her face, I think they'd be taking their life in their hands if they tried. Looks like you're good to go, Baby Bear."

Even with the limousine Libby had arranged to be waiting for them outside, it had taken a level of smooth talking she hadn't known she was capable of to convince Elizabeth Belle to accept her offer of a ride to the airport. Apologizing for the perceived insult of her colleagues' unimaginative presentation had been tricky because she didn't want to give any impression of disloyalty to her own firm. She wasn't trying to steal Lady Belle's business— she was trying to save it. It was a bit of luck that only Alan and Kevin had met with Belle for the presentation, because it allowed her to play the they're-only-men-what-can-you-expect? card. It was a blatantly sexist strategy and she might have felt worse about it not for Kevin's own remarks to her earlier.

Besides, it had worked. She was now in the back of the limousine with Belle. The woman's body language did not radiate openness, but at least she'd agreed to listen.

"Envision a woman in an elegant evening gown making her way down a wide marble staircase, her hand resting on the arm of her handsome, sharply dressed escort. Music—a Viennese waltz—is playing in the background. The camera comes in for a close-up of her face. Her hair is perfectly coiffed. Full lips smiling under a shimmering coat of glossy red lipstick, cheeks glowing with blusher. Blue eyes carefully accented with eyeliner and mascara. All artfully applied but obvious makeup.

"Suddenly intruding on the music is the sound of bickering children. As the woman's smile starts to fade, her perfectly made-up face dissolves into that of the same woman, but now sans makeup and looking very tired. Her hair is a little wild, maybe coming loose from a haphazard ponytail. And instead of a marble staircase she's standing on carpeted stairs, her hand resting on the handle of a vacuum cleaner.

"Cut to a quick shot of two squabbling children wrestling in front of a TV as she walks past on her way to a bathroom. We see her again briefly in her reflection in the bathroom mirror before she opens the medicine cabinet. On the shelves inside are the familiar purple and gold colors of Lady Belle products. A female voice-over says, 'Your life isn't always a ball, and Lady Belle knows you don't need to be the belle of the ball to feel good about yourself.'

"When the cabinet door swings shut again, the face in the mirror is subtly changed. The faint circles under her eyes are gone. Maybe there's a delicate blush of color on her previously pale cheeks. Her eyes are a bit brighter, a little more defined. But nothing dramatic—just better, in a way that at a glance is hard to pin down. Maybe the ponytail that was coming undone before is once again neat and tidy. The voice-over is, 'Lady Belle Cosmetics. For real women, living real lives'."

For a long moment, Elizabeth Belle stared at her, saying nothing. She concentrated on not looking anxious. Poise and self-confidence. That's what a woman like Belle would want to see, and that's what she would show her.

It's a good idea. She used the thought like a mantra, letting the conviction of it shine quietly from her eyes, from her confident—but not overconfident—smile. *It's a great idea. You love this idea!*

Her confidence, which had been on the verge of wavering, returned with a flourish when Belle flipped open her cell phone. "I assume you have Alan's direct number?"

Chapter Twenty

Libby slipped her portable CD player into a gap between two books and glanced around her office one last time before reaching for the box lid. A movement in the doorway caught her eye and she looked over to see Brian standing there.

"I wish you'd quit looking like that," she told him.

"Like what."

"Like somebody died." She tried to smile. "I'm okay. Really. It's a chance for a new beginning, that's all. You know what they say. When God opens a door..."

"Okay, I don't think I was truly worried until you started quoting from *The Sound of Music.*"

Libby's lips quirked. "Sorry. Best I could come up with on short notice. Come on, Brian. It's not that bad. You know I haven't been happy for a while. Not since Alan took over."

"So what are you saying? You wanted to get fired?"

"Of course not."

"If anyone should be fired, it should be—"

"I don't want to see *any*one fired," Libby said, but she couldn't help remembering the brainstorming session last week. She'd suspected then that someone would be taking a fall if they lost this account. At the time, she'd assumed it would be Kevin's head on the block. And who knows, if she hadn't taken it upon herself to intercept an already irritated Elizabeth Belle to present yet another half-baked idea, it might be Kevin packing his office right now instead of her. "And technically I wasn't fired," she reminded him. "Alan let me resign."

"You'll have to forgive me if I find his charity underwhelming," sniped Brian.

"Seriously Brian, I'm fine with this. Or I will be. Right now all I really want is to go home and—I don't know. Toast serendipity with a six-pack of Sam Adams."

Brian stared hard into her eyes for a few seconds, but she managed to keep her I'm-fine-really smile in place. "Think you'll feel like company later?" he asked.

"Sure," she said, as though that were a silly question. "I'll even save a beer for you, how's that?"

"Sounds good," he told her. "But I won't hold it against you if you don't."

When Libby opened the door to Brian later that evening he said without preamble, "You'll be pleased to know the office is all abuzz with the news of your sudden departure."

"So glad I could liven up the afternoon for everyone," she said mildly before returning to her seat on the couch.

"I would have called ahead to make sure you were really up for company," Brian told her, "but I'd already left the office when I realized you still had my cell phone."

"Oops. Sorry." She reached into her T-shirt to fish the tiny phone from between her breasts.

Brian eyed her chest with wary curiosity. "What else do you keep stashed in there? Never mind," he said, evidently changing his mind. "I don't think I want to know. So you got any of that beer left?"

"Of course," Libby told him and stuck her hand down her shirt once again.

"Not funny."

Libby snickered. "It's in the fridge. Help yourself."

"You never did say what happened to your phone," he said when he came back.

"Oh, I forgot it up at Shepherd's place. I'll have to pick up another one."

He sat down in the armchair opposite her. "Why not just get that one when you go back?"

She made a face. "I'm not going all the way back there just for a cell phone."

"Well, no, but—" He looked surprised. "You're finished up there, then?"

"I only went to clear up the mystery and—" She shrugged. "Mystery solved."

"Yeah, but didn't you say there was some stuff you'd meant to bring back with you?"

She thought briefly of the few things she'd left sitting in the hallway. "Nothing I can't live without."

Brian sipped his beer. "Does that mean you've decided what to do with the place?"

"Not much to decide, really. There's no point in letting it sit empty. I gave the lawyer the go-ahead to start drawing up whatever paperwork would be needed." She'd called earlier and left a message on Latham's machine, telling him she'd decided to sell the property after all and would be back in touch to discuss the details.

"You already have a buyer?"

"No, but I don't imagine it will take long. It's a beautiful spot, right on the lake. The cottages need a little sprucing up of course, but it shouldn't take too much to get it back up and running." She took another sip of beer. "And actually I did run into someone when I was up there who seemed pretty interested in buying the place." She hadn't called the Harrisons, not sure she was equipped to handle their enthusiasm given her own mood. She still had Dr. Harrison's business card though, and figured she'd pass on the information to Latham and let him get in touch with them.

"Is that who was out there the other day?"

She stared at him blankly. "What are you talking about?"

"The woman who answered your phone when I called."

"Why would anyone else be answering my phone?" She shook her head. "You must have dialed the wrong number."

"A wrong number who knew who you were? She told me you'd stepped out and offered to give you a message. Which she apparently did not do."

"Someone answered my cell phone and said she was buying the house?"

"No, she said she was *helping* you with the house. Which, now that I think about it, is a very ambiguous phrase. At the time I thought maybe she worked for the lawyer, but—"

"Oh," she said, suddenly realizing what must have happened. "That would have been Rhonda. I gave her the keys to go over there and asked her to kind of keep an eye on the place."

"No, not Rhonda," he said, trying to remember. "That's my sister-in-law's name so I'd have remembered it. It was—Gwen, I think. Something like that. Come on, you must—"

"Quinn?" she said, startled.

"Yeah, Quinn, that's it. Okay, spill it, sister," he demanded, registering her reaction to the name. "Who's Quinn?"

Caught off guard, she heard herself stammering, "She, uh... well, she's, just a, uh—"

"Oh my God." A wide grin split Brian's face. "You slept with her. I *knew* it." He leaned forward in the chair. "Okay, girlfriend, start at the beginning and don't leave anything out. Wait—do we need popcorn for this?"

"What? *No*," she said, flustered by the unbridled glee on his face. "Why would you just assume something like that? Did she tell you we—"

"I don't have to assume what's written all over your face," he told her.

"Well, you can just wipe that damn smirk off yours, because it wasn't like that."

"Are you telling me you didn't sleep with her?"

213

"I—we—" Damn it, how was she supposed to lie to a point-blank question?

"Ha! I knew it." He scooted to the edge of his seat. "Tell Uncle Brian everything," he said, unperturbed by her obvious embarrassment. "Who is she? How did you meet? Did you have to go through all the usual pre-coital lesbian chitchat, or was it just spectacular, spontaneous, mind-blowing sex?"

Wilting against the couch, she clutched a throw pillow to her face to muffle a groan. God, this was so humiliating. She didn't even want to *think* about what he might have said to—

"Wait a minute," she said, dropping the pillow to stare at him. "You *talked* to her? When did you talk to her?"

"I don't know. Sometime Tuesday afternoon."

"And she was there? She was in the house?"

"I don't know where she was. All I know is she answered your phone and—"

"What did she say? *Exactly*."

He related a short conversation, but Libby's mind was racing ahead before he finished talking.

Quinn had come back.

"Well?" prompted Brian when he finished. "You going to clue me in on what's going on in that head of yours or am I supposed to start guessing again?"

She hesitated, but knew she'd already made up her mind. "You're going to think I'm nuts," she began.

214

Chapter Twenty-One

It was a little after two in the morning when Libby finally reached the lake, trading the monotonous hum of blacktop for the crunch of pea gravel as she turned off the highway. The car's headlights swept across the trees as she turned, briefly reflecting off a pair of eyes low to the ground that probably belonged to a raccoon, but might have given her a moment's hesitation if she didn't have more important things to think about.

She slowed to a stop just before the house would have come into view, suddenly afraid to go the rest of the way. This was why she'd refused Brian's offer to come along. As much as she could have used his company on the excruciatingly long drive here, she knew she'd feel like a fool if they arrived only to find Quinn long gone. Not that Brian would ever hold it against her, but she'd rather have her heart break in private. And if Quinn were here—well, three would definitely be a crowd. Closing her eyes she sent up one last heartfelt plea.

Please don't let me be too late.

She let the car roll forward. The house was dark, but there was a truck in the driveway. The sight of it left her limp with relief for only a moment before a burst of adrenaline had her trembling, her heart thumping wildly in her chest.

She was out of the car and trying to open the front door of the house before she realized it was locked, and she no longer had the keys. She hesitated only a moment before knocking on the door. After a moment she tried pounding on the door, but still no one answered.

She glanced over at the truck again, frowning. Would Quinn be sleeping in her truck? If she was, surely she would have heard her when she drove up.

She noticed him then, sitting by the back right tire of Quinn's truck, barely visible except for the white patch of fur on his chest.

"PJ?"

He continued to sit there, waiting until she was coming down the porch steps toward him before he stood and trotted off toward the woods.

"PJ, don't—where is she?" She called after him, frustrated. "PJ!" But he had already vanished behind the trees.

"Damn it, PJ," she cursed under her breath.

He reappeared from the edge of the trees to chastise her with an impatient-sounding bark.

Understanding that he wanted her to follow, she headed toward the trees. The urgency of his barking increased as he ran farther ahead, but once she moved into the cover of trees it quickly became too dark to see much of anything. "PJ, slow down," she called. "I can't even see where I'm *going*."

As if on cue, a light appeared on the porch of the cottage several yards ahead.

The light of the single naked bulb had Quinn squinting as she opened the door to poke her head out onto the porch.

"PJ," she shouted, "if that's you making all that noise, you better have a damn good reason for—" Her complaint died on her lips when she saw Libby emerging from the shadows. They stared mutely at each other for a very long few seconds.

Libby spoke first, a hesitant smile on her face. "I guess that depends on what you call a good reason."

Quinn started to answer, but it took another second to find her tongue. "You're definitely what I'd call a good reason," she managed finally. Libby's blossoming smile seemed to mirror her own relief, but then as quickly as it had appeared it flattened out into a look of astonishment when Libby noticed the changes that had been made during her absence. She swallowed nervously, watching Libby's gaze sweep across the petite, white-picket fence that now surrounded the cottage.

"Did you do this?"

"Uh...yeah." Her baggy white T-shirt and flannel pajama bottoms did little to protect from the frosty night air, but the arms she folded over her chest were aimed at keeping her pounding heart in more than the cold out. She'd spent every waking moment of the past two days with the almost paranoid hope that at any minute she might hear a car driving up and turn around to see Libby getting out of it, but with every hour that passed when it hadn't happened, a little of that hope had slipped away. Seeing Libby standing here now, when she was least prepared for it... Quinn found herself suddenly unsure of everything. Why she'd come back. Why she'd stayed. Most of all, what she'd been doing here while she waited.

"You'd talked about the window boxes the other day," she said, and when Libby's eyes widened anew, realized she hadn't even noticed those until they were mentioned. "And I wasn't exactly sure what you wanted for the fence," she said, certain that it was all wrong. "But if you don't like it I can always—"

"No!" said Libby quickly, looking shocked by the suggestion. "No, I...I love it."

"I know they look kind of stupid right now," she admitted, looking at the empty window boxes again herself.

"It doesn't look stupid," Libby told her. "It looks..." She shook her head slowly, as if at a loss for words. "Perfect. It looks exactly...perfect. I can't believe you did this." Libby's eyes found their way back to Quinn's face. "I can't believe you're here." Her earlier look of astonishment had settled into an almost shy smile that did wonders to settle Quinn's nerves.

"Why don't you come inside."

In the cottage she reached for the portable electric heater she'd picked up to make the place comfortable in the evening and angled it toward Libby. The quiet whir of the heater's fan filled a moment of awkward silence while she found her sweatshirt.

"So when did—" Poking her head through the collar of the sweatshirt she saw Libby staring at the brushes and cans of paint and stain she'd left sitting on the tiny drop-leaf table. She stepped between Libby and the table as if she could make it all disappear simply by blocking it from view, and quickly found herself on the receiving end of Libby's confounded expression.

"What were you planning on doing with all that?"

"I wasn't trying to set up house or anything like that," she assured her. "I was...I don't know. Just looking around. And I remembered you talking about the cottages the other day. About window boxes and...dollhouses.

"I don't have much experience with dollhouses," she admitted, trying to hide her nerves behind an awkward, self-deprecating laugh. "So I wasn't quite sure what you wanted. I mean, the only thing you'd really talked about was the fence and the window boxes. I was kind of winging it on the rest," she said, rubbing the shiny splotch of cheery blue paint daubed on top of the paint can. She'd started-second guessing herself almost as soon as she'd gotten the supplies back here. For all she knew, Libby hated blue. For all she knew, Libby would hate all of it.

"But...why? Why would you do this for me after..." Libby couldn't even finish the question, and the wounded look on her face drove the ache deeper into Quinn's heart.

"Because I thought—hoped—that when you saw it, you'd know it was from me. And that maybe later on when you thought about me—I mean *if* you thought about..." She scrubbed a hand over her face, frustrated that this wasn't coming out the way she'd wanted. "I just didn't want making you cry to be all you had to remember me by," she finished lamely.

"Why would you say that? Why would you even *think* that?"

asked Libby, with a look that told Quinn she was about to insist it wasn't true.

"Rhonda told me you were pretty tore up when you left." It was probably better that Libby knew, that way she wouldn't waste her time trying to make her think she had nothing to feel guilty about.

"And so you just assumed it was because of you?"

"Well, I—" She hesitated, thrown off by what sounded a lot more like impatience than sympathy or even accusation. "I told you I was coming back and I didn't. So I thought...maybe. Yeah."

"Quinn, that's not why I left."

She searched Libby's eyes, suspicious that she was only trying to spare her feelings.

"That was the night I figured out who Shepherd really was. Or thought I did. Turns out I was wrong. About him. About...a lot of things. But that night I was so sure I'd figured out the truth and I...I convinced myself that people I'd trusted, people I'd loved, they'd all lied to me. Had been lying to me my whole life. Not you. It didn't have anything to do with you."

She didn't doubt the sincerity she saw in Libby's eyes, but there was a ghost of sadness mixed in with it that kept her wary.

"But then it was morning, and...you hadn't come back. By that point all I wanted to do was just get the hell out of here. And I didn't think you'd care that I left because...you're right." Libby's features twisted in a painful mix of guilt and remorse. "I didn't think you were coming back. Or that you'd ever intended to. God, I am such an *idiot*."

"You're not—" When Libby turned away, she reached out to snag her arm to pull her back. "You're *not* an idiot, you're— Oh, God, are you crying? Don't cry." She pulled Libby into her arms. "Please don't cry, because then it really will be my fault."

"I'm sorry." Libby's voice was muffled because she had her face pressed against Quinn's shoulder. She lifted her head to draw in a shaky breath. "It's just... I was so scared all the way up here because I knew you were going to be gone. But you're not. You're

219

here." Quinn felt Libby's arms tighten around her, as if needing to prove what she'd said by hanging onto her. "You're really here, and you did all of this just for me and I *am* an idiot. I'm sorry."

"Will you quit *saying* that?" She pushed Libby away to look into her eyes. "You've got nothing to be sorry for, Libby. No, let me finish. I wish I could say you were crazy for thinking I wouldn't come back, but the truth is I don't have such a great track record in that area. Believe me, there are plenty of women who'd say you were right not to trust me. I think that's what scared me the most the other night," she admitted. "You saying that you did. I kept thinking somebody ought to warn you what a mistake you were making. But the only one around who could've said anything was me. And...I couldn't. I didn't want to. Because as much as it scared me...I liked hearing you say it. I liked how it made me feel. Kind of like when you look at me," she said, faltering at what she saw in Libby's eyes. "For most of my life there hasn't been anyone I wanted to turn even halfway around for. But every time I walked away from you, all I could think about was how much I wanted to come back."

She wiped the moisture from Libby's cheek with her thumb. "I guess what I'm trying to say is, if you got a little worked up the other night thinking about too many people letting you down, I can understand that. And I'm sorry I played any part at all in it. But I'd just as soon you not waste any time feeling bad on my account, because in case you can't tell," said she with a shaky smile, "I'm pretty damned happy just to have you here right now. I didn't think I was ever going to see you again."

"I just knew I was going to be too late. I prayed all the way up here that you wouldn't be gone."

"I'm not. I'm right here."

"Yes, you are," whispered Libby, and released a breath that sounded like she'd been holding it for far too long. She raised her face to brush her lips across Quinn's, then lingered to take the kiss deeper.

"You know," Quinn said, when Libby's arms wrapped around her neck, "you're not going to get rid of me by doing that."

"Hey, you had your chance to escape and you didn't take it. So quit stalling and kiss me."

She was too happy to oblige. Hugging Libby to her, she rested her face against the top of Libby's head, sliding her cheek over the silky softness of Libby's hair. "I really did have a good reason for not making it back," she said, wanting Libby to know.

"I'm sure you did," said Libby, sounding unconcerned.

"Don't you want to know—"

"Later." She felt Libby's hands slide under her sweatshirt. "We're going to have a lot to talk about, but later."

Later. Later was probably good, because right now the steady progress of Libby's hands was making it a little hard to concentrate on what she was saying.

"Right now," Libby told her, "I want to make love to you until the sun comes up and then fall asleep in your arms."

The tenderness Quinn saw in her smile drew her in for another slow, sweet kiss.

"And you'd better not plan on going anywhere," Libby warned her, "because I intend to wake up in your arms and start all over again."

"I won't be going anywhere," Quinn promised, and knew it was a promise she could keep. Because finally, she'd come home.

Epilogue

A few days later, seven miles north of Bryantville, New Hampshire

Beth Armstrong trudged up the side of the embankment, cursing the darkness that made it impossible to watch where she was going while simultaneously keeping one eye on her phone. After she narrowly avoided going flat on her face when she tripped over an exposed tree root, she decided she'd gone as far as she dared. Twenty feet below, the hazard lights of her car pulsed in the darkness. Getting back down was going to be infinitely trickier than climbing up, and she didn't need a flat tire *and* a broken ankle to contend with.

Staring at the illuminated face of her cell phone, she held it out in front of her and then lifted it over her head while turning in a narrow circle, but it continued to flash *Searching...*

So much for nationwide coverage.

She took advantage of the slightly different perspective offered by the hillside to study her surroundings. There had to be a town around here somewhere, but there wasn't a light in sight other than the moon overhead that slipped behind a cloud again just as she started back down the hill. She stopped, willing to wait another minute or two to see if it would come out again, and became aware of what sounded like a car approaching. Her eyes scanned the darkness until she spotted the faint glow of headlights coming around a curve about a mile down the road. The headlights vanished for a second, then reappeared a bit closer.

Shit. It would be here in just a minute. She started back down, trying to move faster without breaking her neck, and knew she wasn't going to make it in time.

The headlights came around the curve below and she heard the car slow down, evidently taking notice of the hazard lights she'd left blinking. She paused from her downhill trek to wave her arms.

"Hey!" she shouted, encouraged when the car pulled to a stop next to hers. "Hey! I'm up here! Don't—" She slipped and slid the last few feet on her backside. By the time she'd scrambled to her feet the car was taking off again, its driver apparently having decided whoever set the hazard lights had already been picked up or gone ahead for assistance.

Still shouting, Beth ran out into the road, but her cry for assistance became a horrified gasp when she saw a small dog run out from the trees directly in front of the oncoming car.

If she hadn't already slowed in order to check out that car on the shoulder, Danielle Frasier would have been going too fast to avoid hitting the dog. As it was, she barely had time to hit the brakes when she saw it dart out in front of her. And then it just *sat* there the middle of the road, watching as the car came screeching toward him. Even now, the little animal looked completely unfazed by its own close call. Hell, he looked downright happy about it, she thought, watching his little hind end swaying along with his tail.

She heard someone shouting and looked in the rearview mirror to see a woman running up the road behind her.

"Do you think you can you help me?" Beth asked, happy to see it was another woman getting out of the other car. "I've got a flat tire and I've been sitting here for over an hour."

"I stopped, but it didn't look like there was anyone with the car."

"I know, I saw you from up there," Beth said, indicating the sloping embankment above them. "I'd climbed up to try to get a signal on my cell phone. I didn't think I was going to make it down in time."

"If it wasn't for your dog, I never would have seen you."

"Oh, he's not—" She stopped when the little black-and-white dog came over to sit by her feet.

"That was a pretty dangerous stunt. He could have gotten himself killed." When the other woman crouched down to pet the animal's head, the dog rolled onto his back to invite a brief belly rub. "What's his name?"

"His name? I, uh—well, I really haven't picked one yet," Beth hedged, staring down at the furry little face that seemed to be laughing at her. "But I'm thinking about calling him Angel."

Publications from
Bella Books, Inc.
The best in contemporary lesbian fiction

P.O. Box 10543, Tallahassee, FL 32302
Phone: 800-729-4992
www.bellabooks.com

WITHOUT WARNING: Book one in the Shaken series by KG MacGregor. *Without Warning* is the story of their courageous journey through adversity, and their promise of steadfast love.
ISBN: 978-1-59493-120-8
$13.95

THE CANDIDATE by Tracey Richardson. Presidential candidate Jane Kincaid had always expected the road to the White House would exact a high personal toll. She just never knew how high until forced to choose between her heart and her political destiny.
ISBN: 978-1-59493-133-8
$13.95

TALL IN THE SADDLE by Karin Kallmaker, Barbara Johnson, Therese Szymanski and Julia Watts. The playful quartet that penned the acclaimed *Once Upon A Dyke* and *Stake Through the Heart* are back and now turning to the Wild (and Very Hot) West to bring you another collection of erotically charged, action-packed tales.
ISBN: 978-1-59493-106-2
$15.95

IN THE NAME OF THE FATHER by Gerri Hill. In this highly anticipated sequel to *Hunter's Way*, Dallas Homicide Detectives Tori Hunter and Samantha Kennedy investigate the murder of a Catholic priest who is found naked and strangled to death.
ISBN: 978-1-59493-108-6
$13.95